"Tamora Pierce creates epic worlds populated by girls and women
of bravery, heart, and strength. Her work inspired a generation
of writers and continues to inspire us."
—HOLLY BLACK, #1 *New York Times* bestselling author

"Few authors can slay so effectively with a single sentence—
I mean fist-in-the-air, shouting-at-my-book slay—as Tamora Pierce.
All these years later, I still draw strength from her words."
—MARIE LU, #1 *New York Times* bestselling author

"Tamora Pierce is a pillar, an icon, and an inspiration.
Cracking open one of her marvelous novels always feels like coming home."
—SARAH J. MAAS, #1 *New York Times* bestselling author

"Tamora Pierce is a seminal figure in the fantasy field of writing,
turning out one terrific book after another."
—TERRY BROOKS, *New York Times* bestselling author
of the Sword of Shannara trilogy

"It's impossible to overstate Tamora Pierce's impact on children's literature.
Her tough, wise, and wonderful heroines have inspired generations of readers."
—RAE CARSON, *New York Times* bestselling author

"In the world of YA fantasy, there's before Tamora Pierce, and then after her female
heroes started kicking down the doors (and walls, and other barriers)!"
—BRUCE COVILLE, *New York Times* bestselling author

"Tamora Pierce is a trailblazer for so many fantasy writers, hacking through the old tropes with her narrative machete and showing us that girl-centered adventures are not just possible but amazing."
—RACHEL HARTMAN, *New York Times* bestselling author

"Tamora Pierce's writing is like water from the swiftest, most refreshingly clear, invigorating, and revitalizing river. I return to her books time and time again."
—GARTH NIX, *New York Times* bestselling author

"Tamora Pierce is gloriously unafraid to give her readers joy and laughter along with adventure and struggle, to let us love her characters wholeheartedly and find the best of ourselves in them, and her books never cease to give me happiness and inspiration."
—NAOMI NOVIK, *New York Times* bestselling author

"Tamora Pierce and her brilliant heroines didn't just break down barriers; they smashed them with magical fire."
—KATHERINE ARDEN, author of *The Bear and the Nightingale*

"Whenever I meet someone else who's read Tamora Pierce's books, we share a certain knowingness—that her stories have not only delighted and inspired us, but indelibly shaped our lives."
—CALLIE BATES, author of *The Waking Land*

"Tamora Pierce is the queen of YA fantasy, and we are all happy subjects in her court."
—JESSICA CLUESS, author of *A Shadow Bright and Burning*

"Tamora Pierce is an epic trailblazer in girl-powered, feminist fantasy."
—LAURIE FOREST, author of *The Black Witch*

"Tamora Pierce's novels gave me a different way of seeing the world."
—ALAYA DAWN JOHNSON, award-winning author of *Love Is the Drug*

PRAISE FOR THE
PROTECTOR OF THE SMALL QUARTET

"Pierce once again shows an expertise for creating compelling, page-turning narrative. . . . Old and new readers alike will be won over by Kel."
—*Publishers Weekly*

"[Kel's] exploration of what it means to be both a knight and a woman make[s] her a compelling character."
—*The Horn Book Magazine*

"Kel's world is completely realized in quick, precise detail."
—*Booklist*

"Many books portray girls excelling in traditionally male roles through manipulation and finesse, but Pierce makes Kel sweat for her success through perseverance, hard work, and skill. Readers will appreciate this true example of grrrl power!"
—*SLJ*

"Keladry's a real scrapper and her adventures are truly entertaining."
—*Locus*

"Pierce's Kel is at once a talented warrior and a refreshingly human young woman."
—*VOYA*

TAMORA PIERCE

PAGE

PROTECTOR OF THE SMALL · BOOK TWO

A TORTALL LEGEND

EMBER

Text copyright © 2000 by Tamora Pierce
Cover photographs copyright © 2018 by Howard Huang

All rights reserved. Published in the United States by Ember, an imprint of Random House Children's Books, a division of Penguin Random House LLC, New York. Originally published in hardcover in the United States by Random House Children's Books, New York, in 2000.

Ember and the E colophon are registered trademarks of Penguin Random House LLC.

Visit us on the Web!
GetUnderlined.com

Educators and librarians, for a variety of teaching tools, visit us at RHTeachersLibrarians.com

The Library of Congress has cataloged the hardcover edition of this book as follows:
Pierce, Tamora.
Page / by Tamora Pierce.
p. cm. — (Protector of the small)
Summary: Keladry of Mindelan continues her training to become a squire with the aid of a new maid, the support of her friends, interference from some other pages, and some serious, even dangerous opposition.
ISBN 978-0-679-88915-1 (trade) — ISBN 978-0-679-98915-8 (lib. bdg.) — ISBN 978-0-375-82907-9 (tr. pbk.) — ISBN 978-0-307-43361-9 (ebook)
[1. Knights and knighthood—Fiction. 2. Sex role—Fiction. 3. Fantasy.] I. Title.
PZ7.P61464 Pag 2000 [Fic]—dc21 99-089894

Printed in the United States of America
14 13 12 11
2018 Ember Edition

To Julia Niederhut Muche

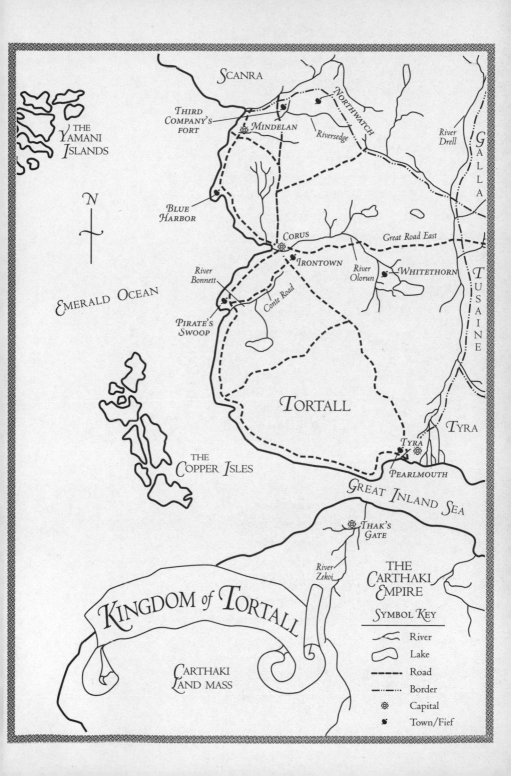

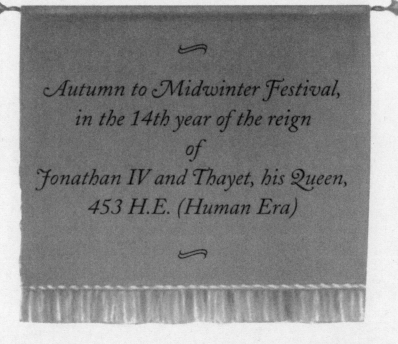

Autumn to Midwinter Festival,
in the 14th year of the reign
of
Jonathan IV and Thayet, his Queen,
453 H.E. (Human Era)

I

PAGE KELADRY

*F*all that year was warm. Heat lay in a blanket over the basin of the River Olorun, where the capital of Tortall covered the banks. No breath of air stirred the pennants and flags on their poles. The river itself was a band of glass, without a breeze anywhere to ruffle its shining surface. Traffic in the city moved as if the air were thick honey. No one with sense cared to rush.

Behind the royal palace, eleven-year-old Keladry of Mindelan stared at the rising ground that led from the training yards to the pages' wing and decided that she had no sense. She felt as if she'd let people beat her with mallets all morning. Surely it was too hot for her to do as she normally did—run up that hill to reach her rooms and bathe. After all, she would be the only one to know if she walked today.

Who would think this cursed harness would make

such a difference? she wondered, reaching under her canvas practice coat to finger broad leather straps. At some point during her first year as page, she had learned that second-, third-, and fourth-years wore weighted harnesses, and that more weights were added every four months, but she had never considered it in terms of herself. Now she wished that she had donned something of the kind in the empty summer months, when she made the daily trek to the palace to keep up her training. If she had, she wouldn't ache so much now.

She wiped her sleeve over her forehead. It's not even like you're carrying a lot of weight, she scolded herself. Eight little disks—maybe two pounds in lead. You trained last year and all summer with lead-weighted weapons, just to build your strength. This can't be *that* different!

But it was. Hand-to-hand combat, staff work, archery, and riding took extra effort with two pounds of lead hanging on her shoulders, chest, and back. I've got to run, she told herself wearily. If I don't move soon, I'll be late to wash and late to lunch, and Lord Wyldon will give me punishment work. So heat or no, I have to go up that hill. I may as well run it.

She waited a moment more, steeling herself. She hated this run. That slowly rising ground was torture on her legs even last spring, when she'd been running it off and on for more than half a year.

No stranger, looking at her, would have thought this disheveled girl was the sort to cause a storm of argument at court. She had a dreamer's quiet hazel eyes, framed in long lashes, and plain brown hair that she wore cropped as short as a boy's. Her nose was small and delicate, her skin tan and dusted with freckles. She was big for a girl of eleven, five feet three inches tall and solidly built. Only someone who looked closely at her calm face would detect a spark in her level gaze, and determination in her mouth and chin.

At last she groaned and began to trot up the hill. Her path took her behind the mews, the kennels, and the forges. Men and women in palace livery and servants' garb waved as she ran past. A woman told some kennel workers, "Looka here—tol' ya she'd be back!"

Kel smiled through pouring sweat. No one had thought that the old-fashioned training master would allow the first-known girl page in over a century to stay after her first year. When Lord Wyldon surprised the world and allowed Kel to stay, many had assumed Kel would "come to her senses" and drop out over the summer holiday.

You'd think by now they'd know I won't quit, she thought as she toiled on up the hill.

She was lurching when she reached the kitchen gardens, her shortcut to the pages' wing. There she had to catch her breath. An upended bucket did for a seat. She inhaled the scents of marjoram, sage, and thyme, massaging her calf muscles. For the hundredth time she wished she could use the palace baths as the boys did, instead of having to go all the way to her room to wash up.

"Hi! You!" cried a male voice from the direction of the kitchens. "Come back with those sausages!"

Kel got to her feet. A cook raced out of the kitchen, waving a meat cleaver. Empty beanpoles, stripped after the harvest, went flying as he crashed through them. Metal flashed as the cleaver chopped through the air. The man doubled back and ran on, plainly chasing something far smaller than he. Once he stumbled; once he dropped the cleaver. On he came, cursing.

The dog he pursued raced toward Kel. A string of fat sausages hung from his jaws. With a last burst of speed, the animal ducked behind Kel.

The cook charged them, cleaver raised. "I'll kill you this time!" he screeched, face crimson with fury.

Kel put her hands on her hips. "Me or the dog?"

"Out of the way, page!" he snarled, circling to her left. "He's stolen his last meal!"

As she turned to keep herself between the man and his prey, Kel glanced behind her. The dog huddled by her seat, gobbling his catch.

"Stop right there," Kel ordered the man.

"Move, or I'll report this to my lord Wyldon," he snapped. "I'll get that mongrel good and proper!"

Kel gathered dog and sausages up in her arms. "You'll do no such thing," she retorted. The dog, knowing what was important, continued to gorge.

"You'll hand that animal over now, my lad, if you know what's right," the servant told her. "He's naught but a thieving stray. He's got to be stopped."

"With a meat cleaver?" demanded Kel.

"If that's what it takes."

"No," she said flatly. "No killing. I'll see to it the dog doesn't steal from you."

"Sausages is worth money! Who's to pay for them? Not me!"

Kel reached instinctively for her belt and sighed, impatient with herself. She didn't wear her purse with training clothes. "Go to Salma Aynnar, in charge of the pages' wing," she said loftily. "Tell her Keladry of Mindelan requests that she pay you the cost of these sausages from my pocket money. And you'd better not overcharge her," she added.

"Kel…Oh, Mithros's"—he looked at her and changed what he'd been about to say—"shield. You're the girl. Being soft-hearted will do you no good, mistress," he informed her. "Be sure I'll get my money. And if I see that animal here again"—he pointed at Kel's armful—"I'll chop him up for cat-meat, see if I won't!"

He thrust his cleaver into his belt and stomped back to the kitchens, muttering. Kel adjusted her hold on the dog and his prize and headed for the pages' wing. "We aren't allowed pets, you know," she informed her passenger. "With my luck, all those sausages will make you sick, and I'll have to clean it up." She passed through an open door into the cool stone halls of the palace. As she trotted along, she examined her armful.

The dog's left ear was only a tatter. He was gray-white for the most part; black splotches adorned the end of his nose, his only whole ear, and his rump. The rest of him was scars, healing scrapes, and staring ribs. His sausages eaten, he peered up into her face with two small, black, triangular eyes and licked her. His tail, broken in two places and healed crookedly, beat her arm.

"I am not your friend," Kel said as she reached her door. "I don't even like you. Don't get attached."

She put him down, expecting him to flee. Instead, the dog sat, tail gently wagging. Kel put her key in the lock and whispered her name, releasing the magic locks that protected her from unwanted visitors. The year before, the boys had welcomed her by ruining her room and writing on her walls, making such protections necessary. While she had made friends among the pages since that time, there were still boys who would play mean tricks to make her leave.

She followed the dog into the two rooms that were her palace home and halted. Two servants awaited her before the hearth. One she knew well: Gower, the long-faced, gloomy man who cleaned her rooms and fetched hot water for washing up and baths. The other was a short, plump, dark girl with crisp black hair worn neatly pinned in a bun. She was quite pretty, with huge brown eyes and full lips. Kel didn't know her, but she was dressed like a servant in a dark skirt and a white blouse and apron. On that hot day she wore the sleeves long and buttoned at the wrist.

Kel waited, uncertain. Gower would surely report the dog to Salma. Kel was trying to decide how much to bribe him not to when he coughed and said, "Excuse me, Page Keladry, but I—we—that is…" He shook his head, ignoring the dog, who sniffed at him. "Might I introduce my niece, Lalasa?"

The girl dipped a curtsy, glancing up at Kel with eyes as frightened as a cornered doe's. She was just an inch taller than Kel, and only a few years older.

"How do you do," Kel said politely. "Gower, I'm in a bit of a rush—"

"A moment, Page Keladry," Gower replied. "Just a moment of your time."

In the year he had waited on her, Gower had never

asked for anything. Kel sat on her bed. "All right." She took off her practice jacket and harness as Gower talked.

His voice was as glum as if he described a funeral. "Lalasa is all alone but for me. I thought she might do well in the palace, and she might, one day, but..."

Kel looked at him under her bangs as she pulled at one of her boots. Suddenly Lalasa was there, her small hands firm around the heel and upper. She drew the boot off carefully.

"She's country-bred, not like these bold city girls," Gower explained. "When city girls act shy, well, men hereabouts think they want to be chased. Lalasa's been... frightened." Lalasa did not meet Kel's eyes as she removed the other boot and Kel's stockings. "If it's this way for her in the palace, the city would be worse," Gower went on. "I thought you might be looking to hire a maid."

Kel blinked at Gower. Pages and squires were allowed to hire their own servants, but having them cost money. While Kel had a tidy sum placed with Salma, against the day that she might get enough free time to visit the markets, she wasn't certain that she could afford a maid. She could write to her parents, who had remained in Corus to present two of Kel's sisters at court that fall. Kel wasn't sure their budget, strained by the costs of formal dresses and the town house, held spare money for a daughter who would never bring them a bride-price.

She was about to explain all this when Lalasa turned her head to look back and up at her uncle. Kel saw a handspan of bruise under her left ear.

Suddenly Kel felt cold. Gently she took Lalasa's right arm and drew it toward her, pushing the sleeve back.

Bruises like fingerprints marked the inside of her forearm.

Lalasa refused to meet her eyes.

"You should report this," Kel told Gower tightly. "This is not right."

"Some are nobles, miss," replied the man firmly. "We're common. And upper servants? They'll get us turned out."

"Then tell me the names and *I'll* report them," she urged. "Salma would help, you know she would. So would Prince Roald."

"But his highness is not everywhere, and others will make our lives a misery," Gower replied. "In the end it's Lalasa's word against that of an upper servant or noble. It's the way of the world, Page Keladry."

Kel heard a whisper and bent down. "What did you say?" she asked.

Lalasa met her eyes and glanced away. "They meant no harm, my lady."

"Grabbing you by the neck so hard it bruised? Of course they meant harm!" snapped Kel.

Gower knelt. "Please, Lady Keladry," he said. "If she's *your* maid, she'll be safe. Your family is in great favor since they brought about the Yamani alliance."

"Please get up," Kel pleaded. No one had knelt to her since she was five. Then the tribute had been to her mother, standing beside her. "Gower, stop it!" I've enough pocket money to pay her for the quarter, she thought hurriedly as she stood and tried to tug the man to his feet. If I explain to Mama and Papa, they'll help, I know they will. "She's hired, all right? *Please* stop that!"

He stared up into her face. "Your word on it?"

"Yes, my word as a Mindelan."

"You won't be sorry, miss," Gower told her as he rose. "Ever."

Kel heard footsteps pound in the hall outside. "Oh, I'm going to be late!" She scribbled a note for Salma, asking for an extra magicked key to Kel's door, a silver noble as a month's wages, and a spare cot for Lalasa to sleep on. She waved the note to dry the ink and gave it to Gower. "About the dog," she began.

"What dog?" Gower asked. He bowed; Lalasa curtsied. They left Kel to get ready for lunch.

Shaking her head at her folly—she didn't need another complication in her life—Kel looked around until she saw the dog. He had jumped onto her bed to nap. "Good for you," she said, and stripped off the rest of her clothes.

A real bath was impossible. She wet her head and scrubbed her face and under her arms, mourning the proper soak that would have eased her aching muscles and made her feel less sticky. Perhaps she could visit the women's baths that night, though it meant she'd have to take time from her after-supper exercises and classwork.

"First day and I'm already behind," she remarked as she struggled into hose and tunic. "Oh, how splendid."

Kel raced into the mess hall that served the pages and squires. All eyes turned toward her; some boys growled. Lunch was the pages' most anticipated meal of the day after a morning's rough-and-tumble in practice. Since none could eat until everyone had arrived, latecomers were never greeted pleasantly.

"I suppose she thinks she's one of us now, so she

doesn't have to be polite anymore." Joren of Stone Mountain's cultured voice was clear over the boys' low mutter.

"Page Keladry." Lord Wyldon of Cavall, the training master, could pitch his voice to carry through a battle or across the hall easily. Kel faced his table, placed on a dais at the front of the room, and bowed. "A knight who is tardy costs lives. Report to me when you have eaten."

Kel bowed again and went to get her food.

"Joren of Stone Mountain." Lord Wyldon's level tone was the same as it had been for Kel. "Good manners are the hallmark of a true knight. You too will report once you have finished."

Kel sighed. She and Joren had not gotten on during her first year as a probationer. She'd hoped that would change now that she was a true page. If Joren was to be punished on her account, she didn't think it would improve his feelings about her.

Once her tray was filled, Kel looked around. Hands waved from a table in the back. She walked over and slid into place among her friends. Nealan of Queenscove poured her fruit juice while other boys passed the honey-pot and butter.

"So, Keladry of Mindelan," said Neal, his slightly husky voice teasing, "not even a full day in your second year, and already you have punishment work lined up. Don't leave it to the last minute, that's what I say!" He was a tall, lanky youth who wore his light brown hair combed back from a widow's peak. His sharp-boned face was lit by green eyes that danced wickedly as he looked at her. He was sixteen, older than the other pages, but only in his second year. He had put aside a university career to become a knight. Neal had taught Kel to know the palace the year before, assisting her with classwork and cheering her worst moods with his tart humor. In return she tried to keep him out of trouble and made him eat his vegetables. It was a strange friendship, but a solid one.

"Neal's just disappointed because he thought he'd be first." The quiet remark had come from black-haired, black-eyed Seaver. He, too, was a second-year page.

"I'm surprised he didn't dump porridge on Lord Wyldon this morning, just to get the jump on the rest of us," joked Cleon. A big, red-headed youth, he was a fourth-year page. "Guess you'll have to wait till next fall, Neal." He smacked the top of Neal's head gently, then went for seconds.

Kel looked to see who else had joined them. There was red-headed Merric of Hollyrose, whose temper was as quick as Cleon's was slow; dark, handsome Faleron of King's Reach, Merric's cousin; and Esmond of Nicoline, whose normal powdering of freckles had thickened over the summer. All were her friends and members of the study group that had met in Neal's room the previous year. With them were three new first-year pages, boys that Cleon, Neal, and Merric had chosen to sponsor. She wasn't sure if they were friends or not. They would have been rude to refuse to sit with their sponsors, and thus with The Girl.

Only one of their company was missing, Prince Roald, but that was expected. Roald, now a fourth-year page, was always careful to slight no one. He had eaten with Kel, Neal, and their group the night before. Today he and the boy he had chosen to sponsor sat with some third-year pages.

Lunch passed quickly, the boys' talk filling Kel's ears. She had little to say. After living in the Yamani Islands for six years, she had picked up Yamani habits, including a reluctance to chatter or let emotions show. Someone had to listen to all that talk.

At last it was time to hand in her tableware and present herself to Lord Wyldon. Joren was already at the dais, waiting. Lord Wyldon always made it clear when he was ready to speak to his charges.

When Kel reached the dais, Joren stepped away from her. Kel sighed inwardly, her face Yamani-blank. Joren and his cronies had done their best to make her leave the year before. For her part, she had declared war on their hazing of the first-years beyond what she felt was reasonable. Interference with Joren and his clique had often turned into fist fights until her friends began to join her. At year's end, there were enough of them to stop Joren's crowd from hazing entirely. Over the summer Kel had let herself hope that Joren would give up now. Glancing at him, she realized her hopes were empty.

Three years older, Joren was just four inches taller than Kel and beautiful. His shoulder-length hair was so blond it was nearly white. It framed pale skin, rosy cheeks, and sky blue eyes set among long, fair lashes. He was one of the best pages in unarmed and weapons combat, although in Kel's opinion he was heavy-handed with his horse.

Well, I've only one more year with him, Kel thought as Lord Wyldon finished cleaning his plate. After he takes his big examination, he'll be a squire and gone most of the year.

Lord Wyldon drained his cup and set it down sharply. His dark eyes, as hard as flint, inspected first Joren, then Kel. Did he regret that he had allowed her to stay? Kel wondered for the thousandth time. Over the summer she had learned that last year the betting among the servants had been twenty to one against Lord Wyldon's allowing her to enter her second year.

Now, looking at Wyldon's hard, clean-shaven face, marred by a scar that stretched from his right eye into his close-cropped brown hair, she wondered why. If she smacked the training master's bald crown would the answer pop out of his mouth? The thought nearly made her laugh aloud, the image was so funny, but her Yamani training held. Her lips didn't quiver; her throat didn't catch. She blessed the Yamanis as the training master drummed his fingers on the table.

"Joren of Stone Mountain, I will have a two-page essay on good manners by Sunday evening," he said. As always, the words came reluctantly from his mouth, as if he felt he might be poorer by giving them away. "Keladry of Mindelan, for your lateness, you will labor in the pages' armory for one bell of time on Sunday afternoon." It was the standard punishment, no more and no less than he gave any other page for tardiness.

She bowed, just as Joren had. They were not permitted to argue.

"You are both dismissed." Lord Wyldon picked up his documents. Joren made sure he beat Kel out of the mess hall. She let him have the lead, since he seemed to think it was important. Once he was out of her way, she ran back to her rooms. She needed to collect her books for the afternoon's classwork.

2

ADJUSTMENTS

*T*he dog was still asleep on her bed. He was not alone.
While Kel had to keep the big shutters locked when she
was out, the small pair over them were open in all weather
so the sparrows that had adopted her could fly in and out.
Three now perched on her coverlet, eyeing the dog with
interest.

"He isn't staying," Kel told the small brown birds. The
dog's tail wagged, though he didn't open his eyes.

One sparrow flew over and perched on her shoulder
with a peep. It was the female who led the flock. A pale
spot on top of her head had earned her the name Crown.
Kel gave the bird a sunflower seed and gathered her books.
Crown flew back to the bed to continue her inspection of
the newcomer.

The palace animals were peculiar. They seemed wiser,
in the human sense, than most other animals. The

difference was caused by a young woman named Daine, the Wildmage, whose magic allowed her to communicate with animals. After she had talked to Kel's gelding Peachblossom, the vicious horse allowed Kel to ride him without making her bleed for the privilege. Even Daine's mere presence affected palace animals permanently. Three months before, Kel's sparrows had led Kel and a troop of hunters to the lair of the giant, human-headed spider monsters called spidrens, though Daine had not been there to ask it of them.

Might Daine help with this dog? Kel wondered as she locked the door behind her.

Neal had been waiting in the corridor. He wrapped an arm around her shoulders. "Come, Mindelan," he said cheerfully, towing her toward the classroom wing. "While you were here riding your evil horse and bending a bow all summer, did you crack a single book?"

"I helped the housekeeper with the accounts," retorted Kel, letting her friend tow her. "Did you bend a bow or ride a horse all summer?"

"Had to," Neal said gloomily as they walked into their first class, reading and writing with the Mithran priest Yayin. "Our master at arms kept after me."

She sat next to him. "We'll make a knight of you yet, Queenscove."

"That's what I'm afraid of," he retorted.

After class Kel returned to her rooms to find that life had suddenly improved. A full tub of hot water awaited her. She could take a real bath while the ugly dog looked on. As she soaked, Kel realized he, too, had been washed. His fine, short fur shone white between scars. He was still homely. His legs were a little bowed, supporting a barrel chest and thin hips. She had already noticed that twice-broken tail and his torn ear. His whole ear was sharp, pointed, and upright on a head shaped like a thick ax blade. That skull looked too big even for his sturdy neck, but the dog lifted it with pride.

"You will never be a beauty," Kel informed him as she dried off. He wagged his absurd tail, as if she'd complimented him.

As she put on a brown shift, orange gown, and stockings—she always wore a dress to supper, in case anyone had forgotten that she *was* a girl—she noticed other welcome changes. Her desk had been neatened, her clothes pressed till not a single wrinkle was left. There was a bowl, empty even of crumbs, and a half-empty water dish: the girl Lalasa had washed *and* fed the dog. She had also found Kel's store of seeds and filled the sparrows' feed and water dishes. No bird droppings could be seen anywhere.

Someone pounded on her door. "Kel, come on!" yelled Neal. "I'm hungry!"

When she opened the door, he poked his head inside. "The cooks say there's ham and blueberry pies, since it's the first day. I love blueberry pie—Mithros, that is the ugliest dog in the world." He stepped inside.

The dog trotted over to sniff him energetically. His crooked tail began to whip. He stood on his hind legs, braced his paws on Neal's long thighs, and rooted at one of the youth's pockets.

"Caught me out, old man, didn't you?" asked Neal with a grin. He crouched, pulling a roll from his pocket, and gave it to the dog. It was gone in three bites. "You know we can't have dogs," he reminded Kel, scratching the animal's rump. "Mithros and Goddess, he is *ugly*."

"You said that already. I know I can't have a dog. Neal, will the Wildmage take him?"

"Daine? Of course," he replied. "She's here—I saw her last night. Ask her after supper."

"Did you maybe want to go with me?" she offered gingerly, afraid that she might cause Neal hurt by asking him along. Last year, he had introduced her to Daine when Kel had needed help with Peachblossom. Kel had seen that Neal was smitten with Daine, though she lived with the mage Numair Salmalín.

"No," he told Kel nobly, and sighed. "It just tries my heart, to see her with that old man."

Kel didn't think Master Numair was so old, but she held her tongue. It did no good to argue with her lovestruck friend.

"Kel, is Neal here?" Merric stuck his head into the room. "Let's be prompt to supper, shall we?" His blue eyes widened. "That's an ugly dog. You know we aren't allowed pets."

"He goes to Daine tonight," Kel snapped. She thrust her friends from the room.

The king joined them for supper, as he had the year before. He ate with Lord Wyldon, then spoke to the pages and the few squires present about the importance of their studies. Kel watched and listened, her face Yamani-smooth. While she owed King Jonathan her duty and her service, she still wasn't sure that she liked him. The king had allowed Lord Wyldon to put Kel on a year's probation, something no other page had to endure. It had not been fair.

Suddenly she remembered something her father had said when the Yamani emperor ordered the execution not only of a band of robbers but of their women and children as well. "Rulers are seldom nice people, Kel," he'd remarked, his eyes sad. "Even good ones make choices that will hurt somebody."

But what if I *want* him to be nice? she asked her father now as she watched her king smile at the eager boys. What if I *want* him to be fair?

"You may *want* anything you like," her mother would have said. "That doesn't mean you'll get it."

She smiled, but she kept it inside. She didn't want the king to think she smiled at him.

As soon as the king had gone, Lord Wyldon called, "Keladry of Mindelan."

Now what? thought Kel, halfway to the door. Has he heard about the dog? She went back to the training master's table.

At least he didn't keep her in suspense. "I understand you have taken a maid into your service," he remarked when she bowed.

Kel heaved an inner sigh of relief. "Yes, my lord."

"You are permitted to do so. However, a servant is a privilege, not a right, in the pages' wing. In addition to your obligations to anyone in your service, you have obligations to me and to the palace." He regarded her levelly, toying with his knife. "She is not to involve herself physically with any page or squire. Her presence is not considered chaperonage for you. If there is a boy in your rooms, the door remains open. If she is ill, you will call and pay a healer. If she cannot read and write, you must teach her. If she misbehaves—is a thief, or lewd, or quarrelsome—you are liable. If she runs off, or stays away overnight without your permission, or disobeys you, do not ask palace guards or servants to find her or to help you to discipline her. That you must do yourself. Am I understood?"

Kel bowed. "Yes, my lord."

"Do your duty by her, and by us," Lord Wyldon said firmly. "You are dismissed."

Kel left, finding that the halls had cleared while they talked. Most of the boys had vanished to begin their studies. Now Kel grabbed the dog and wrapped him in a blanket. "You keep still," she ordered as she carried him down the hall. The chambers where Daine lived were on the floor above the classrooms. The dog struggled on the narrow stair, finally poking his head out of the blanket. He then stopped fighting and gazed around with interest.

He was so bony, and so light! Couldn't she keep him until he'd made up for the meals he had missed? Kel stopped on the landing to blink eyes that stung with tears. She knew she was being silly. Daine would feed him well, and she could heal his wounds. She could talk to him through her magic, and understand his replies. In a day or two the dog wouldn't even remember Kel, he'd be so happy.

Thoroughly miserable and determined to hide it, Kel resumed her climb to the second floor. Walking slowly, she checked engraved name plates on the doors until she found the one that read: "Numair Salmalín, Veralidaine

Sarrasri." Wrestling a hand free of the blanket, Kel knocked.

The door opened. For a moment Kel was confused—she saw no one. A sharp whistle drew her gaze, and the dog's, down to the floor. A young dragon, just two feet tall, was looking up at them. Her scales were dusty blue, her large, slit-pupiled eyes sky blue. She had draped her foot-long tail over a forepaw, like the train on a gown.

"Aren't you pretty," Kel said, admiring the small creature. She had seen the dragon Skysong, nicknamed Kitten, before, though at a distance. "Is Daine about?" Dragons, even very young ones like Kitten, were supposed to be as intelligent as human beings.

The dragon tilted her slender muzzle and voiced a trill, then raised herself on tiptoe to inspect the dog. Kel knelt politely so the two could look at each other.

"Keladry, hello!" the Wildmage said cheerfully as she came to the door. "Welcome back!" She was just three inches taller than Kel and slender, with tumbling smoky curls and grave, blue-gray eyes. She was dressed for rough work in breeches and shirt. Feathers clung to her hair. Her shirt was speckled with bird droppings and a streak of green slime that had to have come from a horse or donkey.

Kel got to her feet and smiled at Daine. "It's good to be back, my lady."

"Who's this?" Daine stretched out her hands.

As Kel handed the dog over, she explained how she had met him. "My maid gave him a bath and some more food, so he doesn't look as bad as he did," she finished. "But I can't keep him. Would you? He likes you already." It was true; the dog was gleefully licking Daine's face. When she set him down, he offered Kitten the same attention. Kitten stepped back with a shrill whistle. Scolded, the dog looked up at Kel and panted, tongue lolling.

"I can *try* to keep him," Daine said, a doubtful look in her eyes. "He needs patching up, and something for worms. He's barely more than a pup." She crouched beside the dog, running her hands over his scrawny frame. "He says his name is Jump."

Kel backed up. "Name him as you like, my lady," she said, clenching her hands behind her back. She was not going to get upset over a dog she'd known less than half a day, and that dog going to the best home in the palace. "Thank you for taking him. If there's anything I can do for you..."

Daine looked up at Kel. "You came almost every day this summer to ride Peachblossom and groom him," the Wildmage said quietly. "You bring him treats, and go easy on the rein, when last year at this time he could look forward to another brutal master or death. And Crown and her flock say that you always stopped by, though you knew Salma was looking after them. It is I who thank you, Keladry, for them. You treat animals as well as you treat human beings." She smiled. "I will try to keep Jump. If you find other animals in need, come to me."

She offered her hand. Kel gripped it gently, mumbled something about appreciation, and fled. She had to stop in the stairwell to collect herself. Daine the Wildmage thought well of *her!*

Suddenly she heard a boy snap, "I don't understand *why* I have to."

She stiffened, her senses alert. Down the steps she went, cat-silent, until she was just around the corner from the ground floor landing.

"It's a page's duty to obey." The perfectly chill voice belonged to Joren.

"You first-year squirts need lessoning." That was Vinson of Genlith, one of Joren's cronies. Kel shook out her shoulders, loosening them up.

"This is a waste of time." The new voice belonged to Joren's closest friend, Zahir ibn Alhaz. Zahir had stopped helping the others to haze new pages late last winter. "We have better things to do."

"What?" demanded Vinson. "Are you afraid of the Lump and her friends?" The Lump, or the Yamani Lump, was their nickname for Kel.

"When you're done with children's games, Joren, let me know," Zahir said. Kel heard steps fade into the distance.

After a moment Joren said tightly, "Get to work, boy."

"But cleaning spilled ink I can't even see—" protested the voice Kel had first heard.

There was a thud. *"We* see it," drawled a new voice belonging to Garvey of Runnerspring. He and Vinson were Joren's chief companions in hazing first-years.

Kel flexed her hands. They knew we didn't expect them to start up the first night of training, she thought angrily. They knew we'd think they were as tired as the rest of us, so they sneaked around and found a victim.

She looked at her clothes. Since she hadn't expected to patrol the halls in search of bullies, she hadn't changed into shirt and breeches after supper. Fighting in a dress would be tricky. Rolling up her skirt, she gathered it at one side and knotted it. I don't care if Oranie thinks that sashes make me look thick-waisted, Kel told herself. Oranie was her sharp-tongued second oldest sister. From now on, that's what I wear.

Kel walked down the last few steps and into the ground floor hall. Ten yards away one of the new first-years, Owen of Jesslaw, lay on the floor. Vinson, Garvey, and Joren stood around him, leaving him nowhere to run.

They turned when they heard Kel's sigh. "I hoped you'd all realized how stupid this is," she remarked coolly.

Joren smiled. "My day is complete," he said. The three older boys moved apart, then closed in on Kel.

Owen struggled to his feet. He was short and chubby, with plump hands and big feet. His tumble of brown curls looked as if somebody had yanked them. His gray eyes were set under brows shaped like question marks laid flat. Confused, he looked from Kel to the fourth-years.

"I'm sure you have classwork," Kel told him, shifting to put a wall at her back. "Get to it. These *boys*"—she put a world of scorn into the word—"and I have a debate to continue."

Owen stayed where he was.

Maybe he doesn't understand, Kel thought. She backed up, to draw the fight away from him.

Garvey came at Kel from the right, punching at her head. She slid away from his punch, grabbed his arm, pushed her right foot forward, and twisted to the left. Garvey went over her hip into Vinson, who'd attacked on her left. Joren, at the center, came in fast as his friends hit the wall. Kel blocked Joren's punch to her middle, but his blow was a feint; his left fist caught her right eye squarely. Kel scissored a leg up and out, slamming her right foot into Joren's knee. Joren hissed and grabbed her hair. Someone else—Vinson—tackled her. Kel let his force throw her into Joren. Down the three of them went in a tumble. Joren let go of her hair, fighting to get out from under her and Vinson. Kel elbowed him in the belly and turned to thrust her other hand into Vinson's face, encouraging him to get off her by pressing his closed eyes with her fingers.

Garvey waded in and grabbed the front of her gown to haul her to her feet. Owen—forgotten until that moment—struck him from behind. Down Garvey went, face-first, chubby Owen clinging monkey-like to his back as Kel rolled out of the way. Owen beat Garvey wildly about the head and shoulders with one hand.

Not much technique, Kel thought as she got to her knees, *But he's got plenty of heart.*

Joren's arm wrapped around her neck, cutting off her air. Vinson attacked her, cursing, his blows nearly as wild as Owen's. Kel's vision was going dark when hands pulled Joren's arm away. Kel gasped for air. Dark breeches and white shirts on her rescuers told her palace servants had put a halt to things.

Two hands wrapped around her arm and drew her to her feet. Kel looked down a couple of inches into Owen of Jesslaw's shining gray eyes. "That was *jolly!*" he said. Apparently a bloody nose and a cut that dripped blood into his ear were not important. "Did you learn to fight like that *here?*"

* * *

"So." Lord Wyldon coldly eyed Kel and Owen. "Already you instruct the new boys in your brawling ways."

"We fell down," Kel replied steadily. She knew this play by heart; so did the training master. First he questioned the senior pages, who claimed they had fallen. Then he questioned her—and, for the first time, the boy who'd been the object of the hazing. No other first-years had stayed to help before.

"Three footmen and a torch boy said you were fighting," Lord Wyldon pointed out.

"They were mistaken, my lord," she replied.

Wyldon drummed his fingers on his desk. Finally he said, "Owen of Jesslaw, you have made a very poor start. Report to Osgar Woodrow at the forge outside the squires' armory for the first bell of time every night after supper for a week. You may cool your passions by sharpening swords." His brown eyes locked on Kel. "As for you, Mindelan— report to Stefan Groomsman at the same hour. He is to find you work pitching hay down from stable lofts."

Clammy sweat broke out between Kel's shoulder blades. "St-stable lofts, my lord. Of course." At training camp before the summer holiday, Lord Wyldon had made Kel climb every day to deal with her fear of heights. Kel bit her lip guiltily: while she had trained all summer, she had not tried to look down from anything higher than a few steps. *I bet he knew,* she thought queasily. *I bet he knew I didn't climb anything on holiday.*

"A final word, Page Keladry." Lord Wyldon stood, bracing his hands on his desk. "This will stop," he said tightly. "There was never so much fighting before you came. It will end *now*."

Maybe you just never heard about all the fights, Kel thought wearily. Big boys picking on little ones just to be mean. Maybe no one made enough of a fuss to bring it to your notice.

From the corner of her eye she saw the red-faced Owen open his mouth. Kel bowed to Wyldon and managed to stumble, banging into the new boy. The training master waited for them to stand at attention once more, then dismissed them.

"Why'd you do that?" demanded Owen when they closed the door behind them. "Why'd you bump me?"

"Because you were about to say something," she replied calmly. "You aren't supposed to say anything except that you fell down. Whatever punishment he gives you, whatever he says, you take it in silence."

"But they started it," he argued. "You were helping out another noble, like we're supposed to, and they waded into you."

Kel sighed. "That's not why I did it."

Turning into their own hallway, Kel and Owen halted. The prince, Neal, Cleon, and Kel's other friends stood there, waiting.

"Good evening, your highness," Kel said.

Prince Roald nodded gravely.

Neal strode over to her. "What on *earth* did you think you were doing? I thought we solved all this last year!"

Kel replied, "We did."

"Then why did you patrol without us? We had a deal. We went with you and we dealt with that lot as a *team*."

"Don't yell at her," Owen snapped. "You should have seen her fight. And they started it."

The prince smiled at him. Roald of Conté was a fourth-year page, quiet and contained, with his father's very blue eyes and black hair that could have come from either of his parents. He was so polite that he appeared stiff, and he made friends with difficulty, but when he spoke, he was listened to. "We have been trying to stop the hazing of first-years," he told Owen. "And I believe I suggested that you study with our group." Roald was Owen's sponsor, charged with teaching him palace ways.

"But there was a *library*, your highness," Owen said. "A *big* one. I was just going to look."

"And I wasn't patrolling," replied Kel. "I had to see Daine. When I came downstairs..." She shrugged.

"And got a black eye for your pains," Neal said with disgust. He reached toward her, green magical fire shimmering around his fingertips.

Kel stepped back. "You'll get in trouble with my lord if you heal something he can see," she pointed out. "Fix Owen's cut."

Now it was the plump boy's turn to step back. "What?" Owen demanded nervously.

"Neal has the healer's Gift of magic," said the prince. "Don't be silly. He can at least make it so that cut and your nose don't hurt as much."

Owen rolled his eyes, but let Neal care for his injuries. The cut in his scalp was shallow; Neal shrank that. "The nose isn't worth troubling with," he told Owen. "It's not broken. Just be careful how you blow it." He looked at Kel with a rueful smile. "Might we at least get *some* classwork done?"

Kel went to her rooms. Gathering her books, she was

trying to remember her assignments when she heard a sound behind her. She whirled, dropping her books. Someone gasped and ducked inside the dressing room.

"Who—?" Kel began, then remembered: Lalasa. She would sleep in the dressing room, like the servants who attended other pages. Kel had seen Lalasa's cot and the wooden screen that gave her privacy when she took her bath. "It's just me."

The older girl peered around the door, then ran forward and knelt to gather Kel's fallen books. "My lady, forgive me, I never meant—" She glanced up at Kel and gasped again. "My lady, your pardon, your poor eye! Who could have done such a thing? Shall I fetch a healer—no, Uncle says only my lord Wyldon may approve healers…A cut of meat, perhaps ice from the ice house if they'll let me have it. Oh, my lady," she wailed, her hands clasped before her.

Kel blinked at her. "It's just a black eye," she said. "Please don't dither at me."

"But it's all swollen! How can you *see?*"

"Badly," admitted Kel. "It'll mend. I've had them before."

"Doesn't it *hurt?*" begged Lalasa. "You act like it's nothing."

Kel shrugged. "It hurts, yes, but not as bad as some I've had. May I have my books, please? I have to study."

Neal stuck his head in the door. "Are you *coming?*" he demanded. "We only have a bell left before bedtime, and half of us are stumped on that catapult mathematics problem. Who's she?"

Kel sighed and introduced Neal to Lalasa. The girl

who had been so outspoken in her dismay went quiet the moment she saw Neal. Silently she backed toward the dressing room, stopping only to curtsy when Kel gave her friend's name.

Why hide? wondered Kel as she left the room with Neal. "Does she know you?" she asked as they went to his rooms.

"No—should she? I mean, I saw her working in the squires' wing once or twice last year. Timid little creature."

His chambers were crowded. With the addition of the first-years to their study group, there was a boy on every surface that might be claimed as a seat. The cluster on the bed shifted, making room for Kel. They were all boys who had gotten her help with mathematics before: it was Kel's favorite subject, and she was good at it.

Who would believe it was just Neal and me a year ago? she thought. I thought we'd never have any friends, what with Lord Wyldon hating him for being fifteen and educated, and me being The Girl.

About to take the offered place, she had an idea. "You know, they do allow study groups to meet in the libraries." She smiled. "I believe there's room for us in the classroom-wing library." Last year Joren and his friends had made life miserable for any first-year who entered the room. It was only right that their group reclaim it for people who wanted to study.

The boys looked at each other, then at Kel. Without a word they gathered their things and streamed out of Neal's room. Owen left skipping to a soft chant of "Books, books, books!"

Neal threw open his arms as if to embrace his now-empty chambers. "What shall I do with all this space in the evenings?" he inquired airily, waving Kel out ahead of him. "Plant a garden, perhaps, begin my eagerly awaited career in sculpting—"

"If I were you, I'd practice my staff work," Kel replied. "You need to."

The bell that signaled the end of their day clanged, and the pages returned to their rooms. By then Kel felt each and every bruise from the fight and from her day's training with that weighted harness. Stiffly she put her books on her desk, noticing a mild, clean scent in the air.

"I fixed willow tea for my lady," explained Lalasa as she poured a cup from the kettle on the hearth. "And Salma gave me a package for you."

Kel looked the package over. It was like others she'd received from an unknown benefactor: a plain canvas wrapper tied with string and a plain label. She undid the knots and pulled the canvas away to reveal a small wooden box.

She wriggled the top off to reveal the contents: a pamphlet and three oval leather balls, each of a size that would fit into her palm. Did her mysterious well-wisher want her to learn to juggle? She picked up a ball, which was heavier than it looked. Kel squeezed it. From the texture, it was filled with sand.

"What on earth?" she muttered, and leafed through the pamphlet. It was hand-lettered and clearly illustrated. Suddenly she began to grin.

"What is it, my lady?" asked the maid.

"Exercises," replied Kel. "For my arms, and my hands." She molded the leather ball in her left hand, squeezing hard. "This is supposed to strengthen my grip." How does he know, or she, what's needed? Kel wondered, scanning the descriptions of the exercises. Last year it had been a good knife, her jar of precious, magicked bruise balm, and a fine tilting saddle for Peachblossom. Now it was more exercises, small ones she could do any time, that would help to build strength in her hands and arms.

Reminded of the bruise balm, Kel took the jar out of her desk and dabbed a little on her swollen eye. The throbbing ache in it began to fade.

I wish I knew who you were, she thought, sipping the tea that Lalasa had made. I would like to thank you—and ask why you do these things for me.

3

BRAWL

The next morning Kel rose before dawn as always. It was not easy. She felt stiff, old, and battered. When she stubbed her toe, she remembered that she could only see through one eye. At least the blackened eye no longer ached so much.

I could have had ice, Kel thought bitterly. But no. I had to be tough. I was mad when I chose this life, she decided as she unlocked her large shutters. I was stark raving mad, and my family was too polite to mention it. That's what living with the Yamanis does to people. They get so well-mannered they won't mention you're crazy.

She opened the shutters wide. Outside lay a small stone-flagged courtyard with a slender, miserable tree at the center. The flock of sparrows perched on its branches headed for Kel, swirling around her in a rustle of feathers and a chorus of peeps. Except during winter, they preferred to sleep outside and join her for seed and water in the short gray time before sunrise. While most of the birds went straight to the dishes, a few landed on her shoulders and arms. Kel gently stroked their heads and breasts with a finger. She had nearly thirty after the spring nesting. Brown-and-tan females and males, the males also sporting black collars, they appeared to see Kel as a source of food and entertainment. They chattered to her constantly, as if they hoped that with enough repetition, this great slow creature would understand them.

She was admiring the male whose pale-spotted head had earned him the name Freckle when something large and white vaulted the windowsill on her blind side. It landed beside her with a thump as the sparrows took to the air. She backed up to look at it properly.

The dog Jump grinned cheerfully at her, tongue lolling. His crooked tail whipped the air briskly.

"Absolutely *not*," Kel said firmly. She pointed to the window. "You live with Daine now! Daine!"

Jump stood on his hind legs and thrust his heavy nose into Kel's hand.

"How did you know to come in here?" Kel leaned out of her window. If she hadn't been so vexed, she would have been impressed—it was four feet from the ground to her sill. She turned to glare at the dog. "Back to Daine, this instant!" she ordered. "Out!"

"*Out?*" a quavering voice inquired. Lalasa stood at the dressing room door. "What did I—"

Kel pointed to Jump.

"Oh. The dog has returned." Lalasa padded out into the main room and poked up the hearth fire, then put a full pot of water over it. "My lady should have roused me. I did not mean to lay abed after my lady was up."

"I wake before dawn," Kel said, going to the corner where she had left her practice glaive. "I practice before I dress." She gave the weapon an experimental swing, making sure there was plenty of clear space in this part of her room. She didn't want to break anything as she exercised.

At least she had gotten some real glaive practice over the summer. While her sisters Adalia and Oranie, young Eastern ladies now, had lost the skills they learned in the Yamani Islands, their mother had trounced Kel every day for a month before Kel's old ability had returned. Kel often thought that Ilane of Mindelan could give even the Shang warriors who taught the pages a real fight with a glaive.

Kel swept the weapon down and held it poised for the cut named "the broom sweeps clean." Her grip was not quite right. She adjusted it and looked up, ready to begin the pattern of movements and strikes that were her practice routine.

Lalasa stood against the wall beside the hearth. Her hands, covered by the large quilted mitts used to lift hot things off the fire, were pressed tight over her mouth. Her eyes were huge.

Now what? Kel wanted to say. She wasn't used to explaining her every move to someone. Instead of scolding, she bit her tongue and made herself think of a lake, quiet and serene on a summer's day. When she had herself under control, she asked, "What's the matter, Lalasa?"

"I—I want to be out of your way, my lady, is all. It's so big. Do you always swing it like that?"

Kel looked at her weapon, confused. It was just a practice glaive, a five-foot-long wooden staff with a lead core, capped by a curved, heavy, dull blade eighteen inches long. "That's what it's for. See, you can wield it like a long-handled ax"—she brought the glaive up overhand and chopped down—"or you can thrust with it." Kel shifted her hands on the staff and lunged. "Or you can cut up with the curved edge." She swung the weapon back to the broom-sweeps-clean position, and stopped. Lalasa was plainly more frightened than ever. "You could learn to use it," offered Kel. "To protect yourself. The Yamani ladies all know how to wield the glaive."

Lalasa shook her head vigorously. Grabbing the pot of hot water, she scuttled into the dressing room with it.

I wish she wasn't so nervous, Kel thought, clearing her heart for the pattern dance. I hope she gets over it.

She put Lalasa from her mind and took her opening position. Step and lunge... Her stiff body protested. She was panting by the time she was done. Next she forced herself through twenty of the floor press-ups that Eda Bell, the Shang Wildcat, had said would strengthen her arms. As she finished, the great bell that summoned all but the deafest nobles from their beds rang. It was the beginning of another palace day.

Kel walked into the dressing room. Hot water steamed in her basin; soap, drying cloth, brush, comb and tooth cleaner were all laid out neatly beside it. Even in here, Lalasa had made things more comfortable. A tall wooden screen hid her bed and the small box that held her belongings. She had found a scarlet rug somewhere, a brazier for heat when it turned cold, and a cloth hanging to cover the privy door. Kel's morning clothes—shirt, canvas breeches, stockings, boots, a canvas jacket—were draped neatly over a stand that Kel had always thought was a hurdle put in her room by mistake.

"Lalasa," she said when she was dressed, "would you like to learn ways to make people let go? Holds, and twists to free your arms, grips that will make them think twice about bothering you? I know some, and—"

Lalasa shook her head so hard that Kel wondered if her brain might rattle. "Please no, my lady," she said in her tiny, scared voice. "It'll be different now, with my having a proper mistress. That's what Uncle said. The nobles don't mess with each other's servants. And I'll be careful. I'll be no trouble to you, my lady, you'll see."

"Hey, *Mindelan!*" someone yelled in the outside hall. "Come on!"

Kel sighed and looked at Jump. He had watched her get ready, his tiny eyes intent. "After breakfast, will you take him to Daine?" she asked. "She's on the floor above the classrooms, with—"

Lalasa was shaking her head again. "My lady, she'll turn me into something. She's uncanny, forever talking to animals and covered with the mess they make…"

Kel was a patient girl, but there was something to Lalasa's meekness that set her teeth on edge. "That's silly," she snapped.

Lalasa stared at the floor.

And here I've frightened her *again*, thought Kel. Now her head ached as much as the rest of her. "Look. Will Gower do it, if you ask him? Take Jump up to Daine?"

Lalasa nodded. "Yes, my lady."

"Then please ask him to." Kel left before she could say anything else.

Lalasa just needs to get used to me, she told herself as she joined the boys headed for the mess hall. She just needs to learn I won't be mean to her. Then she won't be so, so mouse-ish. Please, Goddess.

Neal's first block of Kel's first punch felt every bit as soft and weary as her blow. They both made faces.

"What's the matter, second-years? Tired?" Kel had always thought that Hakuin Seastone, the Shang Horse, was improperly cheerful for a Yamani. Now he circled her and Neal, grinning. He was tall for an Islander, with plump lips and dark, almond-shaped eyes framed with laughlines. His glossy black hair was cropped short on the sides and long on top, so a hank of it always lay against his broad forehead like a comma. He wore plain practice clothes and went barefoot. "Add two pounds of weight to your chests and you act like you carry the world. Put strength into your blocks. I want those punches to mean something! What if you're unhorsed and fighting in mail or plate armor? You'll wish you'd listened to old Hakuin then. Ready, begin. High punch, high block! Middle punch, middle block! Low punch, low block!"

His teaching partner, the Shang Wildcat, peered into Owen's face. She was an older woman, her skin lightly tanned from summer, her close-cropped curls silvery white. "What are you looking at the seniors for?" she asked Owen, pale eyes glinting. "You don't get to look around till you punch like a fighter, not a cook kneading bread."

Kel tried to will more vigor into aching muscles. At breakfast Faleron and Roald had said that everyone was exhausted when they first donned the harness, or when new weights were added, but Kel didn't remember if she had noticed the older pages struggling last year.

"I hear the third day's worse," Neal moaned as the bell rang. It was their signal to lurch to the yard where Lord Wyldon and Sergeant Ezeko drilled them on staff combat.

"I just want to live through today," said Merric as they filed down the hill.

The fourth-years, walking behind them, pushed by the younger pages to take the lead. They did it roughly, yelling, "Oldsters first!" Passing Kel, Joren thrust his elbow back, clipping her black eye. Kel gasped and bent over, covering her throbbing eye.

A cool hand rested on hers, and something flowed through her fingers. The pain vanished. Kel took her hand away, and glared at Neal.

"It still looks nice and puffy and colorful." His voice was dry, his green eyes worried. "Kel, we have to do something about him."

"Yes," she replied, "stay out of his way. Joren's a page for just one more year, and that's what I mean to do."

"She's right." The prince stopped beside them. "If she takes revenge, she's the one who will look bad."

"So there," Kel told Neal, and marched on down to the next practice court. Beneath her calm exterior she wished fiercely that she could pound the meanness out of Joren. Even as she thought it, she knew she would do better to ignore him. Water, she thought, collecting her staff from the shed where it was kept. I am a summer lake on a windless day, clear, cool, and still. Joren is a cloud. All he can do is cast a shadow on my surface. I'll be here long after he's gone. She concentrated on that thought fiercely until Lord Wyldon and the sergeant barked orders for the first series of exercises.

The yard rang with the clack of wood striking wood and yelps from those pages whose fingers got hit. Kel listened to the noise and let it fill her—it worked better than thoughts of a clear lake to clear her head. At least she was less stiff after their time with the two Shangs.

Settled into the rhythm of the first exercise, she looked for the training master. Lord Wyldon watched them from the fence. Keeping his eyes on them, he crouched to scratch the ear of an ugly white dog with black spots.

Kel's attention wavered; Faleron smacked her collarbone with his staff. The force of the blow drove her to her knees as pain shot like lightning through her right side.

"Kel, you didn't block it!" cried Faleron, appalled. "Neal—"

"Back in line, Page Nealan!" Ezeko ordered as he came over. "If there's a break, she'll see a proper healer!" He knelt beside Kel and felt her collarbone, his fingers gentler than his face. He was a barrel-chested black man, a Carthaki veteran who had fled slavery to enter Tortall.

"Just—a bruise, I think," Kel said, gasping for breath. "The—the strap—"

The sergeant pulled her jacket aside, examining the harness. "You took the blow on that?" he demanded. "I don't feel anything broken."

Kel nodded.

"Stupid," Ezeko told her. "You haven't let anybody

land one in months. I don't care how tired you are, pay attention!"

"If we are done fluttering over the girl?" Lord Wyldon demanded, walking over. "Back to work, lads. Can you use the arm?" he asked Kel gruffly.

The emperor's soldiers fight with broken arms, Kel thought, remembering the hard-faced men who defended the Yamani court. It isn't broken, just bruised. *Really* bruised. She nodded, meeting Lord Wyldon's gaze squarely.

He sighed. "Yancen of Irenroha, pair with Faleron." Yancen, a third-year, obeyed. "Mindelan, with Prosper of Tameran." Prosper was a new page. Kel saw what Lord Wyldon intended: she could defend herself against Prosper even with a bad right arm. As Wyldon continued to rearrange the pairs, Kel glanced at the fence where he'd been. Jump noticed her look and wagged his tail.

Neal saw the dog as they were putting their staffs away. "Is that——?" he asked. Lord Wyldon was scratching Jump's spine.

Kel nodded.

"I thought you gave him to Daine," Neal murmured.

"I did," she replied. They walked to the archery courts with the other pages. Lord Wyldon and Sergeant Ezeko brought up the rear, Jump trotting beside them.

"You know, if he doesn't want to stay, Daine won't make him," Neal whispered.

Kel sighed. She *did* know. The Wildmage had refused to change the nature of Kel's contrary mount Peach-blossom. "*That's* why she said she would try to keep Jump," Kel told Neal gloomily as they gathered their bows and quivers of arrows. "Because she thought maybe he wouldn't stay with her."

When she looked around halfway through the archery lesson, the dog was nowhere in sight. Kel took heart. Perhaps Jump had realized Kel wouldn't encourage him.

Perhaps he's off stealing and getting chopped up by that cook, a treacherous voice whispered in her mind. Kel ignored it. She couldn't solve the world's problems, after all. Not yet, at least.

Her relief and worry turned to resentment as the boys reached the pages' stable for their final morning class. Jump sat by the door, scratching one of his scars.

"Go *away*," she muttered as she walked by. "Go back to Daine!"

As she opened the door to Peachblossom's stall, the dog trotted in ahead of her. His jaunty air suggested that a horse of Kel's was a horse of his. Peachblossom instantly put back his ears, retreated until his rump hit the stable wall, and stamped. Jump sat and regarded the horse.

Peachblossom was a horse to regard with care. He was a small destrier who would have been too big for Kel if he had not allowed her to ride him. He was gelded, with strawberry roan markings: reddish brown stockings, face, mane, and tail, and a rusty coat flecked with white. Only three people could handle him without getting bit, Kel, Daine, and the chief hostler, Stefan Groomsman.

"Ignore the dog," she advised the gelding as she stiffly went over him with a brush. "He thinks he belongs to me, but he's mistaken."

Peachblossom snorted disbelief, but he'd found the apple Kel had brought, and he did like the brush.

He stepped away from the wall.

Despite the pain in her shoulder, Kel put the riding saddle on him and mounted up. This week there would be no work with the lance and the heavier tilting saddle. The pages would be riding only, the seniors to show they hadn't gone soft over the holiday, the first-years to show they could manage a horse. It was boring, but as the ache in her shoulder spread, Kel decided boredom was preferable.

At least Jump didn't follow them out, or if he did, he made sure Kel never saw him. She was able to concentrate on putting Peachblossom through his paces until the end-of-morning bell. She returned to the stable and groomed her mount, glad the morning had ended.

Faleron, whose fire chestnut was Peachblossom's neighbor, leaned on the rail between the stalls. "Kel, I'm still not sure about that catapult problem," he confessed, embarrassed. He knew more Tortallan law than any other page, but mathematics came hard for him. "If I fetch it to lunch, would you take a look?"

Kel nodded. "You didn't have to ask, you know."

Faleron grinned. "Mama raised me polite."

In a nearby stall Garvey muttered, "So, Faleron, you're friends with her now because you can have her whenever you want?"

Faleron threw down his brush and went for the other boy. Sore shoulder or no, Kel flew out of the stall. She caught Faleron just a foot from the sneering Garvey and hung on to him, putting all of her weight into it.

The older boy fought her grip. "Gods curse it, Kel, you heard what he said!"

"I heard a fart," Kel said grimly. "You know where those come from. Let it *go*."

Faleron relaxed, but she still kept both hands wrapped around his arm. He was easy-going, but everyone had sore spots. At last Faleron made a rude gesture at Garvey and let Kel pull him away.

They had almost reached their horses when Neal's unmistakable drawl sounded through the stable: "Joren is *so* pretty. Say, Garvey, are you two friends because you can have him?"

Garvey roared and charged, but Joren got to Neal first. Before they landed more than a punch each, Neal's friends, including Kel, attacked them. More boys entered the brawl, kicking and hitting blindly, striking friend as often as foe. Kel nearly fainted when someone's boot hit her bruised collarbone.

Above the din made by boys and frightened horses, Kel heard the sound of breaking wood. Realizing she would never reach Neal, praying he didn't get his silly head broken, she grabbed Merric and Seaver by the collar and backed up, dragging them with her. The press of bodies behind her let up suddenly; she nearly fell over backward.

Startled, she looked around and saw Peachblossom. His teeth firmly sunk into Cleon's jacket, the gelding drew the big youth out of the fray. Prince Roald gripped Owen by both arms to keep him out of the brawl; Roald's horse, the black gelding Shadow, held Faleron by the arm as he slowly pulled him free. Zahir's bay shouldered through the mob, stepping on no one, but forcing them to move away from him and each other.

For a moment a chill ran through Kel. She thought

uneasily, The animals here are *so* strange. Then she shook it off. The harridan who trained the ladies of the Yamani court to defend themselves had always said, "We use the tools at hand." These animals, uncanny or not, were the right tools for this mess.

She thrust Merric and Seaver into a ruined stall and grabbed Cleon's arm. "Peachblossom, can you find Neal?" she asked her horse.

The big gelding released Cleon's jacket, blew scornfully, and waded into the fight. Unlike Zahir's bay, he was not careful of feet or fingers. If they were in the way, Peachblossom stepped on them. Several boys rolled clear to nurse bruises and broken bones.

"You can let go, Kel," said Cleon, his voice dry. He watched Cavall's Heart, Lord Wyldon's dark dun mare, who had also broken out of her stall. She dragged Garvey out of the pile. "Even I'm not stupid enough to argue with horses. Particularly not *these* horses."

Kel glared up at him. Cleon was a fourth-year, but he was also a friend. "I'm glad you're smart enough to realize that much," she told him.

Cleon slapped her cheerfully on the back. "What's the matter, dewdrop? Don't you like men fighting to protect your honor?"

"I can defend my *own* honor, thank you," she replied. "I thought it was Joren's honor at stake. And stop calling me those idiotic nicknames. That joke is dead and rotting." She watched as Jump grabbed Vinson by the ankle, stopping the boy's attempts to kick anyone.

Peachblossom had just seized Neal's jacket, with Neal's shoulder in it, when Lord Wyldon, Sergeant Ezeko, and three stable hands entered. They tossed the buckets of water they carried on the pages. Silence fell.

"I want this place straightened up and these horses groomed afresh." Lord Wyldon's voice, and eyes, were like iron. "That includes Heart. You will then wash and assemble in the mess hall. I will address you further there." He looked them over, pale with fury. "You are a disgrace, the lot of you." He turned on his heel and walked out.

Silently the pages got to work.

By the time they reached the mess hall, Lord Wyldon had worked out their punishment. It included bread-and-water suppers for a week, study alone in their rooms at night, no sweets, and no trips out of the palace until Midwinter. Those pages who already had Sunday afternoon punishment work were to put that off until the general punishment was done. They were all to help carpenters rebuild the stable. Finally, the training master added two more lead weights to the senior pages' harnesses.

The subdued pages went to afternoon classes in nearly complete silence. When it was time to dress for supper, Kel scrambled into her shift and gown, stopping only to demand of Lalasa why Jump hadn't been taken to Daine that morning. When Lalasa, cringing, replied that Gower had carried the dog up to the Wildmage right after breakfast, Kel shook her head. She would have to deal with Jump later.

Still wearing boots and heavy wool stockings under her gown, she went to Neal's room and pounded on his door. He let her in without a word, but protested when she closed the door behind her.

"Do you want everyone hearing what I have to say?" she demanded sharply.

"If the Stump catches you here with the door shut—" The Stump was Neal's nickname for Lord Wyldon.

"He won't." Kel put her fists on her hips and glared at her friend. "You were sixteen last month. You're supposed to know better. Did you honestly think you were *helping* me down there?"

He had the strangest look on his face. "Are you—Kel, the Yamani Lump—are you *yelling* at me?"

"Yes, I am!" Kel snapped. "You didn't solve anything, you just made it worse!"

He sat on his bed. "Maybe, maybe not. I think they'll reconsider, next time they want to start fights over your virtue."

Kel blinked at him. "What has my virtue to do with anything?"

"I'm surprised they didn't try it last year. Oh, I suppose they made dirty little jokes with each other, never mind that a *real* knight is supposed to treat women decently. Maybe they thought saying you're a lump, and not as strong, and on probation, was bad enough."

"Are you making sense yet?" Kel wanted to know. This conversation had taken a very uncomfortable turn.

"But you're still here. Now they're *really* worried. They haven't changed their minds about lady knights just because Wyldon let you stay."

"I didn't expect them to," Kel informed him.

"Well, so, they decided to try new insults today. And talk of different kinds of sex makes people crazy."

"Your point is…?" she asked. Her mother had

explained how babies were made. Nariko had taught the court ladies, including Kel's family, how to preserve their honor from rapists. That didn't seem to be what Neal was talking about.

"See, Kel, if all of a sudden everyone's getting into fights about your virtue, maybe the Stump will get rid of you after all." Neal sighed and finger-combed his hair back from his face.

Fear trickled down Kel's spine like cold water. Could Lord Wyldon change his mind? Who would protest if he did? The king had allowed her to be put on probation in the first place. No doubt if Wyldon told him Kel had to go, the king would agree. "I'm eleven," she said at last. "That's too young to be lying with men, Neal. Much too young."

He inspected a bruise on his wrist, and touched a fingertip to it. A green spark flashed and the bruise faded. "Facts don't matter with Joren and his crowd. Just gossip. Just making your friends angry enough to fight. I reminded them that gossip is a tricky weapon, that's all. It cuts two ways."

Kel sighed. "I still don't think you did me any good. I can take a few insults."

"*You* can—I can't." Neal peered out the door. "Hall's empty. Shoo." As she walked by, he added, "I consider myself chastised."

She stopped and turned back. "What you said about Garvey and Joren—it's not an insult in Yaman. Some men prefer other men. Some women prefer other women." Kel shrugged.

"In the Eastern Lands, people like that pursue their loves privately," replied Neal. "Manly fellows like Joren think it's a deadly insult to be accused of wanting other men."

"That doesn't make sense," Kel said.

"It's still an insult on this side of the Emerald Ocean, my dear. Now, if I may shave before our bread-and-water feast?"

Kel eyed Neal's cheeks and chin. "You don't need to."

Neal sighed. "I live in hope, as the priest said to the princess. If you don't mind?"

Kel went back to her room, shaking her head.

4

WOMAN TALK

*T*heir punishments for the stable fight cooled the hottest tempers. Kel thought just the addition of two more harness weights would have done it. Even the fourth-year pages were not ready for the change, and it was astonishing how much difference an extra pound made. For weeks Kel felt as if her bones had turned to wax. Master Oakbridge, whose etiquette class was at the end of the day, began to hit their desks with his pointer stick to keep them awake. Extra work, given when sleepy pages didn't finish classwork, piled on top of Lord Wyldon's physical penalties.

Bread-and-water suppers did not help. Scant meals on their schedule meant growling bellies. Sometimes Kel thought it was hunger and the prospect of added weights, rather than insults that cut two ways, that made Joren and his friends leave her and her crowd alone.

Two Sundays went to rebuilding the pages' stable. Once that was done, Kel returned to her earlier punishment, forking down hay from a stable loft. For a week she dripped sweat as she pitched hay down fourteen feet to the floor. Her fright turned the distance into miles. Once that week ended, she enjoyed the absence of fear, until the day she was tardy to a class. Lord Wyldon gave her one bell of time to climb to the palace wall and map the ground between it and the temple district.

Every time she was late, or Lord Wyldon found dirt on Peachblossom's tack, or someone noticed she had lit a candle after lights out, the training master found Kel work on heights. Neal was sure it was torture. Kel argued that Lord Wyldon helped her to become a better knight by forcing her to manage her fear. Prince Roald finally tired of the debate and said it was a little of both; he didn't want to hear the subject discussed again.

Every morning and every evening when she opened the large shutters, Jump bounced into her room. Kel's sparrows made a game of it, clinging to the dog's fur and trying to stay on as he leaped. Lalasa also seemed to enjoy it—she gave the dog a treat when no sparrows fell from his back.

No matter how often Gower and Kel took the dog up to Daine, Jump returned, to her room and to the practice courts. Kel dared not speak to him there: she feared that someone would notice and report it. She was lucky that a dog's presence in the palace was not unusual. The place teemed with dogs—ratters, hunting dogs, even ladies' lapdogs. As long as none of their teachers thought Jump belonged to any pages as a pet, he was free to come and go as he pleased.

By the time the leaves turned color, Jump had joined the night-time study group, and Kel had given up on returning him to Daine. What was the use? He always came back, and she knew Lalasa fed him. Instead Kel lit a stick of incense, asking the Great Mother to protect him, and resigned herself to her new companion.

Jump's snores roused Kel one November morning before dawn. She turned him on his side—he only snored on his back—and waited for sleep to return. It didn't. Instead she worried. She had plenty to worry about. Once they had the energy, she and her friends had begun their hall patrols, trying to catch Joren and his cronies harassing a first-year. They'd had no success. Neal and Cleon thought Joren's crowd had given up. Kel wasn't so sure. Her experience of bullies was that if they weren't doing one thing, they were preparing something else.

It's no good fretting, Kel told herself sternly. Whatever it is, you'll put a stop to it, that's all. She just hoped she'd catch them soon. The suspense was like an itch she couldn't scratch.

As soon as she put Joren from her mind, she worried about practice. She had finally gotten used to the weight of the harness. Only a week ago she had started to hit the quintain properly in tilting; only in the last two days had she returned to hitting it correctly on every pass. Just when she'd gotten her skill back, what did Lord Wyldon do but announce a change. In another week he would be replacing the lances of the second-, third-, and fourth-year pages with swords two days a week and axes two days a week. Kel wasn't ready for that.

Had she noticed the senior pages using other weapons

from horseback the year before? She had to smile at the thought. Of course she hadn't. When she concentrated on something, like her long struggle to learn how to tilt, she saw little else.

Her smile vanished. I'll talk it over with Peachblossom, she decided. He may not understand, but perhaps he'll appreciate my making the effort. I just hope I don't bang him with the sword or the ax. I don't think he'll like that.

Was it even worth trying to sleep again now? she wondered, eyes on the light gray sky beyond the open upper shutters. Chances were she would doze off just as the bell rang for the day to start.

She rolled out of bed and carefully opened the lower shutters so she could see. If she lit a candle, Lalasa would be awake within moments, asking if she could serve Kel— and this even though the dressing room door was shut. Kel sighed, quietly, and wished it were as easy to like Lalasa as it was to like Jump. Certainly the girl was useful. She smuggled Jump's food into Kel's room with no one the wiser. She kept things neater than Kel had ever done. If only she laughed more, and talked about things! She relaxed only with the animals, but not Kel. And she mourned each and every tear in Kel's garments as if a friend had died.

If only she wouldn't be so *skittish*, thought Kel, slipping her weighted harness on over her nightgown. She creeps about like a mouse, flinching whenever you look at her, till you just want to give her something to flinch about. She's *afraid* of me. What have I done to deserve it? Only thought about smacking some life into her, and I know she can't hear my thoughts. If she could, she'd know I felt bad just thinking that.

Her job with Kel was safe: Baron Piers and Lady Ilane had sent money for the girl's wages for a year. Kel had paid Lalasa then and there. There was no reason for the girl to think Kel might dismiss her, after receiving a year's wages. She said little to Kel but "Yes, my lady" and "No, my lady," or for a change, "I'll see, my lady." Kel was a friendly girl; it hurt that Lalasa couldn't be easy around her. It was also uncomfortable, tiptoeing about her own rooms for fear she might startle her new companion.

Kel bent to touch her toes and heard a rip. Her nightgown, more than a bit snug around the shoulders these days, had gotten caught under the harness and torn. Wriggling, Kel tried to get a more comfortable fit out of gown and harness. Could leather shrink? The thing had been perfectly comfortable when it was first made.

She touched her toes again. The seam that had ripped a moment ago tore further. She growled a Yamani curse and tugged the harness again.

"My lady, that won't help." Lalasa walked out of the dressing room, a robe clutched over her bed gown.

This time Kel thought a whole string of Yamani curses. Keeping her face calm, she said, "You *really* don't have to be up. You know I won't need you till the bell rings."

Normally something that close to a reprimand would have sent Lalasa scurrying from the room. Now, however, she strode forward, hands outstretched. "If you please, my lady?" She actually touched Kel, sticking her slim fingers under the shoulder straps of the harness and lifting it off.

Lalasa inspected the harness in the very dim light, exploring its seams and joins with her hands. Kel, intrigued, poked up the fire and lit candles.

"I can do nothing about this," the older girl said, putting the harness down. "You need a new one, and that's tanner-work. If my lady pleases?" She motioned, and Kel turned. Lalasa touched the ripped seam between Kel's shoulder blades, then plucked at sleeve holes, collar, and cuffs. She turned Kel and knelt to pull on the gown's hem.

"As I thought," she said at last. "My lady has grown an inch since this was made. I *thought* you had trouble tying your points yesterday."

Kel made a face. "I've been having a cursed time getting my hose up high enough for me to tie them properly," she admitted. "Even my breeches are short."

"It's easy to get new clothing for practice and classes, my lady," Lalasa said. "We just trade the old things for new at the palace tailors'." She stood and glanced at Kel, then coughed lightly into her fist. "Um—my lady, you have grown elsewhere, too."

"My shoulders," Kel said gloomily. "That's why the gown split, and why I can't settle that harness comfortably. My waist's a little smaller, though."

Lalasa shook her head. "Your shoulders *are* filling out, but those aren't the only things."

Kel rubbed her nose. Finally she said, "You know, I understand better when people tell me straight out what they're thinking."

Lalasa's large, dark eyes met hers. She hesitated, then said, "Most girls pray for this, my lady. You're getting them young. I didn't show until I was fourteen." Realizing that

Kel still didn't understand, Lalasa cupped her breasts and let them go.

Flabbergasted, Kel stared at the front of her nightgown. Sure enough, there were two slight bulges in the proper area for such things. When had this happened? They weren't large enough to be visible under her loose clothes, but how could she have missed them when she bathed?

I hurry when I scrub, she thought, fighting the urge to cross her arms and cover her chest. And I'm always thinking about classwork or practice.

A cold thought overbore everything else: They'll never let me hear the end of this. She accepted that as soon as she thought it. There was little she could do about the boys' future comments, except choose her clothes with care and hope her new, inconvenient badges of womanhood grew slowly.

Lalasa ducked her head. "My lady will need breast bands."

"Oh, splendid," Kel replied. "Just what I need—more clothes." She rubbed the back of her neck. "When you get those new things from the tailor? Make sure they're *loose,* all right?"

"Most girls rejoice at this," Lalasa pointed out softly. "They regard it—and their monthly bleeding—as signs they enter womanhood."

"Most girls don't have a covey of boys whacking them with sticks every morning. Most girls don't want to be knights." Kel plopped onto the bed. Jump wriggled until he could stick his blunt head under her hand. "If this keeps up, eventually I can stop wearing dresses to remind them

I'm a girl. I hope it takes a while. A *long* while." She tucked her chin to look at her front. Lalasa muffled a noise with her hands. It sounded remarkably like a laugh. "I'm glad *you* find it funny," Kel told her with a wry grin.

"I have to take my lady's measurements afresh," Lalasa said, going into the dressing room. "And I need to draw coin from Salma to buy cloth," she called as she opened the box where she kept her sewing things. "I can let out many of your personal garments, but nightgowns, and breast bands, and stockings must be paid for from your own purse."

Kel went to her desk and wrote a note to Salma on her message slate. When she had finished, Lalasa approached with a measuring cord. As she slid it around Kel with brisk efficiency, Kel was startled to see they were exactly the same height. She had grown an inch in three months.

"I don't know when I can get that harness let out," she commented.

"Leave it for me when you come for your bath," Lalasa assured her. "I will take it to the tanner."

"You'll need to give him some encouragement," Kel remarked. If people wanted fast work from palace servants, they paid bribes. "In fact—" She wiped out her note to Salma and wrote a fresh one, asking her to give Lalasa Kel's pocket money for the quarter. "This way you don't have to apply to me, and I don't have to apply to her. You can keep it here and draw what's needed." She handed the slate to Lalasa, who held it with a stunned look on her face.

"What is it?" Kel asked, picking up her glaive. The bell would ring soon; she had to start her practice dances.

When Lalasa didn't reply, Kel looked sharply at her. "What's wrong?"

Lalasa was trembling. "Aren't you afraid I will steal it?"

"No," Kel said, trying deep knee bends to loosen her legs. Each bend was marked by another tiny rip. It seemed her nightgown had decided to give up completely. "You didn't run off when I paid you for the year."

"All nobles think that servants steal."

Kel tucked her nightgown's skirt into the side of her loincloth. "People who believe servants will steal usually get servants who do." She swung her glaive. "You never give me any reason to doubt your honesty."

For a moment Lalasa said nothing. Then she uttered a soft "Oh" and set a pot of water over the fire to heat.

For the first time since Kel had taken her as a maid, she stayed in the room as Kel performed the complex swings, thrusts, turns, and rolls of a practice dance. She put out fresh seed for the sparrows and laid out Kel's morning clothes. Only when the water on the hearth began to steam did she collect the pot and take it into the dressing room so Kel could wash when she was done.

That afternoon, in the pages' class on magic, Tkaa the basilisk began to speak of how the Yamanis practiced magic. Knowing of Kel's six years there, he called on her. When Kel mentioned that she had a spirit bag, an amulet created for her by a Yamani shaman, Tkaa asked if she would let the class see it. Kel bowed to him—she had gotten over the strangeness of having an eight-foot-tall gray lizard as a teacher months before—and went to her rooms.

About to turn into the pages' hall, she felt an itch and

halted, making a face. The breastband she had on was crisp new linen, and it itched. She glanced around: no one was there to see. Hiking up her tunic, she scratched her ribs through her shirt.

From the pages' wing she heard a man say, "Don't be shy. If you're nice, I'll get you a better place than working for that crazy Mindelan girl." He spoke quietly, but he couldn't have been far away. "You waste your prettiness toiling after a mad page."

There was a reply, in a female voice far softer than the man's. It was Lalasa and she was frightened. Quickly Kel tugged her tunic over her hips and walked into the pages' wing. A man in servant's clothes had backed Lalasa up against Kel's door. He leaned against it, trapping the maid between his arms. Her eyes were huge as she stared up at him. In one hand she held a brand-new weighted leather harness.

Kel strode forward briskly. "What is your name, and what business do you have with my maid?" she demanded, sharp-voiced. "Step away from her at once." It didn't matter that he was a grown man. She was a noble, and she knew her rights.

He looked at her. He was in his early twenties, with a wiry frame. His dark eyes flashed with annoyance as he drew away from Lalasa and bowed. "I am Hugo Longleigh, if it please you, my lady. We were just having a friendly chat—"

"It didn't look friendly to me. What palace service are you in?" Kel asked.

He frowned, but he dared not defy a noble, even one who was only a page. "I am a clerk in Palace Stores.

We have an understanding, Lalasa and me—"

"My lady, I swear, I was just getting the harness, and he approached me." Lalasa's eyes were frantic. "I wasn't idling and we *don't* have an understanding!"

Kel felt very cold inside. How dare he frighten Lalasa! "If you are in Palace Stores, Hugo Longleigh, then no doubt they miss your work," she said, her hands on her hips. "If you bother Lalasa again, I'll report you. Be about your business." She met his eyes squarely, letting him know he didn't frighten her in the least. He looked like the sort who enjoyed other people's fear.

The man hesitated, then bowed grudgingly and left. Only when he was gone from view did Lalasa say, "My lady, please, I didn't want him and I wasn't lazing about—"

Kel fished out her key and put it in the lock. "I know you weren't." She unlocked the door and went to her desk. "It's plain as the nose on my face that you wanted him a thousand leagues away." She found the shaman bag and tucked it into her belt-purse. "As for idling, you really *don't* have to stay here all the time. Don't you have friends to visit or errands to run?"

Lalasa tugged at the straps of the harness. "I like to stay here. Nobody bothers me but the dog and the birds, and I like them."

"Well, think about it," Kel said. "Honestly, I'm not your jailer. And if that Longleigh comes *near* you again, tell me, understand? I mean it."

Lalasa nodded, but Kel wasn't convinced. There was no time to argue, though—she'd already taken longer on her errand than she should. She ran back to class, thinking every step of the way.

* * *

That night, when she went to her rooms after supper, she brought Neal and left the door open. "I don't care if you don't like it," Kel told Lalasa sternly. "We're going to show you holds that will help you, um, discourage someone from bothering you." Lalasa stared at Neal, who rubbed the delighted Jump on his belly, as if he were an ogre. "At the very least you'll convince them that you meant no when you said no. Page Nealan?" she asked, prodding her friend with her foot.

Neal looked at her, eyes filled with mischief. Something—something odd—filled Kel's chest for a moment. Why did she feel giddy?

"If this isn't friendship, what is?" he asked cheerfully. "After people abuse my poor body all morning in the courts, I'm going to let you bruise me some more." He offered Kel a large, bony hand. It felt uncommonly warm in hers as she pulled him to his feet. Once he was up, she dropped his hand as if it were a hot brick.

"I won't bruise you much. Quit complaining," she ordered. "Lalasa, stand close so you can see what I do." Lalasa circled Neal as if *she* thought he was a hot brick, until she stood behind Kel. "You won't see a thing if you look at the floor," Kel chided her. "Neal, grab my arm and get ready for pain."

When he obeyed, Kel showed Lalasa several ways to get free. She bent Neal's finger back, dug her nail into the crescent at the base of one of his fingernails, pinched the web between his thumb and forefinger with her nails, thrust a fingernail between the veins and tendons of his wrist, and gripped his hand with both of hers, forcing the thumb or little finger against his palm. She made Lalasa try each defense on her, since the maid refused to touch Neal. They showed Lalasa how to turn an attacker's arm until she forced it up behind his back. Next they demonstrated how to stamp on an enemy's instep when she was seized from behind, as well as eye gouges, nose and throat punches, and even the simple knee to the groin. By the time they had walked the cringing Lalasa through it all, an audience had gathered at Kel's open door.

"Where did you *learn* all that?" Owen breathed, his eyes wide.

"Some I learned at the Yamani court," Kel replied calmly, gulping down a cup of water. "Some Eda Bell taught me this summer."

"I'm going to treat you with the reverence I reserve for the Crown Jewels," Roald assured her, his eyes crinkled with mirth.

"Me too," added Seaver and Merric.

"I'll treat you with reverence once you help me with classwork, O moon of mathematical wisdom," said Cleon lazily. He still addressed Kel by flowery names, not having tired of it yet. "And you, girl, take my advice," he added, pointing at Lalasa. "Just carry a lead-weighted baton. Then you don't have to be fancy."

As Lalasa protested that she couldn't pick up a weapon, the pages headed to the library. Neal went to fetch his books while Kel gathered all she needed to study.

"This isn't the end of it," she told Lalasa firmly. "We're going to practice together till I know you can use any of those things."

"That's what I'm afraid of, miss," Lalasa said, sounding as gloomy as her uncle Gower.

"I'll tell you what the Yamanis told me," said Kel as Freckle and Crown flew onto her shoulders. "Fear is a good thing. It means you're paying attention."

"They sound like wonderful people, I'm sure," replied Lalasa meekly.

Kel looked at her. Was that a tiny smile on the older girl's lips? It was.

Feeling rather pleased with herself, Kel went to join her friends.

Showing Lalasa how to defend herself was fun. Making her practice what she'd been shown was another matter. Kel tried it when she returned that night, and the next morning, and again before bedtime. Lalasa squeaked and cringed, or she treated it as a silly game. While Kel was glad the older girl was comfortable enough to joke, Lalasa's behavior at her lessons was exasperating.

She worked her vexation off in the practice courts. When winter arrived with four mortal days of sleet and freezing rain, Kel thought she might scream with impatience at being kept indoors. Riding was put aside. Not even giants or spidrens would raid villages when they could slip and break something, and the movements of their enemies were the measure Lord Wyldon used to define how and when they trained.

The pages moved to the indoor courts for archery, staff fighting, and unarmed combat. Lord Wyldon introduced the first-years to basic sword fighting while the older pages did more complex exercises. During swordplay Kel's mood improved. Wielding a sword from Peachblossom's back had made her feel even stupider than a first-year, if that was possible. It was nice to know that she hadn't forgotten all she'd learned the year before; she just wasn't good at doing it on horseback yet.

The second night of their forced indoor exercise was also Kel's first time that year to wait on Lord Wyldon at supper. She had to manage it for three nights without mistake. Once that was over, she could relax until Midwinter. Serving Lord Wyldon, with his sharp eyes and cold manner, had to be worse than waiting on any noble or wealthy merchant in the palace banquet hall. So long as she could serve those people without spills, they would pay attention to their food and their companions, not to her. For the first time since she had become a page, Kel began to think she might actually enjoy the seven days of feasting on the holiday.

5

MIDWINTER SERVICE

The afternoon before the feast that started the week-long holiday of Midwinter Festival, Kel checked her appearance in the mirror at least five times. Each time she turned away, she was convinced that her gleaming brown hair had gotten mussed, her crimson hose twisted, her crimson shirt bunched under her gold tunic. Only another look in the mirror would convince her that she was as neat and elegant as a page could be.

In the normal course of things she would have been nervous, but she might have been able to calm herself. But her parents' trip back to the Yamani Islands at the end of the fall had been canceled, and they were asked to remain in Corus to help the new Yamani ambassador. The marriage negotiations for Prince Roald and Princess Chisakami had collapsed that summer when the princess died in an earthquake. Now a new imperial Yamani bride must be found, a new marriage contract drawn up. It had taken three years to forge the treaty that marriage to Chisakami would have sealed; it might take another three years for a new treaty to be worked out. Kel's father had worked on the original agreements, which made him invaluable to the ambassador, who had to draw up new ones.

All this mattered to Kel because it meant that her parents, as well as her sisters Adalia and Oranie, would be in the banquet hall that night. Kel wanted her family to be proud of her; she wanted to give them reason to be proud of her. Over the last summer her sisters had been distant and cool, hard at work turning themselves into proper Tortallan noble maidens and desirable wives. Kel wanted her family to be glad she was of Mindelan.

She was about to check her appearance for a sixth time when a knock sounded on the door. Lalasa opened it to admit Merric, Seaver, Esmond, Neal, and Owen, all in their best uniforms. Jump ran up to them in hopes of a game, then realized that they, like Kel, weren't wearing playing clothes. He sniffed each boy as he wagged a dejected tail, then lay down with a sigh. Like Jump, the sparrows seemed to realize they should not land on their two-legged friends. They found perches around the room and watched, chattering.

"Reporting for inspection, general, sir!" barked Seaver as he gave a brisk salute. The boys promptly formed a line, saluted Kel in turn, then stood at attention. All were nervous, even Owen, who would not work in the public hall but on the kitchen stairs, handing dishes from cooks to servers.

Kel put her hands on her hips. "What is this? You came to me because I'm the girl?" she asked, mock indignant.

"Of course not. You just have an eye for these things," replied Neal.

"When it isn't black," Esmond murmured, and grinned.

"And your maid sews good," said Owen, showing a rip in his sleeve.

"I have a maid who sews *well*," Kel told him. Lalasa found her sewing basket and took out needle and thread.

Kel inspected Merric carefully. He was an inch or two shorter than she was these days, she realized. She tweaked his tunic a little straighter on his shoulders. Seaver's shirt collar was awry; she tugged until it showed brightly above his gold tunic. Esmond's clothes were perfect; Neal's hose had to be adjusted, and Kel gave him one of her drying cloths to blot the sweat from his face.

As Lalasa snipped off the thread she had used to mend Owen's sleeve, Cleon burst in red-faced, his shirt-sleeves untied. "Kel, I can't for the life of me get my hair to lay flat," he began, then saw the other boys. Slowly he grinned.

"They said they're reporting for inspection," Kel explained. Fourteen-year-old Cleon was five inches taller than she; Kel dealt with that by climbing onto a chair. "Grab that basin of water and come here," she ordered him. With a comb and enough water, she got his hair in some kind of order.

"Neal, do you know where the Lioness will be sitting?" she asked as she carefully parted Cleon's damp locks. She couldn't wait to catch a glimpse of her hero, the woman knight who was the King's Champion.

"Nowhere," answered Neal. "They're still not letting her talk to you, so she's still refusing to come to the palace."

"They think she'll magic you into getting a shield," Owen remarked angrily.

"Like Kel needs help," Esmond added.

Does this mean I won't see her till I'm a squire? thought Kel, dismayed and angry. It's not fair!

She fought off her disappointment. At least her friends had faith in her ability to gain a shield on her own. She smiled at all of them as she stepped off the chair. "Well, come on," she urged them. "Let's get going."

The pages reported to the servers' room off the banquet hall, where Master Oakbridge waited. He was the palace master of ceremonies as well as the pages' etiquette teacher, a dried-up, fussy man who lived to arrange banquets and decree who preceded whom in processions. Once all of the pages had arrived, he gave them a careful going-over, criticizing and correcting. Only when that was over did he show them the plan of the banquet hall, drawn in chalk on a black slate six feet tall.

They memorized their positions. Kel's post was at the back of the hall, waiting on members of the minor guilds. That suited her perfectly. She didn't want a place where important people would take notice of her, such as the great nobles or the monarchs.

Suddenly the pages heard the royal fanfare: the king and queen had taken their places. Kel and the other servers gathered finger bowls and towels.

"Now," said Master Oakbridge.

Kel walked briskly to her post, taking in as much of the dazzling scene around her as she could. The heavy smells of pine and frankincense drifted in the air. The walls and ceiling were draped in pine branches and freshly cleaned banners. Thousands of candles burned in the huge chandeliers overhead, their light reflected by crystal lusters, the guests' gems, and the mirror-polished armor of the men of the King's Own, who stood in niches along the wall. A glance upward showed her galleries on three sides. On one of these the musicians played, as they would throughout the meal. The others were filled with people who had come to watch the spectacle of the feast.

She waited until she was directly across the hall from the monarchs before she peeked at them. At this distance it was hard to see their features, apart from the king's black beard and the queen's scarlet mouth. Like the guests, they blazed with color, the king in sapphire blue trimmed with silver, the queen in crimson trimmed in gold. Both wore delicate gold crowns glinting with gems on their black hair.

She reached the table where she was to serve, exactly where it had been marked on Oakbridge's slate. There she presented the finger bowl to each of five guild notables and their wives as they rinsed their hands and toweled them dry. On her way to fetch the first course, she looked for people she knew.

Sir Myles, the pages' teacher in history and law and, according to Neal, the king's spymaster, sat with an elegant woman whose dark hair was streaked with gray. From the way he looked at her and kissed her fingers, Kel hoped she was his wife, Eleni. Daine was deep in talk with Lindhall Reed, another of the pages' teachers. Daine's lover, Numair Salmalín, sat closer to the monarchs, beside a Yamani delegate. Neal's father, Duke Baird of Queenscove, sat beside a Yamani man whom Kel recognized as one of the emperor's healers. The green-eyed brunette on Baird's other side had to be Neal's mother; Neal had the look of both his parents. Kel saw her parents, who sat with the Yamani ambassador and his wife, on the king's right hand.

She reached the servers' door. Owen waited for her, his round face pale as he offered Kel the plate with the first meat course. Kel passed him the finger bowl with one hand and took the plate with the other, while Owen lifted the towel from her arm. "Don't look so tense," she murmured. "It'll be over before you know it."

"Not if I kill Master Oakbridge it won't," he replied. "What a fuss pot!"

Kel smiled. "I think it's been tried before, without success."

As Kel returned to her guildsmen, her mother caught her eye. Ilane smiled and waved slightly. Kel's father did the same. Her parents were pleased! Kel replied with the tiniest of bows, then hurried to her table.

Trouble developed as she went for the second fish course. Turning away from Owen, she saw a page across the hall, talking to the people she was serving. She couldn't see who it was. As she returned to her post, the other page moved away. Something about the way he walked told her it was Quinden, a second-year who was a friend of Joren's.

She had given the second fish course to three guests when the man who represented the Lamplighters' Guild leaned forward and said, "Is it true? You're the girl?"

Kel looked down. Her new breasts were invisible under her roomy shirt and tunic. She bowed and said, "It's true, sir."

"It's not decent," the man's wife said huffily, her eyes filled with dislike. "One girl, and all those boys."

"My advice to you, lass, is to go home and hope your parents can make a proper marriage for you," the oldest of the guildfolk informed her. "Ladies have no place bearing arms."

Kel bowed, her face like stone. She wouldn't let them see that her feelings were hurt.

"And tell the master of ceremonies we wish to be served by another," one of the other guildwives said.

Kel bowed again. On her way back to Master Oakbridge, she kept her chin up, though her hands trembled on the tray. Furious thoughts swirled through her brain. Chief among them was that she owed Quinden a pummeling. Now she knew why he'd been at her table: he'd told those merchants exactly who she was.

"What?!" cried Master Oakbridge when she told him. "This is impossible! I have no spare pages! Only the first-years and they haven't a whit of grace…Mithros, I appeal to you," he said, raising eyes and hands to the ceiling. Then he sought out a victim. "Prosper of Tameran, take Keladry's place. If those vulgar busybodies attempt to discuss her with you, keep silent, understand?"

Prosper nodded and shed the apron he'd worn over his uniform. Owen silently handed the next dish to him, with a look on his face as if his favorite dog had died.

"Take over for Prosper, Keladry," Master Oakbridge instructed. "I will assign you a new place tomorrow night."

Kel accepted a platter of meat—pork roasted in honey, apples, and cinnamon, from the smell—to hand to a serving page. Several of them, including Neal, were converging on her from the hall. Kel thought, He's so graceful. Handsome, too.

Why she noticed such things these days mystified her. Last year an approving look from his lively green eyes hadn't made her skin prickle with goosebumps. Was this more womanly stuff, like her growing breasts? she wondered as five pages came at her at once. She stepped just enough to the side that she could hand the plate to Neal first. His hands closed on it; he grinned at her and drew the plate away—and suddenly he was falling. Sauce flew everywhere as he hit the ground.

Kel stared at him. How could he fall? He wasn't clumsy; the floor was dry. The pages who had walked with him reached to help Neal up. The front of his tunic dripped sauce and grease; his shirt and hose, no less crimson than his face, were ruined as well. Kel eyed the other boys around him. Prince Roald had spots on his hose; so did the two third-year pages in that small group. The fifth boy was Garvey. He smirked at her and Neal alike, no spots whatsoever on his clothes. He had gotten out of the way in time, which argued that he knew that Neal would fall, because he had tripped him.

Master Oakbridge clutched his temples and demanded basins of cold water and napkins, so Roald and the two third-years could wipe the spots from their hose.

Garvey took a platter from Teron of Blythdin and returned to the banquet hall.

Master Oakbridge pointed to Teron. "You—take Nealan's station!" he barked. "Nealan, put an apron on and take his place!"

Neal, beet red with humiliation, did as he was told. Kel battled to put her fury with Garvey from her mind, trying vainly to imagine herself as a calm lake. During the third meat course, someone jostled Seaver from behind, making him spill wine on the head of the royal university. In the jam of boys in the serving area, someone hit Owen with an elbow, hard enough to bruise his eye. The young ladies waited on by Faleron whispered and giggled when he brought their food, as if they knew something ridiculous about him. No one had seen if another page had spoken with them, but Faleron told Kel they'd acted perfectly all right during the first two courses.

Now Kel knew why Joren and his cronies had been quiet for weeks. They had planned to embarrass Kel and her friends in the most public way possible. From her quick conversations with her friends, Kel learned they didn't suspect a plot—they blamed it all on bad luck. Serving at banquets was always a mess. This king and queen dined in state rarely, which meant the pages didn't get much experience waiting on people.

By the end of the evening, Master Oakbridge could hardly bring himself to look at his charges. Only when the diners had left and the last empty plates had been given to the servants did he speak to them. "You will all report to my classroom after lunch tomorrow. It seems you require practice."

*   *   *

The second night of the festival, Kel was sent to wait on a table of young, unmarried court ladies. She approached warily: this was the group that had made Faleron so uncomfortable. Kel stopped at the first lady's left hand. "If my lady pleases?" she murmured, offering the finger bowl.

The very fashionable damsel turned. It was Kel's seventeen-year-old sister Adalia, elegant in a gown of leaf green and a gold brocade surcoat with green silk trim. Like many other court ladies, she wore her hair in the pinned-up tumble of curls made fashionable by Queen Thayet. The barest touches of lip color and powder, another royal fashion, warmed her pale skin. Her eyes widened in dismay. "Kel!" she hissed, keeping her voice low. "What are you doing here? Where's the boy we had last night?"

Kel tried to smile, but something in Adie's eyes worried her. "Master Oakbridge had to change the serving order around," she replied softly.

The girl in an amber-colored gown next to her was sixteen-year-old Oranie, the second of Kel's sisters at court that year. "Why didn't you tell him to put you someplace else?" whispered Orie. "*Any*place else?"

"We aren't allowed to turn down assignments," Kel said, keeping her face bland as she offered the finger bowl. Adie rinsed her fingers with quick, nervous movements and quickly dried them. Her face was Yamani-calm, though her movements were not. "What's the problem?" Kel asked.

"The problem," Orie said tightly as she rinsed her own hands, "is that the Nonds are interested in Adie for their second son. Old Lady Florzile is here tonight to look her over." A jerk of Orie's head indicated an old woman dressed in an old-fashioned black gown seated across the room from them. "If she sees us on friendly terms with you, she might well change her mind!" She was so tense that the gold beads that trimmed her brown velvet surcoat trembled.

"We told her we hardly know you, you're so much younger," Adie explained. "She's a conservative, and as rude as a Scanran. She told Papa that girls had no business in combat, ever. You know Papa—he hemmed and gave some diplomatic not-answer. She said she was only interested in me because she was assured I was a proper damsel."

The girl seated next to Oranie leaned over her and inspected Kel from top to toe. "So this is your page sister?" she inquired lazily, and snickered. "Yes, I can see why she isn't concerning herself with marriage—unless she were to marry an ox."

"And I can see why you're still unbetrothed at nineteen, big dowry and all, Doanna of Fenrigh," said the young lady seated next to her. She wore her masses of crinkled black hair pinned under a gold net at the back of her head. Her delicate pink gown, set off by a white velvet surcoat, gave her creamy skin a rosy glow. "Your tongue has cut all your suitors away."

Kel's heart warmed as her sisters looked at the girl in pink and smiled. Moving down the line of young ladies, Kel offered the bowl to Doanna of Fenrigh without looking at her. Doanna hurriedly dipped her fingers and dried them, splashing Kel's tunic as she did so. Kel then offered the bowl to her defender.

The girl rinsed and dried her hands. "I'm Uline of

Hannalof," she murmured as Kel offered the bowl to the girl on her right. "I'm glad to meet you, Keladry."

Kel hid a smile. Once the remaining damsels at the table had used the bowl, Kel stopped behind Uline and whispered, "Thank you" before she returned to the serving area.

When she came back with the first meat course, Doanna looked at her as if she carried a platter of poisons, not venison. "Inform Master Oakbridge that I require another server," she said haughtily. "A male, not an under-bred female who claims to be noble."

Adie and Orie gave the older girl a look that promised trouble. Kel almost felt sorry for Doanna—her older sisters could be quite inventive when it came to revenge. For her own part she could only say, "I'll tell him when you are served, my lady." She resisted the urge to drop a slice of venison on Doanna's silk-clad lap.

Uline smiled up at her as Kel placed venison on her plate. "Forgive Lady Doanna," she said, her voice carrying to the other damsels at the table. "Her mother's family is in trade, and too often Doanna has a shopkeeper's turn of mind."

"Thank you, my lady," Kel replied, glad that Uline had chosen to be on her side. To Adie she whispered as she left, "I hope this Nond boy is worth it."

Adie gave her the tiniest of smiles. "He is, even if the old lady isn't."

When Kel gave Master Oakbridge her tidings, he sighed and looked around frantically. Already Cleon had taken someone's place among the first-years: fish scales added glitter to his gold tunic, and his face was white and set with humiliation. "Jesslaw!" barked Master Oakbridge.

Owen's plump cheeks went as pale as Cleon's. With the air of a boy going to his doom, he came over. He quailed when the master of ceremonies ordered him to serve Kel's group. "Does it have to be girls?" he asked plaintively. "I'm scared of girls."

"You're not scared of me," said Kel, giving him a playful shove.

"But you're practically as good as a fellow, and you don't giggle," objected her friend. "I'd rather scrub pots if it's all the same, Master Oakbridge."

The man grabbed a plate of fish and thrust it into Owen's hands. "Go!" he ordered.

Owen went as Kel took his place in the serving line. Another first-year was sent out when Esmond of Nicoline, caught in a knot of pages and acrobats who were leaving the hall, collided with an armored warrior. The clatter was bad enough, but the man was caught off-guard. He stumbled from his niche and fell over the hapless Esmond, knocking the wind from the boy. Then it was Owen's turn to be replaced when someone—he wasn't sure who—spilled hot soup down his back.

"We still appear to have lessons to learn," Master Oakbridge told the pages grimly before he dismissed them. "My classroom, directly after lunch."

After the banquet the pages ate in silence. Kel was wondering if she could sleep right on the table when Merric growled, "I've had enough! I'm calling Joren out!"

Kel grabbed him as he began to rise. "No," she said flatly. "We are not going to brawl over Midwinter, not one of us!"

"Why not?" hissed Owen. "They started it!"

"It's wrong!" replied Kel. "If we pick a fight, then we're just as bad as them. Combat should be used just to help people who can't defend themselves, period."

"Well, if I don't fight back and they pound on me, then I'm one of the people I should be defending," said Esmond.

Kel, still holding Merric, looked at her freckled year-mate. "Did that even make sense?" she asked Esmond.

He smiled crookedly. "We have to stand up to them, Kel. Otherwise they'll keep doing this to us," he said.

"It's not just that," Roald pointed out. "Midwinter is tiring enough without more etiquette training. They're making it hard for everybody."

"Perhaps you could exercise royal authority—?" suggested Neal carefully. Roald looked down, his mouth tight.

"You know he hates to call on royal privilege," Kel told Neal sternly. "He's trying to be the same as we are." The look of gratitude the prince gave her warmed Kel's heart.

"We still should do something," growled Esmond. "I've never been so humiliated in my life. And that man was heavy." He rubbed his ribs. "I'd like to dump plate armor on them. See how they like it," he added, glaring at Joren and his friends on the other side of the mess hall.

Kel looked at the table, thinking. "All right. They gave up hazing the first-years because there got to be too many of us to fight," she pointed out. "Maybe we should do something like that to make them back off."

"How?" demanded Merric, relaxing in her grip at last.

Kel let go, now that he'd cooled down. "I bet we aren't the only ones who'd want to rest instead of practice bows and serving."

Neal leaned back until he could poke the closest page at the next table. "Hey, Yance!" he whispered. Yancen of Irenroha turned to face him. "Looking forward to more banquet service lessons tomorrow?"

"You do it," whispered Neal as the last pages finished their meal. Joren and his group were still talking eagerly at their table, heads close together.

Kel stared at him, shocked. "I can't!" she replied softly. "I'm just a second-year—I'm not senior enough!"

"All right," said Prince Roald. "Cleon and I are fourth-years, Faleron's third, and Neal's sixteen. We appoint you to speak for us, and we will back you."

Kel met his level blue eyes and saw the prince's mind was made up. He did not like to put himself forward—he seemed to think people would accuse him of abusing his station if he did—but he was every bit as stubborn as his famous parents. Looking at her circle of friends, seeing the same expression on their faces, Kel thought, I guess stubbornness is catching.

She put her dishes away first. The other pages who did not belong to Joren's clique followed suit. Then she walked over to Joren's table with the prince, Neal, and Cleon at her back and the others following them. Standing behind Joren, Kel waited, hands on hips, until he and the others realized they had company and looked at her.

When she was sure that she had everyone's attention, Kel said, "We've had enough accidents and extra hours with Master Oakbridge. It's got to stop."

Joren locked his blue eyes on Kel. Framed in long blond lashes, those eyes were very cold. He remained silent.

Vinson smirked. "Says who?" he demanded.

The rest of the pages closed in around them. "So say we all," replied Kel.

"See here, you lot." Balduin of Disart belonged to neither Joren's group nor Kel's. Though only a third-year, he was fourteen, having started his training at eleven, and he was big. His shoulders were broader than Cleon's; he topped Cleon by an inch. When he leaned in so Joren could see him, the smaller pages in front of him got out of the way. "I figured, if you wanted to waste time and strength on idiot squabbles with her and her friends, well, you were the ones who'd have to find more strength for the practice courts. But now you've let it cut into our free time. It seems to some of us that maybe she's had the right of it all along."

"Any more accidents, and we'll see if we can't make a few of our own happen," said one of the fourth-years. "Something painful and lasting."

"Are you quite finished?" asked Joren quietly.

"No more accidents," said the prince.

"No more accidents," chorused the pages who stood around the table with him.

"Something harsh befalls the next one who causes things," promised Balduin.

"Make sure you can lock your doors and windows," added a fourth-year.

The room went still. The pages who stood remained in their places, watching Joren and the others for some sign. Kel finally got tired of waiting. She leaned in until scant inches separated her nose from Joren's. "Are you hearing us now?" she asked softly.

He blinked, then raised his hand to cover a fake-looking yawn. "I'm too tired to do anything but what my teachers order me," he said at last. "And you are just too rough-and-tumble to bear. We shall stop, but only because we are bored."

They would get nothing further, Kel knew. She moved out of Joren's way, allowing him to rise and go. The other pages streamed out the mess hall doors, many lost to a storm of very real yawns.

It isn't over, Kel thought as she bid her friends good night. We're just forcing them to be sneaky. And Joren... She sighed as she fitted her key to the lock on her door. I don't know if he'll ever stop with me.

On the third night of the holiday, Master Oakbridge found a place for Kel that no one contested. Although by the strictest terms of protocol a second-year page was not senior enough for the duty, Master Oakbridge set her to wait on the archpriestess of the Great Mother Goddess. That old, formidable lady sat with Eda Bell and Hakuin Seastone, the two Shang warriors, and Harailt of Aili, the round-faced and cheerful head of the royal university. Every moment that Kel attended them she was terrified she would do something wrong, but the Shangs made it clear she had their confidence. They kept the old woman and Master Harailt busy. Kel was able to serve and slip away like a ghost.

Neal got her old place with the damsels. "Your sisters are well enough," he said when he sat down to supper with Kel. "But Uline of Hannalof—isn't she a beauty? And kind, too. She asked how you were. She has the prettiest voice…" The rapt look in his eyes was the same as when he'd spoken of his hopeless love for Daine. "Skin like porcelain. And she's reading *Ethical Contrasts of the North and South*. I told you about it—I read parts of it to you last year." He often shared his philosophical books with his friends, who ignored him. "Too bad I couldn't really discuss it with her."

Listening to him, Kel felt her heart sink. "Sounds like you're in love," she commented softly, too tired to eat. "And I believe she isn't even betrothed."

Neal coughed nervously. "It's too early for me to think of such things. It's improper for a page to court anyone. You did like her, didn't you?" he asked, suddenly anxious. "You know I value your opinion, except on philosophy."

Kel made herself smile, though her heart was sinking. What's the matter with me? she wondered, vexed with herself. It's not like I'm in love with him.

Or that he'd ever look at you twice if you were, her sharp-voiced self retorted.

"That's because the philosophy you read me is silly," she told him, trying to sound as boyish as possible. "And yes, Lady Uline is very kind." She's also the sort of girl boys fall in love with, she thought, putting her dishes on her tray. A part of her—the stupid part, she thought crossly—that wanted him to be happy added, "She is very pretty."

"I think of her as luminescent," Neal said, dreamy-eyed. "When the candle light falls on her, she makes the light part of herself, and returns it."

"I'm off," said Kel. "Don't be up too late dreaming." Thoroughly depressed, she returned her tray to the servers and trudged back to her room.

The fourth day of the festival arrived, the time when gifts were exchanged. Remembering that she'd never gotten to the city's markets the year before, Kel had done all her Midwinter shopping over the summer. The only other people she had needed gifts for were Lalasa, who got the customary silver coin for her service, and Owen. He was easy: Kel gave him one of her razor-sharp Yamani throwing stars. Jump got a meaty bone Kel had bargained out of the palace butcher, while her sparrows got dried fruit.

While Kel practiced with her glaive, Lalasa went to fetch gifts left for Kel with Salma. Her uncle Gower returned with her, carrying a large box. It bore the same canvas wrap and plain label as other packages from Kel's unknown benefactor.

When Kel took the package, she nearly dropped it. The thing was heavy. Unwrapping it, she found a rectangular wooden box, beautifully made and polished, with leather carry straps at each end. Burned deep into the top was the legend, "Raven Armory: Serving Tortall's Finest."

Her jaw dropped. Everyone knew of Raven Armory. Boys who stood well enough in Lord Wyldon's graces to have time off in Corus always went to see what the realm's finest armory offered. Few could afford Raven goods unless the item was small, like Zahir's blade-polishing cloth, or the knife Neal wore hidden in his belt buckle.

Kel opened the box. Like any armory, Raven carried supplies for the care of weapons and leather. Inside the box lay polishing cloths; the armory's prized polishing compound, guaranteed to scour away the tiniest flecks of rust or scratches; rust-proofing oil; an oil to preserve and soften leather fittings; sharpening stones in three sizes;

and a bag of sand for cleaning chain mail. It was perfect for a second-year page.

"Who is it?" Kel whispered, staring at the box's contents. Her lips were trembling. In a moment, she knew, she would start to cry, and that was no good. She took a deep breath and held it, staring at the ceiling until she had her feelings—doubt, gratitude, wonder, confusion—under control. "Who sends me these things?"

"Someone who likes you, Page Keladry," said Gower in his usual glum way. "The joys of the season to you, my lady." He bowed and left.

Kel turned to Lalasa. "Has he always been so gloomy?"

The girl looked genuinely startled. "Gloomy? Uncle's in a wonderful mood."

Kel blinked. "A good mood," she repeated, just to be sure she had it right.

"Oh, yes," Lalasa replied, nodding vigorously. "He likes you."

Kel opened her mouth, about to repeat what the older girl had said, and thought the better of it. "I don't know why," she murmured, baffled. "Any more than I know why whoever sends me these things likes me."

"There's plenty of reasons to like you, my lady."

This time, when she stared at Lalasa, the maid kept her eyes lowered. "Thank you," Kel said at last. "I don't mean to sound ungrateful—I just don't understand." She laid her hands on either side of that wonderful box. "Mithros's blessings attend you, whoever you are," she said. "One day I should really like to thank you in person."

Late Winter–Early Spring
454

6

MORE CHANGES

For the new year Lord Wyldon added two more weights to the senior pages' harnesses. For a week or so Kel felt as if she were trying to fight through clinging mud. Her body then adjusted to the added weight.

Lord Wyldon took them on a winter camping trip in February, which made no one happy. Only the first-years were foolish enough to let him hear their complaints. He gave them a blistering lecture about how knights weren't able to choose the conditions under which they traveled, while Kel and the other pages tried to pretend they were invisible.

Neal continued to sigh after Uline of Hannalof. Kel listened, and made soothing noises, and bit her tongue when she wanted to point out that he had said many of the same things about Daine the year before. One night after the pages were supposed to be in bed, she joined their other friends outside Neal's window. They caterwauled the soppiest love ballad they knew while Jump howled accompaniment. When Neal threw open the shutters, only the hapless Cleon was too slow to avoid a bath as Neal dumped a water basin on him. For weeks after that, all one of them had to do was to hum part of that song, and the others would start to grin.

Spring came just as everyone was giving up hope. Even the forlorn tree in Kel's courtyard thrust out a crown of leaves. The sparrows abandoned her room for the outside once more, setting tiny nests in the eaves around the courtyard. Jump proved to have a dismaying love of rolling in the mud. No matter how thickly he coated himself, Lalasa bathed him patiently until he was white again.

To Kel this spring smelled of promise. The big and little examinations were coming; she would be free of Joren, Vinson, Garvey, and Zahir. Sadly she would also lose Prince Roald and Cleon. Knights were already walking the pages' wing, inspecting the fourth-years as possible squires. Most would be gone into service by the time the junior pages left for summer training. A handful always stayed until fall, when knights in the field could return and choose a squire.

Kel tried not to think about that. When she did, she had to wonder what knight would be mad enough to take her into his service. Her dream had been to act as the Lioness's squire, but she saw now that might not be wise. It seemed people still thought the Lioness might give Kel magical aid. Did this mean Lady Alanna would not be able to make Kel her squire for the same reason?

Worse, if she couldn't or wouldn't take Kel, who would?

She put it from her mind. The big examinations were two years away. She had a lot of work to do before then, and worrying about things she had no control over would just drain her strength. She concentrated on studies, on exercises, and on fighting her powerful new feelings for Neal. Feelings, she learned, were hard to fight. She treasured his smiles and compliments and tried not to dwell on the fact that he gave these things to his friend Kel. His dreamy-eyed gazes, poems, and fits of passionate melancholy were for Uline. It was hard not to resent the older girl.

Even as she wrestled with strange new emotions, though, Kel recognized some facts. Uline hadn't the slightest idea of Neal's feelings. The poems stayed in his desk, the gazes and melancholies in the pages' wing. When Kel urged Neal to send Uline a poem, he refused. "I'll enjoy my crush in private, thanks all the same," he told her ruefully. "I prefer that to finding out she and her friends giggle over my poor verses."

"I don't understand," Kel confided to Lalasa the April night before the little examinations. "If he loves her, why doesn't he *do* something? To her he's just another pair of scarlet arms and legs in a gold tunic. She'll never love him if he doesn't make himself known to her."

"Perhaps Master Neal just likes being in love," Lalasa remarked, snipping off a thread. She was letting down Kel's tunics again. "If he puts himself forward and she rejects him, he'll feel the fool."

"I'd do something," grumbled Kel, practicing a headstand. "I'd *make* her fall in love with me."

Lalasa smiled. "Would you, my lady? And what of your own feelings for Master Neal?" She shook out the tunic. "Let's see how this fits."

Kel obeyed, red-faced. Lalasa was right. It was easy to say she'd make Uline love her if she were Neal, but when it came to herself, Kel was terrified to speak up. She would hate it if Neal were no longer comfortable with her. Better to be a coward and still be his friend.

She went to bed with those comforting thoughts. In the morning came the little examinations, when first-, second-, and third-year pages were tested before an audience on the last year's learning and skills. The exams were not considered serious, except to the pages who had to take them. What they did was ready the pages for the big examinations at the end of their fourth year. Those were more difficult tests conducted before a very large audience. The practice had been started fifteen years earlier by King Jonathan's father, in the last year of his reign. With people wondering if Alanna the Lioness had cheated to win her shield, King Roald had wanted to ensure that anyone could see for himself that fourth-year pages knew their work and were fit to be squires.

That night, Kel dreamed of going to the platform to answer the judges' questions, only to find that she was naked. It left her grumpy. She skimped on morning exercises, washed and dressed, fed the birds and Jump, then made her way to the mess hall. Like Kel, her friends were nearly silent over breakfast.

Halfway through the meal, she felt a trickle of wetness in her loincloth. What on *earth?* she thought, appalled. She was too old to wet herself like a baby. Besides, the lit-

tle exams didn't scare her that much! Crimson with humiliation and trying to hide it, she stood and put the last of
her breakfast onto her tray.

"Where are you going?" Neal mumbled, staring at her
with bleary eyes. "We're to report to the examination
room. We can't be late."

"I won't be late," Kel said tightly, feeling more wetness.
Great Goddess, would it soak through to her hose? "I'll
only take a minute." She handed in her tray and raced
back to her room.

Lalasa was brewing her morning tea on the hearth.
"My lady, what—?" she began, startled, as Kel ran by. Kel
ducked into the dressing room and shut the door.
Hurriedly she undid her points and rolled down her hose.
If she'd wet herself, wouldn't she have noticed a feeling in
her bladder? This had come from *nowhere*...

Blood was on her loincloth and inner thighs. She
stared at it, thinking something dreadful was happening.
Then she remembered several talks she'd had with her
mother. This had to be her monthlies, the bleeding that
told every girl she was ready to have babies if she wanted
them.

"Of all times for it to happen," she muttered, wetting a
cloth in her wash basin and scrubbing herself. "First
these"—she meant her breasts—"now this." She had a dull
ache in her abdomen. Was that normal?

Lalasa opened the dressing room door. Looking at
Kel, she saw the problem immediately. "Do you know
what this means?" she asked, opening a dry-goods chest
and drawing out linen and a fresh loincloth.

Kel nodded, still scrubbing.

"Congratulations," Lalasa said. "You've become a woman. It's the Goddess's mark on us, that we bleed every month. You started early, didn't you? Not even twelve. I was thirteen... Have you cramps?"

Kel frowned. "Cramps?"

"An ache, like." Lalasa patted her abdomen.

Kel nodded.

"Willow tea will help. Here." She showed Kel how to fix a linen pad inside her loincloth, to catch the blood. "We can change that at lunchtime."

"I need clean hose, too," Kel said gloomily.

"You look as happy as you did when I pointed out you needed a breastband," the older girl pointed out, her voice gently teasing.

Kel opened her mouth to reply, then closed it. To her intense shame, tears began to roll down her cheeks. She turned away from Lalasa and buried her face in her hands.

"Here, what's this?" Lalasa turned Kel and pulled her mistress's head down to her shoulder—she was two inches shorter than Kel. "Most girls are happy, you know. Please don't cry. You *never* cry. Not when I would be awash in tears from all those bruises, not when that beastly horse steps on your foot—"

"He doesn't mean it," Kel said into that sensible white cotton shoulder.

"Isn't it just like you to stand up for him?"

Kel drew away. "I hate my body doing new things without telling me," she said wetly, and sniffed. She wiped her eyes on the back of her arm.

"Some get the weeps with monthlies, like cramps," Lalasa explained. "It could be worse. My mama got plain mean right before hers."

"Mine gets hungry for sweets," Kel said, adjusting her loincloth impatiently. It now felt as bulky as a diaper. "She ate a whole cake once."

Someone banged loudly on the outer door. "Kel, come on!" bellowed Neal. "We'll be late!"

"Hose." Lalasa dragged out a fresh pair. "I'll tie one leg if you'll do the other."

"Neal, hold on," Kel shouted. "I have to fix something!" She struggled into both hose, then tied the points on her left side while Lalasa did up the right. Before they were half done Neal banged on the door again. "Go without me!" Kel ordered.

"*No!* Come on!"

Points and hose tied, Kel struggled back into her slippers. "Thank you," she told Lalasa warmly. "I'll have that tea when I get back from the tests." She ran to the door and yanked it open.

Neal stood there, red-faced with impatience, ready to knock again. "About time," he said. They trotted down the hall.

"Why are you in such a tearing hurry?" demanded Kel, stopping in the classroom wing to adjust the hose on one leg. "We'll get there."

"You don't understand," Neal said when they ran on. "If you're even a little bit late, the Stump makes you repeat the last year. He did it to two boys three years ago. And if you're *really* late, you have to repeat *all four years.*

Edmund of Rosemark, a year before we started, was that late. He refused to do four more years and went home."

"Why is he so hard on latecomers?" Kel asked.

"You know the Stump. He says tardiness in a knight costs lives."

"You could have gone without me," Kel reminded him. She stopped him and finger-combed his tumbled hair to lie flat. For a dizzying moment, she thought they were close enough to kiss, and swallowed hard.

Neal destroyed her romantic daydream by straightening her collar in his most businesslike way. "I will *not* repeat even the littlest bit of this happy experiment of ours, if that's all the same to you. And I should think you'd feel the same." They walked into the room together, to join the pages already there.

Neal's worries aside, the tests for second-years were every bit as easy as those for the first-years. First they were asked questions based on their classroom learning. Then they were ushered outside to show they had mastered the best part of a second-year's combat lessons. After Neal hammering at her door and fretting that they might be as much as a step behind Lord Wyldon, it was something of a letdown. The examiners, whom Neal had once described as the oldest, fustiest nobles the king could find to judge the pages, seemed to frown a little deeper when Kel was tested. For all that, they couldn't fault her answers, and she passed, just as the other first-, second-, and third-year pages did.

The next week, she and Neal watched the fourth-year examinations in support of the prince and Cleon. These tests, the big exams, were longer and harder than those given to the third-years, but again it was material the fourth-years were expected to know. Everyone passed.

That night, the fourth-year pages moved to the squires' side of the mess hall, to enthusiastic applause from their fellows. Kel, watching Joren, Vinson, Garvey, and Zahir walk away, heaved an inner sigh of relief. Things would be quieter in the pages' wing, of that she was certain.

More knights visited in May, watching the new squires in the practice courts, eating supper with Lord Wyldon as they looked over prospects. Kel had noticed them the year before, but had not much cared who had come. This year they would take people she knew. Lord Imrah of Legann, a bald, pockmarked man with a hawk's-beak nose and pale, intelligent eyes, chose Prince Roald as his squire, to everyone's surprise. In the past the heir had always served his father; it seemed King Jonathan meant to do this as differently as he did everything else.

Kel also got to see her second oldest brother, Inness, who visited for a few days, before he rode north to the Scanran border. He took Cleon with him. Zahir was chosen as squire by the king. Joren went east with Paxton of Nond. Garvey and Vinson, as well as five other new squires, remained in the palace while Lord Wyldon took the pages out to their summer camp.

Summer
454

7

HILL COUNTRY

*T*he year before, the pages had camped in the Royal Forest. This year the training master took them south and east, into the hilly country that lay between Lake Tirragen and the River Drell. Part of Kel's sparrow company, eighteen birds in all, came along while the rest stayed at the palace. No one raised an eyebrow at the small birds' presence: they had followed Kel the previous summer and had proved useful.

In addition to Sergeant Ezeko, the two Shang warriors, Hakuin Seastone and Eda Bell, rode with them. Kel had the idea that Eda, the Shang Wildcat, was her chaperon, just as she had been the year before. When she mentioned it to the older woman, the Wildcat laughed. "Maybe I just want to get out of the palace for two months," she said. "I'm a hillwoman, you know. Born and raised just south of Malven, till I ran off to the Shangs."

She grinned, showing teeth like small white pearls. "I'm my lord Wyldon's local expert."

On their first morning away, Kel woke at her usual hour, before sunrise. Picking her way among blanketed forms in search of the latrine, she froze. Jump was curled up beside Lord Wyldon. As if he knew she was goggling at him, the dog opened one eye, wagged his tail twice, and closed his eye again. Kel cursed him silently all the way to the latrine. What if Lord Wyldon suspected the dog was a pet, not just a friendly stray? Instead of her glaive exercises she did some of the unarmed combat dances, combinations of punches, kicks, and rolls. They helped her burn off part of her fear that somehow Lord Wyldon would know Jump was hers and take the dog away.

At breakfast Neal was the first of her group to notice Lord Wyldon's companion. He choked.

"Queenscove, what is the matter with you?" asked Eda Bell.

Neal managed to point. "Dog."

Lord Wyldon looked at the companion to whom he'd been feeding strips of bacon. "This fellow's been hanging about the yards for months," he said calmly. "Evidently he's taken a liking to us. With Daine in residence, it seems few animals are shy about expressing themselves."

"Horses too," said Sergeant Ezeko. "Only reason I think my Dragonfly doesn't talk to me is because she thinks I'm not smart enough to understand her."

"I can't believe our dog's toadying to the Stump," Neal whispered to Kel and Owen as they washed dishes. "I thought Jump was better than that."

"I don't know," Kel remarked slowly. "It's hard to hate

anyone who likes dogs as much as my lord does."

"Jump's smart. He knows if Lord Wyldon thinks he came to see *him*, he won't send him back," Owen pointed out. "He would if Jump looked to be following one of us."

Whatever the dog's thoughts, he kept up as easily as the sparrows while the pages and teachers rode south. The trees of the Olorun Valley gave way to broad green fields, then to drier country. The riders skirted the edge of the Great Southern Desert, turning east. The Bazhir lived in the desert and made it their own. In the southeastern hill country, people had warred with the Bazhir for generations. Sometimes they chose to get extra income by raiding into Tusaine and Tyra as well.

"Don't get your hopes up," Lord Wyldon said when the subject of hillmen arose over their third night's campfire. "According to the local army commander, the area we're visiting has been scoured of bandits. You'll have to prove your courage against bears, hill lions, and the like."

They finally made camp just north of a tributary of the Drell, the River Hasteren. By then they'd been riding for ten days and were glad to stop for a while. Kel was particularly careful to look after Peachblossom. The heat was hard on the big gelding, though she couldn't say if it affected his mood. Peachblossom was always grumpy.

They camped by a small pond that was cupped between hills and fed by a lively stream. Last year there had been a wooden building for shelter for the pages and a stable for their mounts, though Kel and Eda had slept in the open. This year everyone either put up tents or slept under open sky. Even those who chose to sleep without shelter had to prove to Lord Wyldon they could set up their tents quickly and well. Kel had three tries before the training master was satisfied. Neal had ten.

"I hate tents," he grumbled as they went to gather firewood. "They smell funny and they weigh too much. I'd rather sleep under a tree."

"You may change your mind when dark comes," replied Kel, amused. "That's when the bugs will realize they don't have to go to the inn to dine."

They remained in that spot for a week. Game was scarce there. Lord Wyldon said he wanted to teach them, not spend teaching hours trying to feed them. They rode for a day and built a new camp.

The next morning Lord Wyldon sent groups out in different directions to map terrain and to hunt for supper, each with a senior page in command. Kel was in Faleron's company, along with Neal, Prosper of Tameran, Merric, Owen, and Seaver. Faleron, Merric, Neal, and Owen carried longbows; Kel and the others brought spears. If worse came to worst, they agreed, they could try spear-fishing in the broad creek they followed. Jump came, sniffing along the ground. The sparrows spread out as humans and dog hiked, looking for new and tasty seeds in the brush.

The creek led them into a small, twisting valley edged on one side by sandstone cliffs. "Oh, Kel, look," piped Owen, "a height my lord hasn't made you climb!"

"From your lips to the gods' ears, silly—hush!" Kel told her friend, cuffing him gently on the shoulder.

"Hush," ordered Faleron. "You want to scare off all the game?"

Being quiet as they headed into the valley saved their lives. Three hundred yards along, when they rounded a bend in the cliff wall, the pages found a raider camp. Had they been making noise, the outlaws would have been ready. As it was, Faleron gestured frantically for the pages to back up, but too late. A mangy dog howled the alarm; Jump snarled in answer. The hillmen, who'd been napping, scrambled to their feet.

"Run!" yelled Faleron.

They were a hundred feet down the valley when they heard the pounding of hooves. The bandits rode into view on ugly, rugged horses who looked every bit as mean as their masters. They swept out and around the pages, cutting off their escape route. Jump raced into the fray. He leaped and fastened his jaws on a rider's arm, his weight pulling the man from the saddle. The horse reared, panicked by its master's fall. Two men swerved to avoid them and collided, going down in a tangle of screaming horses. The sparrows arrived, chattering in rage as they flew into the raiders' faces, attacking their eyes.

"Jump, come!" screamed Kel. "Faleron, orders?"

Faleron stared at the riders; his eyes flicked from those on the right to those on the left, uncertain. Kel turned to Neal as the oldest. He was as bewildered as Faleron. Kel looked at the others. Merric, Seaver, and Owen were staring at her.

They had to act—the hillmen were closing in. "Neal, Prosper!" she yelled, naming the two with magical Gifts. "Blind 'em, hide us, confuse 'em, *now!* Bows! One shot, aim for the horses, then fall behind the spears!"

She got her spear up and leveled it at the enemy as Neal blinked and shed his paralysis. Green fire poured from his hands, spreading in streams through the air. It bent and rippled, veiling the pages enough that the enemy couldn't see them to target them. Prosper, their other mage, stared blankly at his spear. Kel grabbed it and yelled, *"Now!"*

Light flared in front of Prosper, white edged with blue. It would blind anyone looking at him, or the people near him, briefly. *"Bows,"* shouted Kel again as Jump scrambled through the dust to reach her.

Faleron, Merric, and Owen set arrows to their strings and loosed as Kel glanced behind them. There was the cliff wall, just twenty feet to their rear. "Fall back to the cliff, bows and mages first, then spears!" she cried. "Who's got the horn?"

"Me," said Faleron, coughing from the dust. He took a swig from his water bottle, spat, and blew the alarm call, then set another arrow on his bowstring.

Beyond the shifting haze of green and white lights that veiled them, Kel saw the hillmen draw back a little. Four of their number were down, maybe dead—three in the pileup Jump had caused, one with an arrow in his throat. Others were rubbing their eyes, flailing at the attacking sparrows, or squinting as they tried to see the pages' exact location. Most were still mounted, except for one man who'd jumped clear of his arrow-shot horse. All were wary.

A pair of bony and scarred dogs crept forward, bellies to the ground. The magic veils affected them less. Jump snarled a challenge.

"Stay with *me*," Kel ordered him softly. To her unmoving friends she hissed, *"Fall back!* Bows and mages first. Get against the cliff—archers, be ready to shoot!"

This time they obeyed, Faleron pausing only long enough to blow the alarm call again. Kel whispered, "You'll take command?" when he lowered the horn.

Faleron shook his head. "You've got the cool head, Kel," he replied, then fell back with the other archers, Neal, and Prosper. Once they reached the cliff, Kel and Seaver backed up, spears lowered. Spears would keep the bandits at a distance if they chose to ride blindly through the magic; Kel's archers could shoot easily if they were rushed. She doubted the stalemate could last, however. Through fading magic she saw that the hillmen were stringing the bows they had grabbed in the rush. Once they learned the magical barriers couldn't stop arrows, the pages were in trouble.

"Neal and Prosper, magic again. Hold it awhile!" she whispered.

Green streamers rolled out of Neal, growing wider, forming scarves that moved in the air. Prosper again released a white blaze; how he kept the pages from being as blinded as the raiders Kel had no idea. From their lessons in the use of visible magic, she knew that he and Neal had obscured the area around them for about sixty feet. She could see that the squinting raiders had shifted to form a half-circle around them at a distance of about seventy feet. For all the enemy knew, the pages could be anywhere behind that curtain of moving light.

Her brain raced: When would help come? Were they even within hearing distance of the camp? They had lost track of how far they had gone.

"Kel, we're at the cliff!" hissed Owen.

She looked back. Now they had protection at their

backs, but it was not much. Peering through the fiery shields again, Kel counted twenty-three raiders and gnawed her lip. The odds were bad. What she wouldn't give for mages other than a healer and a light bringer! But they were what she had. She didn't like to think how much of Neal's and Prosper's strength was going into those screens.

Luckily for the pages, the raiders had no leader to coordinate their attacks and make them more dangerous. Just as good, they seemed to have no mages.

"Archers, get ready," she said calmly. Now she and Seaver were at the cliff. Beyond the magics she heard the bandits arguing their next move. Somewhere nearby she heard the low growl of the raider dogs and the sparrows' furious chatter. She sent a quick prayer up that her small friends wouldn't get hurt.

Her people needed cover for more than just their backs, *now*, while they had a moment to look for it. She scanned the ground to her left. All that lay between them and the bend in the valley where this had started was tumbles of small rocks lower than her waist.

No help there, she thought grimly. She looked right, beyond Faleron, and blinked. Was that a trail?

Her eyes followed a narrow track as it rose along the cliff face. It looked to be a goat trail, too narrow for horses. About forty-five feet up, she saw a dark opening in the stone—a cave, perhaps, a hollow at least. Something more than they had here. The trail went past the cave, but that wasn't a problem. They could hold both ends of the track from there, even if the raiders came down it from above.

She swallowed hard. To defend it, they would have to get to it. They would have to climb.

Kel was thinking at lightning speed. How to do this? If help didn't come soon, someone would get hurt—the odds were too great. They would need a healer then. Neal had to stop wasting magic to hide them from view.

All her thought came in a moment. "Faleron," she whispered, and pointed to the trail. Everyone looked; Faleron nodded. "Just to that cave. You first, then Neal. Neal, soon as you're there, switch to archery. You're going to need your Gift." He opened his mouth to argue; Kel looked at Merric. "You next, then Seaver, Prosper, then Owen. Archers, cover us. Prosper, ease off the continuous light. When a lot of them move in, give 'em a light-burst, but only then." She glanced at the enemy through the veils of light; she saw three of them venture forward. "Now go! I'll bring up the rear!"

They could see the horsemen who had found the courage to advance through Neal's fading light-veils. Owen coolly shot at one. The arrow lodged in his mount's shoulder and the pain-stricken animal reared, trying to shake off its rider. As the man fought for control, colliding with his neighbors, the pages raced for the trail and began to climb. Prosper held on to his magic as Kel had bid him, waiting for the bandits to approach. Halfway up the slope, first Merric, then Owen, got off fresh shots.

Kel looked at the trail, gulped, then ordered, "Jump, come." She backed up, keeping both spears lowered and ready.

The two raider dogs were closing in, hackles up. Jump snarled, then attacked the bigger dog. "Jump!" Kel cried, running to save him. She felt, rather than saw, the second dog leap for her. Lashing out with the spear's butt, she caught the animal lengthwise, knocking it ten feet into a tumble of stones.

She heard yelling and looked up. Three raiders galloped straight at her, swords raised. Two arrows took the one farthest to the right. Sparrows swirled around the middle bandit, darting at his eyes. He screamed, clapping his hands to his face; without direction, his horse spun, panicked.

Kel focused on the man bearing down on her. She barely noted a fresh light-burst or the arrows shot by the archers on the narrow path, which forced the other bandits to keep back. The enemy coming at her raised a short, curved sword. She saw he would be unable to touch her until he was directly alongside. Kel dropped her extra spear out of her way, making sure she wouldn't trip on it. She brought her other spear point-down by her right calf, holding it in the glaive position broom-sweeps-clean. The hillman was almost on her, just five yards, now two—

She stepped forward, to the right of the charging raider, and brought the spear up in a firm, sweeping movement. The leaf-shaped blade, razor-sharp, cut deep into the man's leg before Kel had to dodge the downward sweep of his sword. The man turned his horse and came back at Kel. This time she drove her spear through his belly, where it lodged. Kel scooped up her other spear just as an arrow streaked over her head. Suddenly she felt a track of numbness, then of sharp pain, as a second arrow grazed her outer thigh.

"Drat," she said, wincing. She yelled, "Jump, come!"

Jump, his foe dead, raced up the narrow path. Kel followed, spear out, as more bandits galloped forward. She was ten feet up when they reached the cliff and saw they could not ride after her. One raised his bow, sighting on Kel with a rotted-tooth grin.

White light blazed around her: Prosper's work. The men at the foot of the trail threw up their hands to shield their eyes. Kel backed up, sweating and trembling over the height, not the graze on her thigh. She couldn't watch her feet, as she did when she had to climb stairs. She had to focus on the men at the bottom of the trail, which meant seeing how narrow the path was, and how far she would fall before she hit the ground. That distance only got larger as she carefully sidled upward.

Two raiders dismounted. They meant to follow: their swords were out, their eyes locked on her. She halted and turned to block the trail. Hands steady, she lowered her spear. Her Yamani training helped her to barely contain her fear of the drop just inches from her right foot. Jump walked between her spread legs to stand before her, growling. His muzzle was crimson with blood, a sight guaranteed to make the men think twice.

Then Kel's sparrows arrived, attacking the foe. The bandits yelled and backed off, trying to protect their faces.

"Jump, go *now*," Kel ordered. The dog ran between her legs and on up the trail. Kel pulled her right foot back from the drop, sweat running down her face. If I don't move, they'll shoot me full of arrows right here, and then I'll *really* fall, she told herself. She turned to sidle up the trail, her back against the rock, her eyes on her feet. Two more bursts of light kept the bandits milling and half blind.

Kel didn't even know she'd reached their refuge until

the boys pulled her inside. The sparrows followed, chattering as they found perches on the pages. Off the path, Kel's head cleared. She looked at her friends. Merric was down, an arrow in his left shoulder. Neal crouched beside him, stopping the flow of blood from the wound with his magic.

"What happened?" she asked Faleron.

"They got him when he shot at the ones that were coming after you," he replied, white-faced.

Neal looked up. "It's missed anything vital—Kel, you're hurt!"

"Stay with Merric," she snapped. "It's just a graze." She went to the front of the cave. Seaver was lookout; he lay flat to peer over the ledge. Prosper was beside him, also staying low. He looked exhausted.

"Let up for a bit, Prosper," Kel told him. "Eat something. And thanks." Prosper nodded and crawled away from the opening. He dug in his belt-purse for the dried meat and fruit Lord Wyldon made them carry when they left the palace.

Keeping under cover, Kel had a look outside. The raiders were working up their courage, arguing as they approached the trail that led to the pages' sanctuary. Kel retreated into the cave, using her dagger to hack strips from the hem of her shirt. When she had enough to make a bandage, she tied it firmly around the graze in her leg. "How many arrows have we got?" she demanded.

The archers counted. The answer was not bad, but not good either. "From now on, pick your shots," she told them. "Think twice before you do shoot. Faleron, did you blow the horn while I was out there?"

He gave her a shaky grin. "Of course. I take it you were thinking of other things."

Kel smiled ruefully. "I believe I was. Crown?"

While Faleron went to the opening and sounded the distress call yet again, the single-spot female sparrow flew over to perch on Kel's hand. There was red on her beak and tiny claws, and a war-like gleam in her round black eyes. "Crown, it may be they can't hear the horn, back at camp," Kel explained. "Will you fetch help?"

Crown peeped. Away she flew, two males and a female with her.

"Next time maybe we should bring paper and ink," suggested Owen. "They could carry messages."

Kel went over to crouch beside Merric and Neal. "All this noise you're making, I can't think," she teased the red-headed boy gently.

Merric smiled tightly at her. Normally pale-skinned, now he was so white that his freckles looked like paint on wax. Sweat rolled down his face. "We're in enough of a spot without me yelling," he said tightly. "Besides, it's not so bad. Neal stopped most of the ouch."

"Can you do more than stop the ouch?" Kel whispered to Neal.

He shook his head, shamefaced. "I don't have the training," he replied.

"But you can heal," she began.

"Within limits. I was to start learning about arrow, knife, and sword wounds this year, if I'd stayed."

Kel shook her head. "You should get proper training!" she said indignantly.

Neal made a face. "When?" he wanted to know. "Most

people either go for knight or for healer, not both."

Kel began to argue, then closed her mouth. The hurt that showed in his eyes for just a moment made her feel like a brute. "Sorry, Neal," she said ruefully.

"That's all right." He smiled crookedly. "Gods know I keep thinking I was crack-brained to leave the university."

"But if you hadn't, I'd be a lot worse off now," Merric reminded him. "I like you where you are, thanks."

Kel gripped Neal's shoulder in another, silent apology, and went back to the entrance. "Why don't you rest in back?" she suggested to Seaver. "I'll spell you for a time." He nodded and passed his bow to her. Kel took his position, lying flat so only the top of her head showed when she peered out. Looking gave her the sweats, but she made herself do it. She had to know if the outlaws would give up, or keep coming. Right now they seemed to be arguing, but a couple looked at the trail as if they were of a mind to climb it.

Go ahead, she thought coldly. You won't get far.

Two did try. Kel shot one man in the collarbone—it was hard to sight from this awkward angle. Owen, who had come to watch beside her, rose on his knees and shot the second man through the eye. An arrow soared over his head just as he lay flat again. As Kel scolded him for making a target of himself, she heard the sound of horses at the gallop. It was the entire company of pages and teachers, armed for battle, with Lord Wyldon in the lead. The raiders fled.

Kel sent the unwounded pages down to Lord Wyldon, then helped the two Shangs improvise a stretcher and lower Merric to the ground. "We can do the same for you," Hakuin offered. "You *are* hurt."

Kel shook her head: she had her pride. "I'll climb down." She let them and Neal go first, however, and sent Jump after them. Only when she stepped onto the path did she realize that by waiting until last she had created an audience for her descent.

She closed her eyes for a moment, trying to think herself stone, then faced the cliff. At least this time she didn't have to negotiate the path while keeping anyone below in view. The worst this audience could do was laugh. She did hear some chuckles as she sidled along, one eye on the ground just ahead of her right foot, her nose as close to the cliff face as she could put it.

At last she was down. Peachblossom and Jump both nuzzled her; the sparrows swirled around her, but did not land. *They* know what's coming, Kel thought weakly. She waved her dog and horse off, then threw up.

When she stood, wiping her mouth on her sleeve, she turned to face a dark dun horse's inquiring eye. "Well, Page Keladry," the dun's rider, Lord Wyldon, said dryly, "now you realize combat isn't woman's work. I hope you've thought better of this experiment of yours, now that you've seen blood."

"Sir, that isn't fair," protested Owen.

Kel closed her eyes, thinking, not for the first time, Why don't I have friends who know when to be silent?

"What is not fair, Owen of Jesslaw?" demanded Lord Wyldon.

Kel tried to signal Owen to hush, but the plump boy's eyes were fixed on the training master. "Sir, you talk like

Kel couldn't handle the fighting. She's the one who saved our bacon. Sir," he added, in case he wasn't sufficiently polite. "She's just sick from the climbing. The fight didn't bother her, even when she killed that man." He pointed to the raider who lay nearby, Kel's spear in his belly.

I wish he hadn't reminded me, Kel thought. She unhooked her canteen from her belt with trembling fingers, unstoppered it, and poured water over her head. She also took a gulp and swilled it around to clean her mouth, then spat it out.

Faleron spoke up. "We might be dead but for Kel, my lord. I froze when they came at us. Kel's the one with the cool head. She found that cave when we all thought we were trapped."

The other members of their hunting party chorused agreement.

Lord Wyldon's mare shifted on her feet, as if she reflected her master's uncertainty. Finally Wyldon said, "We'll take Merric to the army post for treatment and shift our camp there. I want a word with the district commander"—Kel had the feeling that word would not be "blessings"—"and then I expect a report from each of you. Page Keladry?"

"Sir?" she asked, looking at him. It was impossible to tell what he thought; his clean-carved face was emotionless.

"Mount up," Lord Wyldon ordered.

Kel looked at Peachblossom, who wore only a halter. There hadn't been time to saddle him before they left camp, she realized. Wyldon had simply taken the horses of the missing pages to keep them from being stolen while they were away.

She led the gelding to a stone and climbed onto his broad back. "Try not to spill me," she whispered. "You're slippery."

His ears flicked back and forward in acknowledgment. He did seem careful not to dump her as Lord Wyldon gave the command to ride out. He also didn't object as those sparrows who couldn't fit on Kel or Neal settled onto his mane.

Looking at them, Kel recalled how valiantly the birds had fought. Were any hurt or dead? She did a count and sighed with relief. Eighteen sparrows had come south with her. Eighteen rode with them now.

As they rode out of the little valley, Kel realized it was her twelfth birthday. She couldn't help it—she began to laugh. Remembering the man she had killed, she got hold of herself before she started to cry. Hysterics—that's all I need for them to think I've gone completely female, she thought, biting the inside of her cheek until it bled. And what's *wrong* with being hysterical, if no one is hurt by it and it makes you feel better? I'll just wait and have my hysterics where no one will see or hear me.

Owen rode up beside her, keeping a watchful eye on Peachblossom. "Are you all right?" he asked, his gray eyes worried. "It was a jolly fight, except for you and Merric getting hurt and us not knowing if we would die and all."

Kel looked at him for a moment, startled, then shook her head in admiration. "It won't bother you that we left dead men back there."

"Never a bit," he said cheerfully. "They were bandits. I *hate* bandits. They killed my mother. I'm going to be a knight and hunt bandits for real. You could hunt 'em with me," he offered with a generous smile. "With you and me at the job, there won't be a bandit in the country in ten years."

8

MESSAGES

*T*he healer at the army outpost was able to patch Merric up and to teach Neal a few new tricks. Neal had time to master them as the pages spent the remainder of the summer camp at the outpost, housed in one of the barracks. Lord Wyldon made sure that they helped the captain, who had claimed the district was cleared of bandits, to actually do the work. It wasn't as jolly, as Owen put it, as the valley fight. The pages were carefully watched and never allowed to be anything but backup archers and scouts. They were paired with soldiers, who made them keep quiet and out of the way.

Kel agreed with Owen, bandits should be caught and taken before the law. Still, she also saw the poverty in their camps. Only the best fighters owned shirts without holes; their children were naked, hollow-eyed, and big-bellied with hunger. Despite the rivers and lakes in the area, the pages were told, this was the second year of a drought. Farmers who couldn't pay their rent were thrown off their farms. Many thought banditry was the only way to feed their families, but their victims were as poor as they. There were no easy answers, and Kel was glad to ride north and put it out of her mind for the time being.

Whatever Lord Wyldon thought of her taking command in the Battle of the Cliff, as her friends had named it, he kept it to himself. Those who thought they could tease the pages who had let The Girl take over were corrected in a series of quick, quiet fights. Kel told her friends they weren't doing her any favors by settling matters that way; her friends ignored her.

On their arrival in Corus, they disbanded for two months. Kel, Lalasa, and Jump went to Kel's parents' house in the city, which they and the house servants had to themselves. Kel's parents, Adie, and Orie were away on the summer visits paid by nobility, particularly when nobility had daughters to marry off. Kel did get to spend the last two weeks of September with them when they returned. There was no mistaking her parents' pride—Eda Bell, it seemed, had written to tell them what their daughter had done over the summer.

They took Kel to supper at one of the city's finest eating-houses to honor her. Over the meal they got the tale of the fight and its aftermath from Kel, listening intently and embracing her at its end. They also drew the events of Kel's second year from her, asking questions that showed a great deal of interest. She only left out two major occurrences, and those she told her mother as her father left their private parlor to settle the bill.

Ilane smoothed Kel's hair with a gentle hand. "My poor dear! Breasts and monthlies in the same year, and you not even twelve. Was it very upsetting?"

Kel nodded. "I don't *need* 'em, Mama," she pointed out. "I'm not looking to have babies, ever."

"I don't recall the gods ever asking women if we want these things," her mother pointed out.

Kel sighed. "No, I suppose not. How old were you when all that happened?"

"I didn't start monthlies until I was fourteen—the healer told Mama it was because I was such a beanpole. Mama said she wasn't much of a healer." Ilane smiled at the memory. Kel did, too: her grandmother would not let anyone speak ill of her children. "I didn't have much of a bosom until I got pregnant," Ilane went on. "Your sister Patricine, though, she developed at twelve." As Kel's father returned, Ilane added, "Remember—you may be able to do so, but no one can force you to have babies. You do have a choice in these things. I'll get you a charm to ward off pregnancy until you are ready for it."

"Ready for what?" asked Baron Piers, holding the parlor door for his wife and daughter. Kel and Ilane shook their heads, and changed the subject.

After two quiet months in the city, Kel's return to her palace rooms was like coming home. Even though she had visited her sparrows and Peachblossom every day, and trained in the practice courts, it was still good to settle in at the pages' wing. After she and Lalasa finished unpacking, Kel flung herself on the bed with a happy sigh.

"I dread the ruction," Lalasa commented as she

rearranged the animals' food dishes, "but you're glad to be back with all these noisy menfolk, aren't you, my lady?"

"They don't mean any harm," Kel replied without thinking.

"Not this lot," said Lalasa darkly.

Kel sat up. "You'd tell me if anyone bothered you, right?" she demanded.

Lalasa smiled. "What, your crowd? They're as good-hearted a bunch of lads as ever I saw."

At that moment Owen peered in through the open door. "Kel, you're back!" Running down the hall, he yelled, "She's here already!"

A year before, Lalasa would have squeaked and fled to the dressing room. Now she sat in the window seat, laughing softly as she stitched on a shirt.

Owen raced back with two boys, first-years, in tow. "Say, Kel, will my lord let me sponsor my cousins? One of my cousins? This is Iden of Vikison Lake, and Warric of Mandash. They're both my cousins. This is the tremendous girl I told you about, Keladry of Mindelan."

Kel rose and bowed, trying not to grin at Owen's tumbling chatter. When she straightened, she was startled to see his eyes bulge. "Mithros's spear, Kel!" he exclaimed. "When did you turn into a real girl?"

"You said she was a girl already," muttered one of his cousins—was it Iden or Warric? Kel hadn't gotten them straight.

"But not a girl-girl, with a chest and all!" protested Owen.

Kel looked down. That summer Lalasa had talked her into donning lighter shirts than her palace wear. These were still cotton, but thinner, and they draped like silk—as Owen had noticed. "I've been a girl for a while, Owen," Kel informed him.

"I never realized," her too-outspoken friend replied. "It's not like you've got melons or anything, they're just noticeable."

"Master Owen!" Lalasa cried. "Think shame to yourself for saying such things!"

To his cousins Owen said, "That's Lalasa, Kel's maid. She sews, and she knows all kinds of ways to hurt you." To Kel and Lalasa he added, "I wasn't trying to be *rude*."

"You can be rude without trying," Neal drawled from the doorway. "The Stump would penalize you for talking so loud and free." He looked at Kel, his cheeks pink. "It's your own fault for encouraging him when he was a first-year, you know. Now he thinks he's a human being."

Owen threw himself at Neal. They tussled briefly before they found seats. Kel, meanwhile, wished herself at the bottom of the ocean. Of all the subjects she didn't want discussed around Neal, her bosom had to be at the top of the list. She could barely look at him.

"I was thinking maybe I could sponsor Iden and you could sponsor Warric, Kel," Owen suggested, tipping his chair back until it leaned against the wall. Now it was his cousins' turn to blush.

"He never learned tact, Lady Keladry," one of the new boys explained. "His papa—my uncle—he's every bit as bad."

"Then I will stay away from Jesslaw," Neal said firmly. "It must be a madhouse."

"You've no idea," said the other first-year with feeling.

"I'd like to sponsor Warric," Kel said. The boys looked at her. "But I'm not going to. Somebody very wise once said it wouldn't do me much good to be sponsored by someone at the bottom of Lord Wyldon's list." She smiled crookedly at Neal, who had told her that; he nodded soberly. Kel went on, "It's the same here. You'll do better with someone my lord likes."

Boys continued to drop by over the course of the afternoon: Seaver, Esmond, Merric, Faleron (a glorious fourth-year now), Prosper. Yancen of Irenroha even stopped in. Lalasa disappeared, and returned bearing a basket of pastries and a pitcher of juice. The pages welcomed her with cheers. Lads, she told Kel, were *always* hungry.

Once the others had gone to wash up for supper, Kel turned to Lalasa. "There, you see?" she asked. "They aren't so bad after all."

Lalasa's smile had a bitter edge. "They're boys," she replied at last. "I doubt they'll be so sweet when they're men."

"You have to start looking at the bright side of things, Lalasa," Kel told her sternly.

Now Lalasa really did smile. "If I'm with you long enough, my lady, I don't see how I can escape it."

Once cleaned up, the pages joined Lord Wyldon in the hall outside, to choose sponsors for the newcomers. Owen took Iden, as he had threatened. Merric, after a nudge from Kel, picked Warric.

Then came supper, and Lord Wyldon's speech advising all of them to enjoy their last day of freedom. Afterward Kel remembered that her harness was at the leatherworkers still. She'd dropped it off a week before, to have it let out—it had gone tight on her shoulders over the summer. Now was a good time to retrieve it. She might not have another free hour for months.

She was cutting through the palace grounds, the harness over her shoulder, when she saw a nobleman with a sheaf of papers in his hand. He was tall, heavyset, and pale-skinned even at the end of summer, with brown hair that continually flopped into his eyes. Kel recognized Sir Gareth the Younger, the king's closest adviser and friend.

In his turn, he seemed to know her station if not her name. "You're one of the pages, aren't you?" he asked, brown eyes alert.

Kel bowed.

"Wonderful. Take this to the king for me, will you?" He handed over a sheet of paper. "He's scrying at the top of Balor's Needle. Don't be nervous," he added, misunderstanding the look on Kel's face. "He isn't doing anything that can't be interrupted."

Kel bowed again, trying not to show that she was frightened. She had to do it, she realized as he walked away. She was a page; pages ran such errands when requested to.

But the Needle! she thought, wiping sweat from her forehead. She forced herself to turn and walk steadily down the path. Balor's Needle was an architectural marvel, soaring a hundred feet over the palace roofs. Sightseers, mages, and astronomers went there because it lifted them clear of magical residues and ordinary smokes from palace and town, granting them a view of the entire valley where Corus lay. From there mages could scry, or see, places and other mages at a distance; powerful mages could actually speak to their colleagues.

She walked into the courtyard before the tower entrance. There were two ways up. One was an iron outer stair, which twined around the tower on the outside, with no walls to protect the climber. People on dares and would-be suicides went that way. The outer stair was a beautiful thing, decorative iron wrought in lacy shapes and far stronger than it looked. Kel would admire it only at a distance. She went through the open doors in the base and found the inner stair. It was the twin of the one outside, except that it wound in the opposite direction. There was a magical reason for that, something to do with balancing forces, but Kel couldn't remember what it was.

Like the outdoor stair, this one sported only a thin railing between the climber and open space. All of the inner tower was hollow. Light came from an immense candle-and-crystal chandelier fifty feet up: servants changed the candles by lowering it. Kel stared at the chandelier, transfixed, then forced herself to look at the stair.

I can do this, she told herself, folding and re-folding Sir Gareth's message. Of course I can! It's a stair. I'll just keep my eyes on the steps and the wall. It'll be easier than the climb to that cave, when I had to watch those bandits.

For all her brave thoughts, it was the knowledge that this message was for the king that got her moving. Gritting her teeth so hard she could hear them creak, Kel stepped onto the inner stair. Slowly, doggedly, she began to climb.

Like the outer stairs, these were ornamental iron, wrought in the shape of flowers. If she looked down, she saw the gaps in the steps, and open air below. A couple of mistakes showed Kel that her best course was to focus on the corner where stair met wall. When she halted to rest— she was in good shape, but the stair was steep and seemingly endless—she did so with her eyes closed.

After what felt like years, she stepped onto a level wooden floor, blessedly solid underfoot. She walked through open doors and onto a stone platform. The way to the outer stair was an opening in the platform beside the door—Kel looked quickly away from it and wiped sweat from her face. The wind that blustered up here made it feel cold on her skin.

"Yes?" The king had heard her arrive: he left the waist-high railing to walk over to her. "What is it?" As Kel straightened from her bow and the king saw her face, he smiled. "It's Keladry of Mindelan, isn't it? I've been hearing about you, young lady."

Little of it good, I'll bet, Kel thought. She murmured the polite phrase, "Your majesty is kind to remember me."

"Is there a message? Though I see you're not in uniform yet."

"My lord Gareth of Naxen knew me for a page, sire." She handed the message over. The wind whipped at it. The king gripped the paper tightly and called a ball of light from the air so he could read. The sun had just set, and natural light was fading quickly.

Kel looked around. She could stare across distances if she didn't look down. At such times she felt no fear, only appreciation of the beauty before her. Ahead lay the hills that separated the capital from Port Caynn. Still, steady glows of light identified houses and inns. Moving globes would be the lanterns of travelers. Darker masses in the growing twilight were groves of trees and the Royal Forest itself. It was like a tapestry of the land at dusk, if anyone had cared enough about only light and shadow to weave such a thing.

"This could have waited until morning," the king remarked dryly, tucking the paper into his belt-purse. "That's Gary, though—never put off what can be done right now. This is for you," he added, offering a coin to Kel. "For your courtesy. There is no return message."

Kel thanked him and bowed, tucking the coin in her pocket. She turned to go, and stopped. The opening to the outer stair was just a foot to her left. The stair itself fell away so steeply that Kel could see rooftops below. Her ears buzzed; her head swam. She forced herself to take a step, then another, until she passed through the open doors. Inside, the first thing she saw was the great hollow space on the other side of the platform. Dizziness overcame her. She backed up against the wall by the door and clung to it, trying to tear her eyes from the chandelier's streams of light.

This is ridiculous, she told herself repeatedly. You climb up and down trees. You climbed down from the cave. Just look where the stair meets the wall. Stop goggling at the space, look at the wall! You're going to count to three and take a step. One, two, three.

She couldn't take the step. Nothing she thought helped. She could not force herself onto the stair.

She did not know how long she stood there, trembling and sweating, trying to get her courage together. It was too long, she knew, because the thing that broke through her fright was the king saying, "Page Keladry, look at me right now." Firm hands drew her from the wall's protection, turning her until she stared into the king's face. "It's the height, isn't it? Don't be ashamed, my dear, it's perfectly natural. You can't get the queen up here for love or money. Now, listen to me. I can arrange it so your body will take you down without your mind being any the wiser. I don't recommend it—in that state someone else might order you to kill your king—" He grinned, inviting her to share the joke. Kel tried to smile. "In any case," he continued, "I think it's best for you right now, but you must be willing. I swear on the heads of my children that this is the only thing you will do under this spell, and that once you are on the ground, the spell will be gone. Will you accept that? Are you willing?"

Kel squeaked, "Yes, sire."

"Never agree to this from anyone else unless you are sure of them," the king told her.

She nodded.

"If you like, I could have a talisman made which will help you to deal with this fear." He folded his hands and waited for her reply.

Kel swallowed twice—terror had dried her mouth to paper—before she could say, "No, thank you, sire. What if I lost it? I—I am learning how to do this. Truly I am. It's just such a long way down."

The king nodded. "Very well." Blue fire glinted around his fingertips. "You will feel as if you'd lost track for a moment, but you'll be on the ground." He pressed cool fingertips to Kel's forehead.

She blinked, and found herself at the foot of that

impossible stair. She looked up. The king was leaning over the platform rail, checking to see that she had made it down safely.

"Thank you, sire!" she called. He waved and walked back outside.

Kel trudged back to her rooms in a black mood. She had never forgotten that the king had allowed Lord Wyldon to put her on probation. It was the king who had ordered Alanna the Lioness to have nothing to do with Kel. I'm really finished now, she told herself bitterly. Oh, he was nice enough up there, but he'll soon think the better of *that*. He'll go straight to Lord Wyldon and say he was right, I'm not as good as the boys, send me home. I'll never be a squire or a knight—they won't even wait to see if I fail the great examinations!

And I would be a danger. What if I froze like that someday with people in my care? I could get them killed, because I can't control myself.

Thoroughly depressed, she reached the pages' wing and saw that her door was open. She heard her friends' voices. Kel straightened her tunic and tried to rub color into ice-pale cheeks. She wouldn't say anything about this.

Kel waited all night, but no word came from Lord Wyldon. Somehow she got through the next day— helping friends who were sponsors show the first-years around—and the day after that, when training commenced. Fighting practice helped—with four new weights on her harness, she barely had the strength to think about her weapons and her horse, let alone Balor's Needle. She nearly dozed off in afternoon classes.

That night, the king came to supper as he did every

year to look them over and talk to them briefly. He dined with Lord Wyldon on the dais, then urged the pages to pursue their studies and train hard. In years before, he had left the mess hall before the pages could even rise to bow to him. This year he did not. He waited until they were on their feet, then said, "Might I see Keladry of Mindelan? The rest of you may go."

Kel felt her skin go numb. This was it, she realized. She was about to be dismissed. Blindly, leaving her tray on the table, she walked to the dais. Jump followed, tail wagging.

When she reached the dais, Lord Wyldon and the king were seated. Their page—Yancen, Kel noted—had cleared away everything but a pitcher and three cups, which Lord Wyldon was filling. As Kel bowed to the men, the king raised his brows.

"Pages weren't allowed pets in my day," he commented. "Have a seat, Keladry." He waved her to an empty chair. Kel looked at Lord Wyldon, startled.

He gave her the tiniest of nods and told King Jonathan, "The dog's not a pet, sire—he's a palace stray who attached himself to the pages. I see no harm, if he doesn't distract them. He earned his way several times over during the incident I told you of."

While Lord Wyldon talked, Kel eased herself into the empty chair. Surely if they were going to dismiss her, she ought to be standing. Her nervousness grew when Lord Wyldon put one of the cups before her. It contained grape juice with a touch of spice in it, she discovered as she sipped. She had to grip it with both hands to keep the men from seeing that she trembled.

The king was gently tugging Jump's lone ear, a trick the dog loved. "Yes, that incident. Page Keladry, Lord Wyldon told me what passed this summer between your group and the bandits. I would like to hear the story from your own lips, if you would." The king leaned back in his chair, his very blue eyes on Kel's face. "You were a hunting party, I believe?"

"Just as you told it to me," murmured Lord Wyldon.

She didn't disobey, exactly. She did neglect to mention that the older boys had been too surprised to make the instant decisions that would mean their survival. She told it as if they all had agreed on their course of action—which they had, given a moment to think. Of course Lord Wyldon knew differently. They hadn't even thought to check each other's stories until he'd already talked to Faleron and Neal at the army post. Perhaps the king suspected the truth, too, but he said nothing while she spoke of those frenzied moments on the ground, and the scramble to reach and defend the cave until help could arrive.

When she was done, the king shook his head. "Amazing." He bent to scratch Jump's head: the dog had gone to sleep, his chin on the king's foot. "Certainly you earned all the table scraps you can eat for the rest of your life, eh, boy?" Jump's tail beat lazily on the floor. To Kel the king said, "Your parents tell me you saw this kind of thing in the Yamani Islands."

Kel nodded. "Yes, sire. The land's so mountainous that it's impossible to round up all their bandits. Sometimes they think they can attack the emperor's train when he's on progress, and the company gets strung out between valleys. And you know about their problems from the sea. If it isn't Scanra, it's Jindazhen in the west. You almost get used to surprises." Wyldon's brows twitched, and Kel bowed her head. She didn't want the training master to think she was a babbler. "Begging your majesty's pardon."

"Not that the Yamanis would say any of this," replied the king. "They keep their troubles to themselves." He sighed. "A proud people... And you are much like them, Page Keladry. Lord Wyldon tells me you work hard to overcome your fear of heights." Kel was afraid to look up, afraid this was the moment when he sent her away. Instead the king told her, "I admire someone who tries to master something which defeats other people all the time. Keep up the good work."

She knew a dismissal when she heard it—and this was not the dismissal she had expected. In her rush to get to her feet, she almost knocked her chair over. Somehow she managed to bow and leave the mess hall without tripping. Her friends waited outside.

"What did he want?" demanded Neal. "You were in there forever!"

Kel sagged against the wall. "He wanted to hear about the fight, about how we handled those bandits."

"Gods," mumbled Faleron, covering his face.

"I told him how you led us to the cave, and kept blowing the horn for help," Kel said, hoping he wouldn't be offended. "And how Neal and Prosper made it hard to see us, and what we all did in the fight. And he mentioned the Yamanis, and then he told me I could go."

"Better you than me," commented Merric, shaking his

head. "Talking to royalty makes me sweat. We'd better get to that book Master Yayin gave us if we're to read the first chapter by morning."

"There's something I don't understand," remarked Seaver as they headed down the hall. "Why assign a book about a war fought two hundred years ago?" His confusion was understandable. Master Yayin always gave them books that were literature, reports, poetry, or histories in which battles were seldom mentioned. The pages were certain that changes in their teaching were made only for the most sinister motives.

Neal drew to the rear of the pack and pulled Kel aside as the others turned into the pages' wing. Just the touch of his hand made Kel giddy.

"I saw your face when you went up there," he commented softly as he let her go. "You look like you were climbing Executioner's Hill. What did you expect?"

She hadn't told him about her experience with Balor's Needle. She did so now, keeping her voice low.

"Silly!" Neal said with a grin, cuffing her head gently. "The king doesn't think you have to be perfect—*you're* the only one who's dolt enough to expect that!"

"I'd *like* to be perfect," Kel said plaintively as they followed their friends. "It would be nice."

"And so daunting for the rest of us, trust me," Neal assured her. "So why do *you* think we've been assigned a book about old battles?"

"You mean there has to be a reason for the masters to give us hard work?" she retorted. "I thought that was their idea of fun."

Yayin's change to the kind of reading that Owen classified as "jolly" was not the only difference in how they were taught that fall. The next evening, as the pages and a handful of squires finished supper, Lord Wyldon stepped up to the podium.

"I would like to announce a change in our present schedule. Sunday nights, during the first bell after supper, I wish the fourth-year pages to report here. We will explore combat tactics—how to use ground to your advantage in the positioning of troops, which types of weapon achieve certain effects in battle, and so on." He held up a hand; the pages stifled their groans. "This is not a course on which you will receive marks; it is required only for the fourth-years, though any other pages or even squires who wish to attend will be welcome. Sunday evening, the first bell after supper. You are dismissed."

"As if we *needed* more studies," Seaver grumbled to Prosper.

Neal ran his fingers through his hair, thinking. "Well?" Kel asked him. "I want to go, at least to see what it's like."

"I think I'd like to go, too," he replied, surprising her. "I wonder why they're doing this? Usually they leave that kind of teaching for knight-masters and squires. Of course, the army has an actual school for officers, to teach battle tactics and strategy."

"Tactics *and* strategy? I thought they were the same thing," Kel commented.

Neal shook his head, a comma of hair flipping into his eyes. Kel longed to touch it but kept her hands locked behind her.

"Tactics, my dear girl, is what you did with those bandits. It's immediate planning for the immediate problem.

Strategy is the long view, the movement of armies and a plan that covers an entire battle or war." Seeing her inquiring look, Neal grinned, shamefaced. "My mother's father was one of old King Jasson's generals. He used to tell me about their battles, and all the things that went wrong."

Owen drifted back to walk with them. "Things go wrong?" he asked, startled.

"Grandfather Emry said once the battle starts, *everything* goes wrong," Neal told him. "You plan strategy and tactics ahead so they won't go as wrong as they could."

"Your grandfather was Emry of Haryse?" cried Owen, delighted. "He's a hero!"

"Yes," Neal said dryly, making a face, "I know."

Sunday night came. Faleron attended the new class—as a fourth-year he had to. Neal, Kel, Owen, Merric, and Esmond went out of curiosity. They found something totally different from their other lessons. Lord Wyldon had servants set up a model on a table: it showed the city of Port Legann during the climactic battle of the Immortals War. Metal figures shaped like soldiers, knights, immortals, ships, and catapults were placed to show the positions of each. Daine and the king were there, too. They explained how troops were employed, and asked the pages to suggest why certain types of soldiery had been put in one spot and not another. They learned that Daine had seen the area around the city, mapping enemy positions from dragonback. The thought of flying made Kel feel sick, but she could see that Daine's work had given the Tortallans a tremendous advantage.

The next bell rang too soon. Some pages complained and would have stayed, but Lord Wyldon asked them if they had completed their classwork. By then enough assignments had gone half-done that only Neal had no extra work; they were sent back to their rooms to study.

"Boring," announced Merric with a yawn as they left the mess hall. "I can put the time to better use." Kel shook her head. How could anyone describe the lesson as boring? She would have been happy if it had gone on all night.

Kel was still preoccupied by the battle of Port Legann during her dawn exercise with Lalasa. Would it have been different if relief forces from the Copper Isles had beat the queen's army to the city? Kel let her maid grab her wrist as she tried to see it in her mind. The next thing she knew, she was flying through the air. Only a quick twist saved her from slamming into the door full-force.

Lalasa gasped and knelt beside Kel in a panic. "My lady, I'm sorry, I'm sorry!" she cried. "I never meant it! My lady, I swear, I'll never do such a thing again, only don't dismiss me!" She covered her face with her hands and wept.

Kel took a moment to catch her breath. When she did, she began to laugh. "Stop it, Lalasa, you goose!" she ordered. "That was wonderful! You caught me just as you should have. I won't dismiss you—*please* stop crying."

Lalasa lowered her hands, gazing at Kel with eyes that swam in tears. "You're laughing?" she asked, and sniffed.

"That was *very* good," Kel told her. "You did it exactly right. I'm proud of you!"

"Proud?" Lalasa repeated in a whisper. "But—my lady—I threw you into a door. After all your kindnesses, and teaching me when I've hardly been grateful…"

"What I've been teaching you, among other things, is how to throw me into doors." Kel grinned as she got to her feet.

"Some nobles would kill a servant for doing that. You know it's so, my lady!"

"I do," Kel said grimly. "Nobles like that aren't worthy of the title. How could I punish you for doing what I want you to do? Only think how silly I would look." She helped her maid up. "Now you can use this to protect yourself, so the only men who end up hugging you are the ones you *want* to hug you."

Lalasa smiled crookedly. "That will be some time in coming."

Kel put a hand on the older girl's shoulder. "I wish you would tell me," she said, making her voice as gentle as she could. "What put you off men so bad?"

Lalasa shook her head as she fished her handkerchief from her pocket. "It's nothing, my lady. I *am* sorry I threw you, even if I'm allowed to."

"I'm glad you did. Otherwise how am I to know if you've got the hold and the leverage right?" Kel pointed out. "And—oh, drat." The first bell of the day began to ring. She looked around, to find Lalasa was offering her the weighted harness. Kel looked at it and sighed. She still wasn't used to the new weights. Most of the other pages didn't put theirs on until after breakfast. Couldn't she wait until then just today?

One day leads to another, she told herself wearily. Next thing you know, the boys will get used to it first, and I won't be able to keep up. She took the harness from Lalasa and let its weight slide over her shoulders.

Autumn 454–
Winter 455

9

AUTUMN
ADJUSTMENTS

*A*fter two years, Kel could go through her morning classes in her sleep, and sometimes she did. Hand-to-hand combat with Hakuin Seastone and Eda Bell was first. Then came weapons training starting with staffs in the autumn. Archery class followed weapons, then tilting. None of the pages ever expected anything new. In the fourth week of Kel's third year, however, Lord Wyldon turned creative.

In weapons class, their teachers announced a new program. The first- and second-years were to continue staff practice. The third- and fourth-year pages were to learn how to fight in groups of different sizes. The combinations would change from day to day: three third-years against two fourth-years, four fourth-years against five third-years, or simple battle, one-on-one. They were allowed to use any of their usual weapons, not just staffs.

They could even resort to Shang kicks, punches, and throws in a tight spot. The Shang warriors would record points for each combat. When the senior pages were put in groups, one page would be put in command of each side. If the members of a group looked to someone who was not the appointed leader for orders, their side would lose points.

"One day you will be leading peasants who don't know a sword from a rock. You will have to do your best with them," Lord Wyldon explained on the first day they tried this new practice. "Or soldiers, or other knights, or simply your own squire. Learn to give commands, and learn to take them. Learn to know where the other members of your force are, and learn to command forces of different sizes. Now, get to it!"

"Seniors get to do all the jolly things," Owen complained as they walked to archery practice that first day.

Neal glared at the chubby second-year with all the royal disdain of a vexed lion. He was limping from a staff blow to the knee. "You are a bloody-minded savage," he informed Owen sternly. "I hope you are kidnapped by centaurs."

Kel liked archery. In two years she had gone from holding and drawing the bow wrong to hitting the target's center on every shot. She had just collected her bow and quiver when she heard the archery master call, "The following will come with me." He walked over to the right side of the yard, where the target by the fence had been moved fifty yards beyond those the pages normally shot at. He named a group that included Kel, Neal, Quinden, Merric, Faleron, Yancen, Balduin of Disart, another fourth-year, and Quinden's friend Dermid of Josu's Dirk.

"You people ought to be better," the archery master informed them. "My lord has said it, and I agree. You'll improve by Midwinter or I'll know why. Once you start hitting the more distant target, I'll let you play with these."

Any crossness Kel felt at being forced to work harder when she was already doing well evaporated when she saw the arrows the archery master held. Until now they had shot as if they hunted deer or game birds. These new arrows were armor-piercing broadheads and needleheads, barbed heads, even the ones that made an eerie, whistling sound as they flew. Some were made to pierce a Stormwing's metal feathers or a Coldfang's thick hide.

"Each has a different weight, and will fly different. You'll learn to adjust for each arrow," the archery master told them. "And we'll do a bit with fire arrows. They fly different, too. In the normal way of things you'd leave this kind of work to archers under your command, but times are hardly normal, are they? All these immortals, three dangerous neighbors on edge—and who might they be?" he demanded, gazing sharply at Quinden.

"Carthak, Scanra, and the Copper Isles, sir," replied the boy quietly.

"Very good. You don't know what those enemies may get up to, or what will be asked of you. Now, start shooting. The sooner you hit that target, the sooner you get to play with the pretties."

"If they've changed things 'round in tilting, I'm going to stick my head in a rain barrel and drown myself," Faleron muttered to Kel as they reported to the stables.

Kel and Peachblossom were the first rider and mount

to get into line at the third-years' quintain. Rather than wait for the others, Kel whispered for Peachblossom to charge, and leveled her lance at the target shield. She hit it just right: the quintain dummy pivoted halfway, letting girl and horse thunder by without the sandbag smacking either one. Kel smiled—she loved a good, solid strike—and was about to return to her place in the third-year line when Lord Wyldon yelled, "Stay there, Mindelan!"

He rode toward her at a brisk trot. Kel waited, trying to guess what he wanted. She'd hit the target; Peachblossom was perfectly saddled; she held her weighted lance at the right angle—and why was he carrying a bowl and a brush?

"You're getting complacent, Mindelan," he announced as he trotted by.

"Com—what, sir?" she asked, confused.

"Smug. Comfortable. You think you can hit the target anywhere and it's good, so long as you don't earn a buffet with the sandbag. At your level"—he leaned close to the target shield and painted a round black dot the size of Kel's palm at its center—"you should hit this every time. I *expect* you to hit it every time. You may start now."

Why pick on me? I hit the target every time, and I'm just twelve, thought Kel as she rode back to the line. Only a couple fourth-years hit it as regularly as I do.

The third-years moved to let her at the front. Her friends looked startled; Quinden and his friends smirked. "Who put a wasp in the Stump's loincloth?" Neal muttered as she passed him.

What made Kel really grumpy was that the training master was right: she was getting smug. As long as she hit within the target circle, she felt she'd done all she needed. She ought to strive to improve, not just coast. If Lord Wyldon thought she could hit a dot she couldn't even see from this end of the tilting field, she would try.

She brought Peachblossom up to the starting mark and whispered, "Go faster." He picked his feet up in a trot, then a restrained gallop, not the headlong thundering pace that was his response to the command, "Charge." If she was to hit precisely, she would do better if they took a little more time to reach the quintain.

Kel lowered her lance across Peachblossom's shoulders and aimed for that small dot on the shield. She missed, though she did hit the shield, and wasn't clouted by the sandbag.

"Sloppy," commented Lord Wyldon as she rode past him. He'd dismounted to lean against the fence, where he could see the impact of lance on shield clearly. He was scratching Jump's ear.

I hope he bites you, Kel thought grimly as she rode to take her place in the third-years' line.

In the end, Lord Wyldon required only two fourth-years—Faleron and Yancen—and Kel to hit that dot at the target's center. "I hate it when he thinks up new things," Yancen told Faleron in Kel's hearing.

Kel agreed with him completely.

On the last day of that week, Kel's lance hit the black dot and shattered, the impact and crash making her wrist ache. Shaking her hand, she rode back to the barrel and selected a practice lance. Without lead weights such as she'd had in her old one, the lance was feather-light in her grip. When she next rode at the target, she forgot the new weight and raised her lance point far too high. Before she could lower it, she rode right by the quintain, scraping the target shield. The sandbag thwacked her back soundly, her first buffet in over a year. She heard pages laughing as she returned to the line.

She missed the target on her next charge as well. Determined to hit it, she lowered her lance so hard on her third charge that it bounced off her saddle to rap Peachblossom between the ears. Startled, the big gelding reared. Kel dropped her lance and hung on, praying her mount wouldn't fall backward. Peachblossom wheeled frantically to save himself from that very fate. At last Kel got him under control and on all four feet. She dismounted to collect her fallen lance, and trudged back to the line on foot, leading her mount. She would have dragged the weapon like her eight-year-old nephew if she hadn't known Lord Wyldon would give her a punishment job for it.

"What is the matter with you today?" demanded Lord Wyldon. "This head-in-the-clouds act will get you killed in the field, do you understand that? You dare not daydream with a weapon in your hand, or under you." He pointed to Peachblossom. "*That* is a weapon, in case you hadn't noticed."

Peachblossom's head darted out quickly, like a snake's. The training master was quicker. The gelding's teeth closed on empty air where Lord Wyldon's finger had been.

"My lord, I'd like permission to take this to the smithy," Kel said, hefting the lance. "It's too light."

Wyldon blinked at her. "What?"

"Surely my lord knew that Page Keladry has lead weights in all of her practice weapons," commented Neal, who stood nearby. He looked the spirit of mischief.

Kel glared at him. Neal ignored her. He usually did.

"Queenscove, do not try me," Wyldon said, clear warning in his voice. His eyes were on Kel. To her he stated, "You use weighted practice weapons."

Kel made no reply.

"How long have you done this?"

How could she forget? On the day the first-years began to train with the lance, Joren had made sure that Kel got a lance three times heavier than the normal ones. "Since the first week on lance, my lord," Kel replied evenly.

"All of your weapons, not the lance alone?" he inquired. Neal had told him all, but it seemed he wanted to hear it from Kel.

"It was too strange after a while, going from a weighted lance to a lighter staff and practice sword and ax," she explained. "It works better if they're weighted, too."

Lord Wyldon hooked his fingers in his belt, frowning. As usual, there was no reading his handsome, stern face. At last he sighed. "Tend your mount first. Do not be late for lunch," he ordered.

Kel thanked him and bowed, but he had already turned to Neal. "Clearly you have too much time on your hands," he told Neal. "You may take the next five runs at the quintain, beginning now."

Kel heard Neal say, "Yes, your lordship, immediately, your lordship," as she led Peachblossom away.

"One day he won't let his tongue get him in so much

trouble," she told the horse as she groomed him. "I hope it happens before he dies of old age." Peachblossom whickered, and nudged Kel with his nose. He was uninterested in Neal, except as something to bite, and he preferred to bite apples and sugar lumps. He seemed to think Kel was hiding a treat.

After leaving her new lance to be weighted, Kel returned to her rooms. The noon bell had not yet rung, and she meant to sit in her bath and soak for a while before she had to dress for lunch.

Entering her rooms, she found that Lalasa had company. The stranger was a young woman Lalasa's age, blond and brown-eyed with a soft, round face and strong shoulders. She curtsied gracefully to Kel, who tried to remember where she had seen this woman before.

"Lady, this is my friend Tian—Tianine Plowman," Lalasa said nervously. "She is maid to your sister Adalia."

Kel nodded, relieved. "I thought I recognized you," she admitted. "Is my sister all right?" She couldn't think of any other reason that Adie's maid would come here, unless she was visiting Lalasa.

"She is well, and atwitter over the ball to be held in four days' time at Nond House," said Tian. "She sent me to ask, would you allow Lalasa to serve her? She will pay Lalasa for her time, and of course you would get half. My lady wishes Lalasa to sew for her."

"Is that what you would like?" Kel asked Lalasa.

The maid nodded eagerly. "I do love to sew, my lady. And you won't need more work on your hems or seams for at least a week." Her eyes danced at the small joke.

"I don't grow *that* fast, thank you," Kel said.

Lalasa nudged Tian. The blond woman smiled at her and told Kel, "If it pleases your ladyship, Lady Oranie also wishes to give work to Lalasa, with the same arrangements for pay. To be honest, m'lady, I think others will ask Lalasa to sew for them when they see her work."

"And I'd be sure to do my own work first," added Lalasa. "I wouldn't shirk at all, I promise."

"I don't mind," Kel told her and her friend. "You know I'd like to see you get out and about more."

Tian curtsied to her again and told Lalasa, "This afternoon, then?" Lalasa nodded. "Thank you, my lady," Tian said, and left the room.

Lalasa closed the door behind her and twirled giddily. Suddenly she halted. "You'll see, my lady," she told Kel gravely. "I'll earn you a bit of money, and put some away for myself. Maybe a shop of my own, though that's looking a bit high, perhaps."

"You really like sewing, don't you?" asked Kel, who hated it.

Lalasa nodded. "I'm better than a lot of the maids that serve the young court ladies, Tian says. And it's peaceful. Just you, and the cloth, and getting everything just right."

Kel thought of those moments on Peachblossom's back when she lowered her lance at the quintain, and knew in the feel of the horse, and the weapon, and her arm, that she had it perfectly. "I see what you mean," she murmured. More firmly she said, "But look here—you have to keep what you earn. I don't want it."

Lalasa stared at her. "But most nobles take half at least. Some take almost everything!"

Kel began to strip off her tunic and shirt. "I'm not

most nobles, remember? Is my bath ready?"

"Yes, of course," Lalasa replied, taking Kel's practice clothes. "But, my lady, I wouldn't feel right, with you paying me a wage, and giving me this chance." Lalasa's joy had fallen away, leaving her anxious again.

Kel hated to see that. "All right," she said, against her will. "But I'm putting it away for a dowry or a shop or whatever you like. You remember that."

"You say so now," Lalasa replied, her tone very older-sisterly. "Just wait till you need to buy armor and suchlike."

Kel met the older girl's eyes. "Do you really believe that of me?"

Lalasa opened her mouth to reply, then closed it again. She looked away from Kel's gaze. "No, miss. Not really. And I thank you."

"You're welcome." Shaking her head, Kel walked into the dressing room and climbed into the waiting bath. "I'm glad you have a friend."

"Isn't Tian nice?" Lalasa took Kel's afternoon clothes from the wardrobe. "So clever, and friendly. She really thinks other ladies will ask me to sew for them, and pay well for it."

"She's a lady's maid, so she ought to know." Kel put her head back with a grateful sigh. "If I doze off, wake me when the noon bell rings."

That night, Kel went out after supper to retrieve her lance and take it to Peachblossom's stable, where she placed it with her gear. She was trotting up the sloping, torch-lined road to the palace when someone called, "Hullo—is that Keladry of Mindelan?"

Kel looked around and saw a big man in the stable that housed the horses of the King's Own. She knew that broad, red-cheeked face with its cap of black curls and bright dark eyes. "My lord, good evening," she said, bowing to Raoul of Goldenlake and Malorie's Peak, Knight Commander of the King's Own. "It's a pleasure to see you."

He walked over, tucking riding gloves into his belt. "Good to see you, too, youngster," he said with a kind smile. "Mithros bless me, *you've* grown."

Kel smiled at him. She had added almost two more inches since Midwinter, but there was still quite a gap between her height, nearly five feet and six inches, and his six feet and one inch. "I believe I have, my lord."

"Going to the palace? If you don't mind, I'll come along."

"I'd be honored, sir," Kel replied.

They walked slowly up the hill. "How goes training?" he asked. "Are you still riding that huge gelding—what's his name—Peony?"

"Peachblossom, my lord. Yes, I am." Kel explained her current training schedule, including the new things Lord Wyldon had begun. Lord Raoul asked questions that drew more details from her.

"The thing is, I don't know why he's changing things," Kel admitted.

"I think Wyldon got a scare when you and your friends stumbled into that bandit camp." Correctly guessing the reason that Kel stopped to gape at him, the big man grinned and said, "The whole court's heard about it by now. Anyway, if seven pages had gotten slaughtered, he would have felt responsible. Never mind that the district commander lied about the area being cleared of bandits. They found out he was taking payoffs, did they tell you?" Lord Raoul spoke as he might to a noble his own age.

Kel shook her head. "I still don't see how it would make Lord Wyldon change the training, though."

"He didn't teach you youngsters how to manage when there's no adult in command, is my guess. He's trying to make up for that now. To be honest, I couldn't have done what you did when I was a page. Wyldon's already taught you plenty." The big knight began to chuckle. "Gods, but those free fight sessions must be a mess!"

Kel hid a smile. They *were* messy, with fighters not always knowing where to step and whom to look at. "Is battle like that for real, sir?"

He thought about that for a moment. "It can be," he said at last. "Battle plans go to pieces, as they're teaching you. It depends on the discipline of the people you lead. See, the problem is, knights used to operate alone. We're trained to independence. For centuries the lone knight enforced what law he chose. If he had any help, it was local peasants. With them not knowing their foot from their elbow, you can see where a knight might prefer to fight alone."

Kel could indeed.

"These days, knights have to work with others. You might be put with a squad of the Queen's Riders, or an infantry company, or even a naval crew. *I* was trained to think only for myself, and look at me—acting as general for three companies of the King's Own. We never fight in strengths less than a squad of ten. I learned command on the fly, and wish I'd had more lessons on it as a lad."

Kel nodded. What he said made a great deal of sense. She liked Lord Raoul. At the end of her first year he had led men of the King's Own and pages in a mission to clean up a nest of spidrens in the Royal Forest. She had admired his skill as commander and fighter then, and he had made it clear he thought her talented.

They strolled into the palace, entering a kind of indoor courtyard, with a fountain at the center and trees in pots around the edges. Lord Raoul sat on a bench and motioned for Kel to sit by him. They sat without talking for a while, watching the fountain. It was Lord Raoul who broke the silence. "I hear you and your friends declared war on hazing."

Only six years at the Yamani court, with its iron discipline, kept her quiet. Kel fought to be stone, waiting until she was sure of her self-control before she dared to ask, "How did you hear that, sir?"

Raoul grinned. "The Knight Commander has sources in the palace," he commented, all too innocently. "I hear things. I understand some of last spring's squires were the focus of your campaign?"

Kel looked down, her face as smooth and emotionless as marble. "I couldn't say, my lord."

"Oh, don't start my-lording me, youngster," he said cheerfully. "Didn't anybody tell you a palace is like a sieve? Servants talk, families talk, boys talk, and nobles talk. If people stopped talking around here, the walls would fall in. There'd be no wind to hold them up. So tell me, now that the worst of them are gone, have you given up your no-hazing patrols?"

"No," she replied, startled. "Plenty of pages believe in it still. You can't stop it all. We just want the bullies to back off." She didn't tell him that this year, when her group had found anything suspicious, the other pages had left rather than fight.

"I see. And who's this?"

Kel looked up as Jump trotted in from the outside. He must have gone looking for her. "That's Jump," she said, getting to her feet. "I guess he got worried when I didn't come back." Remembering they weren't allowed pets, she said hurriedly, "He's sort of a mascot, you see. He looks after all of us."

"I've heard of Jump," the big knight said, fishing a strip of jerked beef from a pocket and offering it to the dog. "Wyldon said he accounted for three riders and a dog in that mess this summer. Now that I've got a look at him, I'm surprised he only brought down three." Jump took the strip of dried meat in his front teeth, daintily, and began to gnaw on it.

"I really should do some work tonight," Kel said regretfully. She'd never felt so comfortable around an adult as she did with this man, unless it was her parents or her oldest brother, Anders.

Lord Raoul stood. "Of course. I'm glad we had a chance to talk, Keladry." He smiled at her. "Keep up the good work." He turned and walked out of the room, into the night.

"That's a nice man," Kel told Jump. "I wish more were like him." Jump wagged his battered tail, still gnawing on his jerked beef. "Let's go," Kel said, and headed back to the pages' wing.

10

THE SQUIRES RETURN

*T*he next night Kel was in line for supper when she saw more faces at the squires' tables. The number of squires who lived on the floor above the pages' wing had been growing slowly as autumn went on. Kel barely knew those who had come in before, but tonight she recognized two faces: Cleon and Garvey.

"One good, one bad," Merric remarked from behind Kel.

"Do I have to close my eyes to guess which?" Owen wanted to know.

When they went to their usual table, Cleon walked over. "It's about time," Neal said when the redheaded squire slid onto the bench next to him. "We thought they would leave you in the north all winter. You would have come back as an icicle."

"A really *big* icicle," added Seaver.

After seeing Lord Raoul, Kel knew that Cleon wasn't *that* big, but he certainly seemed to be headed that way. She smiled at him. He seized one of her hands. "Kel, my rose, my pearl," he said, attempting a player's yearning stare, "my life has been a desert drear without the light of your eyes. I knew it not until just this moment, when my soul opened like a flower in the rain."

Kel yanked her hand free. "Stop that, you oaf," she told him, but she grinned despite her stern tone. She had missed Cleon's colorful way of speaking to her.

"It's not right," Seaver announced abruptly.

"What's not right?" Neal asked.

"When Cleon talks to us, he doesn't do that." Seaver frowned at Cleon. "You don't call us 'rose' or 'pearl.' If you don't talk to us like that, you shouldn't do it to her."

"She's as good as us," added Owen. "You don't have to treat her like a *girl*."

Kel hid her face in her hands.

"But she *is* a girl," protested Cleon. "A tall, glorious sunrise of a girl, a—" He stopped, blinked, and, astonishingly, turned red. "Sorry, Kel."

"I know you're just funning," she reassured him. "How's Inness?"

Cleon hit his forehead. "I keep forgetting he's your brother," he explained as the others grinned. "He's nice."

"And Kel's not?" demanded Owen, outraged.

"I can't win," Cleon muttered. "He's quiet like you, Kel. And he's a mean hand with a sword. I'm learning a lot from him."

"Good," Neal told him sternly. "I hope he manages you with a whip and a chair, like a wild animal in a show."

"He hardly ever uses the whip," Cleon replied in his loftiest tone. "I am so much better than his last squire."

When Lord Wyldon arrived, Cleon had to return to the squires' tables. After supper he caught up to Kel just as she was about to enter her room. "I hope you don't mind what I said before," he said gruffly, not meeting her eyes. "I wasn't making fun *of* you. You know what I mean."

What's this? wondered Kel. "I'm surprised they said anything," she replied. "They never minded your foolery before."

"I know," he said. Oddly, he added, "Neither did I."

Addressing him slowly in case, like a skittish horse, he took alarm and bolted, she said, "You talked to me that way while you were making me earn my way as a first-year. Maybe they thought you were trying to haze me again, even though I'm a third-year?"

"That's silly," he said, crossing his arms.

Kel shrugged. "Maybe. Are you coming to study tonight?"

His face lit with a grin. Suddenly he looked like his old self again. "That's right. We're supposed to do reports on our time with our masters for Sir Myles, and mine's only half-done." He walked away, halted, and turned. "We meet in the usual place?"

Kel smiled warmly at him. "You haven't been gone *that* long, Cleon of Kennan."

He looked at her wide-eyed for a moment, as if she had startled him. Once again he turned red. "You look— fit, Kel," he remarked. Then he trotted off.

Fit, she thought, shaking her head as she unlocked her door. Why would he care if I look *fit* or not?

*   *   *

Winter began with a mild storm that left two inches of snow on the ground, not enough for training to be moved inside. The day after the snow fell Kel was on her way back to her rooms at the end of morning classes when someone hailed her. She halted and looked up. There, at the door to the pages' wing, stood Joren of Stone Mountain. He was an ice prince in a blue tunic over a white shirt and hose, his pale blond hair caught back in a horse-tail. Looking at Kel, he actually smiled.

She waited, her face Yamani-smooth, her breath forming clouds on the chill air. What did he want?

Joren folded his arms over his chest. "You look cold," he offered.

"I'm not," Kel replied flatly. She did not feel like conversing with him.

"Listen, Keladry..." He looked down, as if trying to decide what to say. At last he looked up, and gave her a disarming smile. "We got off on the wrong foot."

Is that what you call it? wondered Kel. She continued to wait, her hands clasped loosely before her.

"I—allowed myself to be influenced by the prejudices of others," he explained, still smiling prettily. "And I was reared in a, a rough-and-tumble home, not a cultured place like this." His graceful hand-wave took in the palace that surrounded them. "Sir Paxton, my knight-master, was quite firm about my usual behavior. He gave me cause to think, and to review the things I have said and done."

Kel's mind raced. She supposed it was possible. But he didn't learn in the two years we fought him, telling him that he couldn't thump everyone he had a mind to, her cooler self whispered. How could that change in the seven months he's been a squire?

"What I am trying to say," Joren went on at last, when she was silent for too long, "is that I would like to start fresh with you. If I may."

"Of course you may," she said pleasantly, her eyes on his. "We'll have a fresh start, just as you like, Squire Joren. And now, if you'll excuse me"—she bowed quite correctly, not an inch deeper than protocol demanded—"I must wash up." She walked by him, all her senses alert to the rabbit punch to the back, or the boot in her behind.

"I would like to be friends," he said.

Kel turned to give him her best, most meaningless, social smile. "That would be pleasant," she said, and left him.

Now, what do you suppose that was about? she wondered as she scrubbed. She sighed. She really didn't need him to complicate her life at this point.

That night she was in her room, writing to her nephew before she went to study with her friends, when someone knocked on her door. Kel continued to write as Lalasa answered it. There was a puzzled note in Lalasa's voice when she said, "You have visitors, my lady."

Kel turned, about to demand that she be left in peace to finish her letter. Iden and Warric, Owen's first-year cousins, stood in the doorway, looking very embarrassed. Both held staffs. They didn't try to pet Jump or greet the sparrows who lit on their shoulders, even when Crown perched on top of Warric's staff and began to preen.

"You ask," Iden murmured to his cousin.

Warric punched him gently. "No, you."

Kel sighed. Lalasa had returned to her sewing. "One of you say something, or go away," she advised. "I've classwork yet tonight, and so do you."

"Sergeant Ezeko says *he* should just impale himself on the staff, he's so bad with it," Iden announced, pushing Warric. "My lord told me I'd do better to plant mine and hope a tree grows out of it."

"We're hopeless," announced Warric.

"You're like butter with the staff, butter with no cow hairs in it, all smooth and clean," Iden continued. "Owen said we should stop bothering him because he's no hand with it, either, and you're the best."

"And you never get mad, or yell," Warric finished. "Owen and Merric do."

Lalasa ducked her head to hide a smile as Kel stood. "You want me to help you?" Kel asked. She thought, but didn't add, Even though I'm The Girl?

"If you don't mind," said Iden, hope in his large hazel eyes.

"Just some pointers, so we quit getting our fingers broke," Warric supplied. Kel glanced at his hands—they were covered with bruises, and one finger was swollen.

"Well, you can't start that way," she remarked, and opened the desk drawer where she kept the bruise balm. "Come here, both of you," she ordered as she removed the top. "Let's see your hands."

Both lads' hands were mottled with training bruises. Kel dabbed balm on the worst, nodding as the swellings went down and purple marks faded. "Now," she ordered when she had put the balm away, "show me what you're doing."

She saw the problems immediately. No matter how often she positioned Warric's hands on his staff, he let them slide closer together as he practiced. Iden's stance was bad, even weak; a blow would knock him aside. Using her belt-knife, Kel roughened the wood on Warric's staff at the spots where his hands should be most of the time. Then she marked the floor with chalk to show Iden where to put his feet. She suggested that he take one step out of his stance and another to return to it, starting first with the left foot, then the right, and continue doing only that. Her idea was to make the position feel natural. While he stepped, Kel turned back to Warric.

After he had practiced strikes and blocks for a brief time, stopping often to reposition his hands correctly, she said, "Do it slow. As you're doing each thing, check that your hands are always where they should be."

He swung his staff in the high strike position, moving it with a dancer's slow grace. "But we're supposed to go fast," he pointed out.

"You will, in the practice court. But you do the thing I used to, where I was so in love with swinging a weapon that I didn't care about the exact way to do it. I got my fingers broken before I learned to stop thinking how good I must look, do it slow, and make sure my hands were where they ought to be." She didn't mention she'd been six at the time. If Warric had studied with tough old Nariko, the Yamani emperor's armsmistress, he would be further along, too.

She watched carefully as the boy went through each movement, pushing his hands back into place whenever they moved off the rough areas where he had to grip. When he lost his stance, she stepped behind him to correct the placing of his feet.

"It doesn't *feel* right," Kel heard Iden complain as she positioned Warric.

Lalasa replied, "It didn't to me at first, either. No, your toes point out." Kel glanced over in time to see Lalasa kneel beside Iden. She moved his feet into the correct position and held them in place with her hands as she explained, "They have to point straight ahead on that foot. Try the block now."

Iden obeyed. "But they *want* to point out," he protested.

"And your belly wants sweets. You shouldn't give your body what it wants all the time," Lalasa said.

Warric looked at Kel, startled. She winked and said, "Try that low block again. Hold your stance."

"You know what my lady suggested?" Lalasa asked Iden. "She said whenever you aren't doing anything, just assume that stance and hold it for a count of ten."

"Any old time?" inquired the boy.

Lalasa nodded gravely. "When I get up in the morning, or I'm in line in the servants' mess, or at the draper's waiting for a clerk, I just stand like that and count. The more I did it, the more natural it got. My lady says I do much better now."

"She does," affirmed Kel. "She threw me all the way to the door this week." The boys stared at Lalasa, awed.

The first bell of the night rang, telling pages to start

classwork if they hadn't done so already. As Kel opened the door for her guests, Iden asked, "Would you mind doing a little bit with us tomorrow, like you did tonight?"

"For a while?" added Warric.

"Just till we get it," Iden promised.

Kel sighed inwardly. She hated to lose the little time she had to herself, but they were gazing at her like starved puppies. Only a monster would refuse, she thought. "I'll be happy to," she replied, thinking, Sometimes even knights have to tell white lies.

"You'll see!" she heard Iden tell Warric as they went to put their staffs away. "We'll be good in no time!"

I wish I had such faith in my skill as a teacher, thought Kel. She collected her books. "Thank you for helping, Lalasa."

"I just told him what you told me," the maid said, picking up her sewing again.

Kel shook her head and left for the library.

The weeks between the squires' return and Midwinter evaporated. In that time, Iden and Warric became regular visitors to Kel's room, a source of entertainment that the sparrows, Jump, and Lalasa seemed to enjoy. Cleon taught her a sword thrust and twist good for parting a man from his dagger. The archery master allowed the advanced group to try shooting with broadhead arrows. For the first time Kel was granted a free afternoon to go into the city. Lalasa stopped lowering the hems of Kel's present set of page uniforms, and got her new ones. Kel was five feet seven in her stocking feet at the age of twelve and a half.

Joren said hello quite pleasantly, not just to Kel, but to

her friends as well. One evening he was so bold as to come to the library they had claimed for their study group to get a book. No one knew what to make of it.

Midwinter came, and with it the time for what Neal called "our ordeal by etiquette," the Midwinter banquets. As they had the year before, Kel's friends came to her and Lalasa for a last-minute inspection before they reported to Master Oakbridge. This year it was Owen's turn to be the cool veteran, and Iden's and Warric's to fret that they might actually be called on to serve.

Again Kel was assigned to wait on Danayne, Archpriestess of the Moon of Truth temple in Corus, and those who sat with her: Eda Bell and Hakuin Seastone, and Master Harailt of Aili, dean of the royal university. The Shangs and Master Harailt greeted her with pleasure; Master Harailt inquired about her studies. The Archpriestess said nothing, but then she'd said barely a word to her companions the year before.

Kel was returning for the second fish course when a young woman moved into her path. It was Uline of Hannalof, elegant in petal-pink brocade. She wore her curly hair in a net decorated with moonstones. "Keladry, I wanted to say hello. How are you?"

Kel smiled. "I'm quite well, thank you. And you look very grand!" She was startled to discover that Uline, who was eighteen or so, was Kel's height exactly.

Uline blushed and smoothed her skirts. "Thank you." She looked Kel over. "How goes it? Do they treat you well, those pages?"

"As well as they treat anyone," Kel replied. "It's a rough-and-tumble world, compared to that of the ladies."

"I don't know about that," replied Uline. "This summer I was invited to become one of the royal ladies. That has its rough-and-tumble moments."

"Congratulations," Kel said, and meant it. While the queen had many ladies-in-waiting, only one group was called "the royal ladies." It was made up of fifteen or so young women of noble birth who could wait on Queen Thayet at state functions, keep up with her on horseback, and use weapons in combat, bows for the most part. "That is, I hope you feel you should be congratulated."

Uline giggled. "Back in October, when I broke my arm, I wasn't sure. Now it seems all right. Of course, if you ever see me after riding twenty miles in the rain—well, don't ask me then, all right?"

Kel smiled and bowed.

Uline curtsied. "I'll leave you to your chores. By the way—who is that handsome young man, the one with the green eyes? He looks a bit old to be a page."

Kel made herself say, "Nealan of Queenscove. He didn't start until he was fifteen. He's eighteen now."

"My goodness, how odd," Uline remarked. "Still, don't you think he's handsome?"

"Very," Kel replied. I won't get upset if she falls in love with him, she told herself. Uline's very nice and they would make a fine couple.

Uline sighed. "A pity we're announcing the betrothal tonight. Oh, well—I do love Kieran, and at least the wedding isn't for another year."

"Kieran?" asked Kel, baffled.

"Kieran haMinch," Uline replied. "He's handsome, too, though his eyes are brown, not green. I do love green eyes. Maybe I'll flirt with this Neal." Her own eyes shone as she watched him.

"Wouldn't—" Kel began to say, but the words stuck in her mouth. She swallowed and tried again. "Wouldn't it be, well, not nice to flirt with somebody you don't want to fall in love with?"

Uline sighed. "I suppose it would," she admitted. "Well, I'll dream I flirted with him. Or you could flirt with him for me."

"I think I could flirt about as well as my gelding dances," Kel said frankly. "I'd best get to work."

Uline rested a hand on her arm. "I'm glad it's going well," she said, her eyes kind. "When you come to the big examinations, I'll be in the audience, cheering."

Kel thanked Uline and returned to the room where the serving pages waited. She wondered if she ought to tell Neal that his heart's desire was betrothed, but she thought the better of it. Let someone else ruin his life.

It's not as if he'll ever look at *you,* she told herself as the freed pages trudged to their supper after the banquet. You're the same as another boy to him. You—

"Clumsy idiot!" she heard an all-too-familiar voice cry from a connecting hallway. "Do you know what this tunic cost me?"

She said nothing to her companions, but turned into the corridor. Joren had a footman by the arm. The man still clutched a pitcher; at their feet was a puddle of liquid.

The moment Joren saw Kel, he released the footman and backed away, both hands raised to show he wouldn't grab the man again. "My apologies," he told the man. To Kel he said, "Old habits die hard, don't they?" His rueful smile invited her to share his amusement. When she said nothing, Joren gave the man a silver coin and strolled away.

"What was that about?" Neal demanded.

Kel turned. All of her friends were arrayed at her back. "He says he's changed."

"I suppose he could have changed," Neal said dryly. "I myself have noticed my growing resemblance to a daffodil." The other pages snorted.

Kel eyed her friend. "You do look yellow around the edges," she told him, her face quite serious. "I hadn't wanted to bring it up."

"We daffodils like to have things brought up," Neal said, slinging an arm around her shoulders. "It reminds us of spring."

"Does dung remind you of spring, too, Princess Flower?" Cleon demanded irritably. "You needn't manhandle our Kel like that."

Kel peeled Neal's arm away. "Thanks, but no thanks," she told him, hoping he didn't notice that her breath came quicker, or that her heart pounded like a drum. "I don't want to crush your petals."

"Crush mine all you like, fair lady," Cleon told her, putting an arm around her shoulders in Neal's stead.

Owen wriggled between Kel and Neal and wrapped an arm around Kel's waist. "Me too," he said, grinning up at her.

Kel worked herself free, chuckling. The banquets weren't much fun, but she liked how the boys got silly at Midwinter. You can only be grim and determined to achieve your goals for so long, she thought as they walked into the pages' mess together. After that, you just have to joke around for a while.

"Say, Neal," Owen said as they got into line to be served, "Uline of Hannalof looks *beautiful.*"

"She is not for me," Neal said gravely. Everyone turned to look at him. "She's betrothed to Kieran haMinch—they're announcing it this week. She'll brighten their gloomy northern castles like the moon. Now, the *queen*—she was more than beautiful tonight. Did you see her, in that white gown embroidered in scarlet? The jewels in her hair, like stars in the midnight sky? No other country has a queen to compare. And she has the deadly core of a Sirajit sword, beauty and death in one splendid woman." His eyes were misty as he considered Queen Thayet. "Murdon Fielding, the Sage of Cría, wrote, 'Squire, give thy queen thy purest love. Let her be the living emblem of the power of the Goddess. Her beauteous countenance will be thy guide, her favor and thanks your payment. Let her—'"

Someone passed Kel one of the long, thin loaves of bread served with soup. Before Neal could go on, his friends attacked him with the loaves, battering him until the bread fell to pieces.

Neal brushed crumbs off his clothes and fixed them with his loftiest glare. "Soulless, heartless pages that you are," he said, "I ignore you." He cut ahead of them in line so he could be served first.

Once again Kel's mysterious benefactor surprised her with a costly, useful holiday gift. That summer she had received riding gloves and gauntlets made of beautifully worked leather; in the fall it had been shooting gloves and arm guards to protect her clothes from her bowstring. Now it was a pair of large saddlebags, well made but ordinary enough on the outside, and fitted with large and small compartments. She found things in those compartments: flint and steel, an oiled pouch full of tinder; small iron pots and a plate and bowl set, all of which fit together; a hank of light, strong rope; tooth-cleaning powder; a tidy sewing kit; hooks and line for fishing; and a curious fanlike creation that, when opened up, was revealed to be a waterproof hat.

"Whoever it is, they're driving me mad," Kel told Lalasa. "I can't begin to thank them at this point, and I've no idea who it is!"

"Whoever it is, they want you to keep doing what you're doing," Lalasa said.

"I just wish I *knew*," grumbled Kel. "I hate mysteries. Why does this person like me so much? Who could it hurt if I knew who it was?" When she'd gotten the gloves and arm guards, she realized that her unknown friend knew what size Kel was, but Lalasa swore no one had approached her. Kel had given up on that line of thinking. After all, her changing sizes were noted by the palace tailors so they could supply Lalasa. It would be easy enough for someone who knew the palace to ask the tailors for Kel's measurements.

This Midwinter, Kel made only one vow to keep in the new year. Being allowed to visit the city before the holiday had made her see that she wasn't getting as many punishments as she had in her first two years. She was rarely tardy, she'd learned how to clean her gear to Lord

Wyldon's satisfaction, and she never got into fights anymore. Without punishment work to force her onto heights, there was nothing to help Kel overcome her fear.

If she wanted to defeat it, she would have to face it herself, on a regular basis. She doubted that anyone would send her up Balor's Needle again, but what if she had to take a note to the watch captain on the walls? She was certain that come summer, Lord Wyldon would resume sending her up on heights. She had better practice before then.

Thus, every night after supper, Kel went on a walk. One night she might go to the immense, pillared gallery that stretched around the main entrance hall and map the lower floor, including every potted tree and bench. Another night might see her in one of the watchtowers, forcing herself to note which points of light below were fixed and which moved. She climbed trees in the gardens. On her days off she sought a balcony and mapped the portion of the grounds visible from there, or the land between the outer wall and the city.

It had been easier when she did these things under Lord Wyldon's orders. An order had to be obeyed; she didn't have to think beyond that. When it was her own doing, she was always tempted to skip a day, or just glance down, then get back to the ground. Kel had to force herself to keep her vow. She was better at it some days than others.

Her daily training followed the path set that autumn. After Midwinter Lord Wyldon added to their harnesses once again. Kel adjusted to the new weight more quickly than before, which meant she was exhausted by its drag on her chest and shoulders for just over a week. By the time two weeks had passed, she didn't notice the fresh weight.

On days that were nice enough to allow the pages to practice tilting, Kel hit the black spot on the target shield with every pass. In January Lord Wyldon moved six of the fourth-year pages who could reliably hit the target to Kel's quintain and changed Kel's program. Now she had a harder target—a ring of wood about a foot in diameter, hung from a cord attached to a long rod.

This was very different from what Kel was used to. She believed the training master was trying to make her lose her mind. The circle bobbed and swayed in every puff of air. She felt as if she chased a butterfly with her lance.

"Adversity builds character?" Neal suggested one bitter morning when she was taking a breather.

She looked at Peachblossom. "Bite him," she ordered. The gelding, as contrary as a cat, blew at her.

"All right, how's this? He knows you're far better than most of us, and he's trying to make you better still." When Kel blinked at him, Neal shrugged. "Or we could go back to him being a Stump who lives to torture you. I like that one better anyway."

In weapons practice, Lord Wyldon began exercises in city fighting. He would take the seniors to an empty section of the palace, or to a collection of outbuildings on the grounds, and put them to work. In pairs, in groups, or alone, they chased one another, hiding behind doors and corners, sparring furiously when they encountered the "enemy." Kel, in command of five pages one February morning, routed a group of seven that included Yancen, Balduin, and Neal, by making them split their force.

When Hakuin and Eda declared her side the winner, Lord Wyldon was silent for a very long moment. There was no telling what he thought, or what the tone in his voice meant when he said at last, "Very good, Page Keladry."

It was his first compliment. She knew she would remember it every day of her life.

One March Sunday, Kel climbed the curtain wall. She wasn't sure how long she had been sketching the ground between the palace's Least Gate and Corus when she realized she had company. Joren was draped on a merlon beside her, very much at his ease.

"I thought you were afraid of heights," he remarked when she looked at him.

Kel let no hint of her uncertainty, confusion, and irritation with him show through her Yamani facade. "I am," she replied at last, and went back to her mapping.

"You don't look it."

"Well, that's something," she said dryly, rubbing out a crooked line.

"If you're afraid, why do this?" he asked, at his most reasonable. "They won't test you on it at the big *or* little exams."

"My lord will, the next time he gives me punishment work," Kel informed him. "Or the gods will, the next time I'm supposed to help someone in trouble and they're on a height, or we have to climb to escape danger."

For a while he said nothing, but she knew he was still there, still watching her. "Why do any of this?" he wanted to know. "It isn't at all needful. Did someone tell you that you had no chance to marry?"

Kel's hand jerked, smearing charcoal over her notes. She made a face and rubbed it out.

Joren went on, "It's not true. You'd be a pretty thing, in the right clothes and after you'd lost some weight. After you stopped working so your arms are like a blacksmith's. You'd make a fine wife for one of those big fellows— Cleon, for instance. He seems fond of you. How about Lord Raoul? He can afford a wife. You could settle down and raise young giants." He smiled as Kel looked at him, but the smile didn't reach his eyes.

When she was five and her mother had saved the Yamanis' most sacred artifacts from pirates, the emperor made her family part of his inner circle. Suddenly Kel's family was sought by all kinds of people. Children who had laughed at Kel and called her a hulking barbarian now fought for the honor of sitting with her. They gave her presents and invited her to their homes. Kel heard two of them say privately that their parents had ordered them to befriend the emperor's pets so the emperor might favor *their* families. The smiles of those children, and their parents, never reached their eyes, either.

"It's so good of you to concern yourself with my marriage prospects," Kel replied evenly. "Has it occurred to you I don't want to marry?" Neal, she thought suddenly and horribly. If Neal asked me...

He never will, replied her coldly practical self. He falls in love with beauties.

"Nonsense," Joren was saying comfortably. "All women care about marriage. Even the Lioness scraped up a husband, though she had to dig through the middens of Corus to do it."

Surely the King's Champion had married only because she had wanted to. "If you say so," Kel replied. She went back to her mapping.

"Think about it," Joren said, clapping her on the shoulder. "One battle too many, and you'll be scarred for life. No man will want you then." He ambled off, whistling.

Kel shook her head. Maybe he'll be a great knight one day—maybe, she thought. But first, he'd better get his head out of his behind. And he'd better let me be.

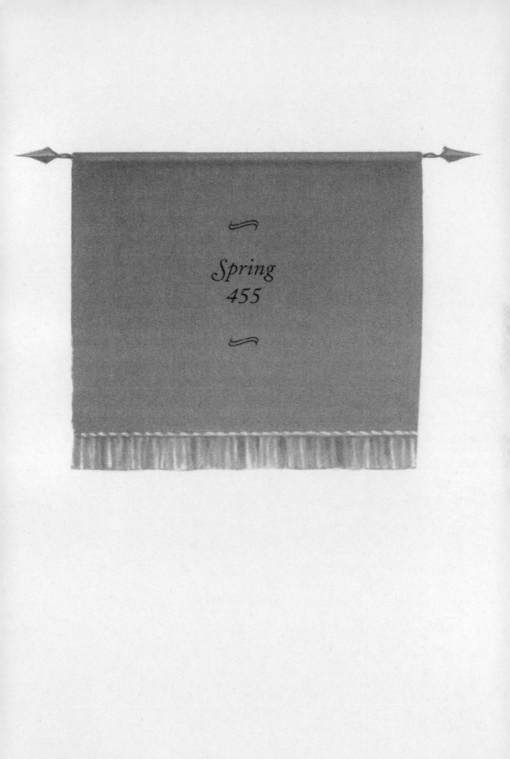

Spring
455

II

UNPLEASANT REALITIES

One evening in late March a sparrow flew into the library where Kel and her friends studied. The bird—the female named Peg for her missing foot—landed on Kel's shoulder and chattered angrily.

"Aren't they supposed to be asleep?" Neal asked.

Kel sighed. "She's probably locked out and can't get to the courtyard." If the sparrows were flying inside, they sometimes got trapped when the doors were closed. With the way to the courtyard, and Kel's open shutter, barred, they usually waited for Kel by her door, fluffing up their feathers and looking the picture of sparrow misery.

Kel got to her feet. "Jump, stay," she ordered. Jump, who slept with his blocky head on Cleon's foot, opened his eyes and snorted. He had no intention of moving.

Cleon didn't look at her as he said, "You want company?"

Kel smiled. "I'm just going to let her into the courtyard. I'll only be a moment." Walking out she told Peg, "I don't see why you couldn't wait till I came home, if Lalasa didn't hear you. Or does sitting on the stones make your stump hurt?" She crossed the pages' corridor into the short hall that led to the outer door. Cool air, not cold, brushed her cheeks—the door was open. "Peg, why in Mithros's name—" Kel began, vexed.

Then a muffled curse, furious sparrow chatter, and the sound of a tussle reached her ears. "You'll pay for that trick, wench!" someone growled. "Call these birds off!"

Kel's instinct was to dash out and halt whatever was going on, but Lord Wyldon's training gripped her hard. Fighting the urge to run, she slid to the open door and carefully leaned around it, moving slowly. A quick movement would attract the eye of anyone in the courtyard.

Her open window was just ten feet away. Vinson stood there, grappling with Lalasa. From the wreckage of the sewing basket on the ground, Kel guessed Lalasa had been working in the window seat when Vinson came by. Now he fought to keep a hand over her mouth while her fingers scrabbled over his arm, looking for tender places to pinch. The sparrows attacked furiously, making Vinson duck their claws as he tried to wedge Lalasa's hands under his free arm. He was lucky the sparrows were half-blind at night, or they could have damaged him badly. As it was, he bled from a dozen peck-marks on his face.

White fury blazed in Kel's heart. She stalked forward, battling to keep her feelings in hand as she said coldly, "Unhand my maid." Lalasa's eyes widened. Peg, a cautious bird, fled Kel's shoulder for the safety of the room.

The sparrows attacking Vinson did the same.

Vinson half-turned to look at her, still holding Lalasa. Kel could see the furrowed gouges of a woman's fingernails down the older boy's face. "If I were you, Lump, I'd walk away right now." He used the nickname she rarely heard these days.

Kel didn't argue. Pivoting on her right foot, she furled her left leg up to her inner thigh and snapped the foot out. Rather than shatter Vinson's kneecap, she hit just above it, where the thigh muscle narrowed. He lurched, knocking Lalasa against the window frame, then let go. Lalasa scrambled back inside Kel's room, tears streaming down her face.

Kel took another step toward Vinson, doubling her fists. For the first time she could understand how someone in a rage might do murder. "How dare you touch an unwilling woman?" she asked.

He swallowed and took another step away from her, unable to rest any weight on the leg she'd kicked. "You're wrong, Mindelan," he said, licking his lips nervously. "The wench has been eyeing me for weeks. They all do it—bed men to earn extra coin over their wages."

"Liar." Kel slapped him. Last year Vinson had been almost a hand taller than she was. Now she was a scant inch shorter, and her build was more solid. Vinson was gangly and he exercised only in the practice courts. "I know her and I know you. Those scratches alone condemn you." She slapped him again. He had to challenge her; no knight could allow anyone to strike him without a fight. When he did, she would teach him a few lessons, then turn him in to Lord Wyldon.

Vinson backed up another step. He was in the wrong in every way. By palace law the maids were to be left alone: violators were brought before the chamberlain. In chivalry, servants were under a master's protection and could not be interfered with unless the master gave permission. No one would argue with Kel's dueling over this.

"You will regret your treatment of me," Vinson said. His voice shook. His face was pale and sweaty around its scratches. "My family is powerful at court."

Kel advanced until they were inches apart. "You are a coward," she told him, soft-voiced. "You knew you could frighten her—that's why you picked her. What kind of knight preys on serving girls? Where is your honor?"

"Just because I won't brawl with you doesn't mean I have no honor!" he blustered. "I—I refuse to get in trouble over a wench who is no better than she should be!"

Kel lifted her hand to slap him again. Vinson flinched, raising his arm to protect his face. He didn't run only because she had backed him against the wall.

She turned away, disgusted. "I'm reporting this," she said, striding toward the courtyard door.

"My lady, no!" cried Lalasa. She lunged out of the window to grab Kel's sleeve. "Don't tell." She wiped her eyes. "They'll talk until I've no reputation, that's how things are in servants' hall." She hung on to Kel with both hands and lowered her voice. "Nobles can make a girl's life a misery—they always do. Please don't report this!"

Kel wanted to argue, but Lalasa made sense. As Kel had just seen, she couldn't be everywhere. Who could say an enemy wouldn't lie in wait for Lalasa in places that Kel could not be?

Still, Kel owed her maid loyalty and protection. "He must be reported," she told Lalasa quietly. "He'll do it again."

"Please, my lady," pleaded Lalasa, "put yourself in my shoes! You'll get me in trouble. His kind can make it hard for servants. He speaks to his mother, who speaks to the chamberlain, who speaks to a steward, who puts my uncle out of work. How will you know it was done? How will you know it even came because of this? In two years you'll be gone, and Uncle and I will still be here. *Listen* to me."

Kel looked for Vinson: he'd stolen away. She tried to still her mind, to think. She certainly knew of nobles who forced themselves on serving women. No one put a halt to it. Within their own fiefdoms, nobles could do as they pleased. Even the priestesses of the Goddess, sworn to protect women and girls from just this kind of thing, might hesitate to offend a lord. Vinson's family was connected to powerful houses throughout the realm. The saying was that if anything was needed, Genliths would supply it. When all else was said and done, Kel *would* be gone in two years, to serve whatever knight would take her for a squire. She'd be hard put to defend Lalasa and Gower then.

Lalasa sensed that Kel was not about to charge after Vinson. She relaxed her hold on Kel's arm. "If I'd been on my feet, I could have done something," she commented, and blew her nose. "He had me all twisted around. I could hardly get at him."

Kel looked at her and remembered what she had seen: Lalasa's hands groping for a nerve, any nerve, in Vinson's imprisoning arm, and the bloody furrows on Vinson's face. "I am so proud of you," she said warmly, patting Lalasa's shoulder. "He's going to hurt for a long time—he won't dare take those marks to a healer." And I'd like to see him explain the scratches to Lord Wyldon, she thought. "I don't know if I could have done as well from that position." She inspected Lalasa. "Did he hit you? Hurt you in any way?"

Lalasa made a face. "I've bruises where he grabbed me. He would've gotten to hitting sooner or later—they all do." Kel stared at her, appalled. Lalasa turned her face away. "My dad, my brothers all hit their women."

Kel realized she was hearing bleak truth. "I thought Gower said you were alone—wait. Does *he* hit you?"

Lalasa shook her head and smiled, her lips trembling. "Dad always said Uncle had strange ideas, learnt up here in the north. He's not, not chirpy, like some, but he's the gentlest soul. He was the only one left..." She took a breath. "Raiders came in from the Copper Isles and burned our village out. They missed me—Dad sent me to the river to wash clothes."

"So you came here."

Lalasa nodded. "Uncle Gower told me the king's palace is a fine place to work. And so it is—I couldn't ask for kinder friends than Tian, and Uncle. It's just—" She shrugged. "No place is perfect."

Kel rubbed her temples. "Use the bruise balm," she suggested. "You won't need a lot." She turned.

Lalasa grabbed her arm again. "You're not—" she began, eyes wide.

Kel smiled grimly. "I won't report him, but I have to make sure he doesn't forget."

Lalasa's eyes searched Kel's face. At last she released her mistress.

"Next time you want to sew in the window?" said Kel. "Come get Jump. He'll see to it you're not bothered."

She went back into the pages' wing, walked straight to Vinson's room, and knocked sharply. "Don't make me say what I've come to say out here in the hall," she called.

Vinson opened the door, his face sullen. "What?" He didn't invite her in.

Kel put a hand on the door and leaned into the opening, making sure he could see her clearly. "If I hear of you bothering any female, not just her, I'll take you before the court of the Goddess. I'll risk making an enemy of the pack that whelped you."

Vinson blanched under his scratches and pimples. A man convicted of hurting women in the Goddess's court faced harsh penalties; those for actual rape were the worst of all. The temples maintained their own warriors to enforce the Goddess's law.

"I never want to see the wench again," he snapped, his voice cracking. "I'd give anything never to see *you*." He slammed the door.

Kel let him do it. He would keep quiet now, she suspected. One thing was certain, though—*she* must not forget. That her servant was harassed without real punishment was a reproach. Nobles were supposed to protect their servants. Lalasa had done well by her. She had to hold up her end of the arrangement.

She had trouble nodding off that night. She couldn't get rid of her anger with Vinson and with a world in which servants didn't matter. It wasn't right.

If she had gone into her usual deep sleep right away, she might never have heard sounds in the dressing room.

Tonight she did. She went around the screen that hid Lalasa's bed to find the older girl crying.

"Now, what's this?" Kel demanded, worried. "Lalasa, what's wrong?" She sat on the bed. "Please don't cry."

Lalasa buried her head in Kel's shoulder. "When he grabbed me, I hoped you would come," she said, her voice thick. "I'd no right, but I hoped. And you did!"

Kel patted her awkwardly. "You have every right," she said. "I'm honor-bound to protect you."

"And you did, you did!" cried Lalasa. "The look on your face—"

"Maybe I should report this after all," Kel suggested. "It's not right, letting him off when you're so scared."

"It's not that," Lalasa replied, shaking her head and sitting up straight. She wiped her eyes on her sleeve. "Not that, not much, anyway." She sniffed. "I never knew anybody who'd fight for me, never. When my bro—a man, a man hurt me, when I was little, and my parents said I lied. He was more important to them. But you—you faced down a noble for me!"

Kel looked down, hiding shock and fury. Lalasa's own brother had hurt her, and her parents had done nothing? They'd as good as told their daughter that she didn't matter!

At last, when she could trust her voice, Kel cleared her throat and said, "Vinson's not much of a noble."

"But I knew you would, if you found out." Lalasa clung to one of Kel's hands. "Since I've come to your service, I never felt so safe."

"Well, it's nothing to *cry* over," Kel said.

Lalasa chuckled and wiped her eyes again. "You're so

strong," she said, a little envy in her voice. "I wish I was like you. I wager no one ever grabbed you in your life."

Kel bent her head for a moment as memory flooded her. "My brother Conal held me off a balcony when I was four. I forget what I'd done to annoy him," she said quietly. "He was always hitting me or pushing me. This time he got caught—one of the maids was in the garden and heard me screaming."

"What a brute!" Lalasa cried, indignant.

"I'd never seen Papa so angry. He almost disowned Conal. He said he *would* disown Conal if he heard of anything else like that." Kel smiled bitterly. "I think the worst part, other than my being scared of heights now...The worst part is that Conal doesn't even remember. I asked him when we came back from the Islands."

"No wonder you hate bullies," whispered Lalasa. "No wonder you learned to fight."

Kel took a deep breath and let it out, thrusting the hard memories away. "Are you going to be able to sleep now?" she asked.

"Yes, forgive me," replied Lalasa, releasing Kel's hand. "I'm sorry I woke you."

"You didn't." Kel got to her feet. "I was awake. But you should sleep—all the sewing you do these days, you've earned your rest."

"And you haven't, I suppose," Lalasa teased.

"Sleep well, Lalasa."

"Thank you, my lady." As Kel reached the dressing room door she heard her maid say, quietly but firmly, "I *knew* you would come."

*   *   *

A week later Vinson was gone with his knight-master. Somehow he'd gotten a healer to tend the marks on his face; Kel would have liked to know what story he'd told. She suspected he'd had to hurt his face with something else, to cover the marks—it was an old trick.

Soon after Vinson's departure, Cleon reported to the study group with a glum face. "This is it," he announced. "I'm off at dawn. We're going back north." To Kel he said, "Sir Inness said to tell you we'll be visiting at Mindelan, if you've anything to send home."

"I have a letter to Anders," she said. "Shall I get it?"

"I'll go with you, if it's all the same," Cleon said. "I need to pack yet tonight." He said his farewells to his other friends, tugged Neal's ear "for luck," he claimed, and followed Kel back to her rooms.

Tian and Lalasa sat in the window seat, doing fine embroidery. Kel waved for them to stay where they were and found her letter on her desk. Quickly she signed and sealed it, and gave it to Cleon.

He turned it over in his hands, glanced at the two maids, and asked, "So, Kel, will you miss me?"

She smiled at him. "I missed you last year. Our group always loses a bit of madness when you're away."

"Here I thought Neal supplies all you could want, and that little scrapper Owen more than you need. Well." For a moment he looked at her, then at the maids, then at the letter. Suddenly he hugged Kel tight; as suddenly he let her go. "Don't break anything while I'm gone," he advised, and fled.

Kel shook her head as the door closed behind the big

squire. Owen would say he was treating me like a *girl* again, she thought, amused.

"You've made a conquest," Tian remarked slyly.

Kel looked at her and Lalasa. They were giggling. "Cleon? He just hates leaving."

"Of course, my lady," Lalasa replied, as meek as a mouse.

Kel sighed, and returned to the study group. At least the boys weren't always seeing romance whenever a male and female touched hands.

Joren, Garvey, and their knight-masters left a week later. More squires trickled out of the mess hall one at a time, until only the pages remained. It was spring. The business of the realm was picking up.

For this year's little examinations, Neal stuck to Kel like a burr from the moment they met at breakfast. "I won't risk you being late, and I won't be late waiting for you, either," he said as Kel gave her shiny brown locks a last combing. "Neither of us will repeat a day of this living doom if I have anything to say about it."

"Stop pacing," Kel ordered. "You'll wear out the floor. Is your tunic straight?" Briskly she tugged the back of his tunic until it hung properly. She was never sure if she was glad that her role as unofficial inspector gave her an excuse to touch him. "So tell me," she began as they walked to the exam waiting room, "is it worth all this struggle? You could have been a healer by now, with a university credential and friends your own age. Aren't you sorry to have missed that?"

She'd expected him to joke, or to be sarcastic, but he actually gave her question some thought. "The physical training, well, I couldn't be a knight without it, and I started late. Nothing would change that. It's true, at the university I never would have spent time with anyone so much younger than me. I would definitely have lost something then. These little fellows here aren't always testing each other like males of my advanced years." He bowed, and Kel smiled. "And I wouldn't give up *your* friendship for all the healer's credentials in the world."

"Me?" she demanded, astonished.

They walked into the waiting room, the first pages there. "You," Neal said, leaning against the wall and crossing his arms. "You are an education, Keladry of Mindelan."

Kel put her hands on her hips. "I'm not sure that's a compliment."

Neal grinned. "Neither am I," he teased.

As Seaver, Merric, and Owen came in, Kel pointed at Neal. "You will pay for that, on the practice courts," she informed him.

Owen promptly went over and clapped Neal on the shoulder. "It was good knowing you," he told the older boy solemnly.

The little examinations went as they had done in the last two years. The questions were all ones each page could answer easily, based on material that had been covered in detail during the year. It was almost a letdown.

The following week the pages attended the big examinations in support of Faleron and Yancen of Irenroha, who was voted "a good sort, if not one of us," by the study group. That night the fourth-years rose from their tables to walk to the squires' side of the room as their comrades applauded and cheered. There was a special dessert and entertainment to celebrate their promotion.

"Next year is our turn," Neal commented softly to Kel.

His words made her heart thud alarmingly. They were now fourth-year pages.

Summer 455 –
Spring 456

12

VANISHING YEAR

Summer camp that year was tame. There were no spidren nests, no outlaws. Lord Wyldon took them north, on a sixteen-day ride into the mountains around fiefs Aili, Stone Mountain, and Dunlath. In the mountains they lived in caves, hunted, fished, climbed rocks, and practiced the ever-vital skill of mapping. Lord Wyldon didn't have to search to find heights for Kel to climb. In this rugged country there were cliffs everywhere. Kel handled them: the weeks of practice since Midwinter had been a good idea. She did not spend her thirteenth birthday throwing up due to fright. She decided that this was a good thing.

I'll be a squire on my fourteenth birthday, she thought that night as she drifted off to sleep.

Their training in command and battle continued, with the pages divided into small groups and set at each other in hard terrain. For three days they had guests, acquaintances of Lord Wyldon from a summer camp the year before Kel had arrived: fifteen-year-old Lady Maura of Dunlath, her knight-guardian Sir Douglass of Veldine, a ten-foot-tall, aqua-skinned ogre named Iakoju, and a pack of wolves. The wolves moved among the pages as if mingling with humans were natural. Their gaze was steady and intelligent, making the hair on Kel's arms stand on end. Lord Wyldon spoke to their leader, Brokefang, as if he expected the great animal to understand him. Worse, Brokefang acted as if he *did* understand.

Kel's sparrows and Jump, who should have avoided the uncanny pack, were quite comfortable with them. During the nights the wolves stayed near the pages' camp, Jump slept with them; the sparrows rode on the animals until their departure.

The break in routine was a lesson in battles. Lady Maura and Iakoju showed the pages how Daine, Numair, and a force of knights, soldiers, animals, immortals, and Maura herself had overthrown Maura's treasonous sister and the Carthaki mages who helped her. Lady Maura explained the battle as coolly as a general while Iakoju drew maps and showed the movements of the odd army that had freed Dunlath. The fact that the wolves helped the ogre to move the stones used to show the forces' positions made Kel shiver.

"I don't know why it bothers me in wolves and not in sparrows or dogs," she confessed to her friends after the lady and her escort had gone.

"Maybe because wolves have no reason to like us," drawled Seaver.

Afterward they discovered that someone had raided their stores of dried meat and fruit. By the look of the tracks, a wolf had done it. Lord Wyldon examined a tuft of fur left by the marauder and shook his head. "Short Snout," he muttered under his breath.

A week after the pages went home for the summer, Kel was grooming Peachblossom when a voice said, "I hope he'll get on with the next page as well as he did with you, m'lady."

She turned. Stefan Groomsman leaned against the stable's back wall, chewing a straw.

"Beg pardon?" Kel asked.

"Maybe Daine will get him to obey his next master like he does you." There was hope in the hostler's bulging blue eyes. "Or do you mean to buy him yourself?"

The practice was common: they could buy the horses lent to them by the Crown once they became squires. Otherwise their knight-masters supplied their horses, and those they had ridden were left for new pages.

"I wish I could," Kel whispered, blinking eyes that suddenly burned. Presenting her sisters at court, opening the town house, paying Kel's expenses and the school fees of her brothers and sisters had strained her parents' finances. Even a troublesome destrier was expensive, and there was the added cost of feeding and housing him. Buying Peachblossom was out of the question.

Stefan cleared his throat. He was more comfortable with horses than with people, but he'd been kind to Kel for Peachblossom's sake. "You've gentled him considerable, miss. Long as his next master don't use the spur, I think he'll get on. You prob'ly saved his life, taking him on like you did."

Kel hid her face against Peachblossom's neck. What would she do without him? No other horse would give her that same fearful, gleeful sense of riding an avalanche. She envied the gelding his freedom to be mean. Sometimes she told herself that Peachblossom was her temper, her *true* temper under all her Yamani manners.

She made herself smile at Stefan. "Well, we have one more year," she said. "We'll just make it a good one." She heard a whine and looked down. Jump peered up at her, his twice-broken tail waving slowly. "At least I'll be able to keep Jump, don't you think?"

Stefan nodded. "Just about all the knights keep dogs. You ever seen the elk and wolfhounds my lord breeds?"

Kel wasn't sure whom he meant. "My lord—?" she asked.

"Him as is your training master, miss. Fief Cavall breeds the finest dogs in the realm. It's no wonder my lord's turned a blind eye to that chap." He nodded at Jump. "He's that fond of dogs, and however beauteous your lad may be, anyone with an eye can tell he's a fine dog under them scars."

Kel smiled. Only Stefan would call a scarred, stocky, one-eared, small-eyed, chisel-headed brawler like Jump "beauteous."

She saw Peachblossom's eyelid lower and grabbed the reins, just as he lunged for Jump. Pulling his head back up, she scolded, "What do you care if he gets compliments? He's a dog." She told Stefan, "It's like he understands what we say."

The hostler grinned. "When new horses come in from outside, I find myself thinking they're stupid. That's the palace these days." He was headed for the door when he thought of something. "You know, Lady Kel, if your knight-master is one what keeps close to court, I'll see to it you stay with Peachblossom. I know that's not likely, but it's something."

Kel grimaced as he left. Was this what she had to look forward to? Either she lost her horse, or she kept him because she'd been chosen by a palace knight, someone like Sir Gareth of Naxen or Sir Myles, who spent his days among documents. There were worse fates, she supposed. She liked Sir Myles, whose comments and quiet jokes had lightened her bleakest days, but serving a knight who rode a desk, not a destrier, was not in her dreams of protecting the helpless.

Kel's two-month holiday passed quickly, as it always did. Stefan gave her permission to ride Peachblossom into the Royal Forest, if she didn't go too far. Kel took Jump and the sparrows, and tried out her mystery well-wisher's latest gift, a beautifully made bow and quiver full of arrows. Several times she brought Stefan small game like rabbits and partridges as a thank-you.

The brightest spot was two weeks spent with her parents in Port Caynn, picnicking on beaches and in the countryside. With Adalia to marry at Midwinter and Oranie betrothed, both to husbands they helped to choose, Piers and Ilane of Mindelan wanted time with Kel. She practiced glaive skills with her mother and talked late into the night with her father, telling him all she had learned about battles. The three reminisced about the Yamani Islands and talked about the negotiations for a new Yamani treaty and an imperial bride for Prince Roald.

On their ride back to Corus, Ilane asked, "Are you frightened of the big exams?"

Kel shook her head. "The worst part is having people watch—well, and the judges don't seem that friendly," she admitted. "But I've sat in on the big exams, and the questions on learning and showing your physical training just aren't that hard. Neal's more scared than I am. He's afraid that we're going to be a sneeze late, and have to do this year—or worse, the whole thing—over again."

"I shouldn't think you'd be late on such a day," Ilane remarked, amused.

"Nor do I, but that's Neal for you," Kel replied, shaking her head.

Training began again. There were new first-years to meet, and the nightly hazing patrols to resume. Lord Wyldon handed out weights to the senior pages, and set new, more vexing targets for Kel to tilt at after she mastered the lightweight ring. He then shifted other fourth-years to the ring once they were able to hit the small black dot on the quintain target.

Requests for Lalasa's services as a seamstress poured in as ladies readied for the court social season. Counting the part of Lalasa's earnings that she was saving, Kel realized that her maid's goal of her own shop might be reached soon. She might even have enough money by the time Kel entered a knight-master's service. Kel wouldn't be leaving her to fend for herself.

The training season was a week old when Iden and Warric reported to Kel's room immediately after supper. With them were three first-years. "We told them how good you two are at helping," Iden explained.

Kel and Lalasa traded looks, Kel's resigned, Lalasa's amused. Extra training with staffs resumed in Kel's rooms.

In November, before the squires returned, Lord Wyldon, Sergeant Ezeko, and the two Shangs took the pages into the Royal Forest, where they camped overnight. In the morning, the pages were split into two groups. One, led by Seaver, hiked beside a broad, brisk stream until they were out of sight of the rest. They would assemble, pick weapons and blunt-tipped arrows, and coat them with red chalk, as Seaver explained what position each of his "men" held. The other group was taken to a huge pile of boulders upstream. This was their castle, which they would defend against Seaver's marauders. They, too, used red chalk to coat the edges of their weapons and arrows. Eda Bell and Hakuin Seastone would judge if a page was still "alive" according to the red marks on clothes or skin.

To everyone's astonishment, Lord Wyldon chose Kel to command the defending force. She trudged around the rocks, scratching her head, then climbed nervously to their heights to inspect their surroundings. There was no moat to keep enemies from taking her rock castle from the rear. She had the stream on one side, which meant that approach was moderately safe. She immediately put her first-years to building noise-traps of dry branches to give warning of the enemy's advance. She chose Neal, Quinden, and Warric and posted them as lookouts farther away. For a moment she thought Quinden would refuse her orders, but the moment passed. He vanished into the trees. The adults left, too, fading into the trees to watch. She wished she had their skill at moving silently through dry leaves.

If she had learned anything in hill country, it was the benefits of high ground. She positioned her archers on the stone heights, in those spots where trees didn't obscure their view of the ground. The pages who wielded staffs she placed on stones that raised them just above the ground, to give them the advantage. Before she took an observation post for herself, she assembled Jump and the sparrows on a rock too small for a human.

"This is a game," she explained, a little embarrassed that her teammates could hear her talking to animals. "It's for fun. Well, not fun, exactly, but—never mind." She glanced around, in case Lord Wyldon had appeared to scowl at her. He was nowhere in view. "You stay right here. Don't move. Don't help." Then she climbed to her own vantage point high on the rocks.

Instead of looking down, which made her sweat, she closed her eyes and listened for the crunch of leaves over the stream's rush. Twice she told the boys in her command to be quiet. For the most part, though, they took her instructions as seriously as if they were at war.

Kel opened her eyes when an arrow struck a tree stump halfway between her vantage point and the archers. She jumped down and inspected it: a purple thread around the shaft marked it as Neal's. The enemy had just passed him. Kel alerted her warriors on that line of approach. She made sure that the others kept their positions. "Don't get into the fight," she told them firmly. "Watch the trees—

Seaver might split his people up. You archers, shoot carefully. You don't want to hurt anyone you hit, and we don't have more arrows once yours are gone."

That should have been everything until Seaver's force reached hers, but Kel was still uncomfortable. She took a last tour of the level where the staff men were, then circled again on her height. She was still fidgeting when the rattle of a noise-trap met her ears. Looking to the rear of her "castle," she saw a small group of pages creeping through the trees.

They got around Quinden, she thought, and alerted the sentries on that side with hand signs. One of them was Owen, who lay flat on a high stone, a selection of cloth balls beside him. Instead of the clear, deadly jelly called blazebalm, used in real combat, the balls held a fist-sized clump of dirt, leaves, and red chalk. When the attackers came within range, he lobbed the balls at them with deadly accuracy. They burst when they hit, leaving his victims covered with dirt and red dust. As "killed men" they sat on the forest floor in disgust.

When they attacked in the rear, Seaver led his main group in a charge at the front.

By Owen's terms it wasn't a jolly fight—he complained later there was far too much thinking and calls of "You, out!" by the adults—but it was brisk. Kel moved from post to post, making sure there were no more surprises and that everyone obeyed orders. Seaver's attack was defeated at every turn. When only three of his "men" were left, they tried to retreat. Kel sent her staff men to capture them, winning a total victory.

Afterward they cooked lunch, and the adults reviewed

their performance. Several boys received punishment labor for refusing to stay dead after an adult decreed them so. Quinden was given twice that amount of work for not warning Kel when Seaver's second group passed him. When she glanced at him, surprised—she'd honestly thought they'd sneaked around him—Quinden sneered at her.

The last of Joren's legacy, Kel thought as she scrubbed her dishes. I'll be glad when I'm a squire and don't have to deal with *that* anymore.

Two days after their return, squires began to appear in the mess hall. Once again Prince Roald stayed at Port Legann in the south. Joren returned, Vinson, Faleron, Garvey, Yancen—but no Cleon. In December Kel got a letter from him, addressed to her but written for the entire study group. Sir Inness had chosen to remain in the north, training villagers in self-defense. They wouldn't come to the palace until the spring.

With the start of winter, Kel's year appeared to melt away. She could remember the passage of time if she thought about it. Once again she waited on the Archpriestess and her companions over Midwinter. She exchanged gifts and received them. There was a beautifully made longsword from her benefactor, one that was the envy of her friends. Lalasa surprised her with a long coat, quilted with down for warmth, containing a number of useful pockets. It was in Kel's favorite color, russet red. Neal gave her a book of Tortallan maps, while Kel gave him a history of his famous grandfather's battles. There were gifts of clothes and money from her family, a drawing of Jump from Seaver, and small gifts from her other friends. Kel gave Owen some of her precious bruise balm—of all the pages, she told him in her accompanying note, he needed it the most. Seaver and Merric each got one of her lucky Yamani cat figures. For the rest she had gotten sweets, knowing they would appreciate those on cold winter nights.

She could remember what she learned in Sunday night battle lessons without trouble: they continued to fascinate her. Lord Wyldon chose battles with immortals, sea raiders, and Scanrans to cover that winter, to give his students an understanding of the methods preferred by the enemies they would have to fight most as knights.

More weights were added to their harnesses in January. No sooner had the senior pages adjusted to them than Lord Wyldon set the fourth-years to tilting at each other. This was unusual: normally, tilting at a human target was left for knight-masters to teach. As far as Kel was concerned, the worst part of it was realizing she was trying to skewer one of her friends with her well-padded lance. She learned to concentrate on the shield. If she looked at her opponent's face, too often it was she who went flying from the saddle.

Classroom work after Midwinter was harder to recall, except for the day that a debate between Quinden and two first-years turned into a shouting match. The subject had been one that would be raised at the nobles' congress in the spring, whether new laws should be made to give commoners the right to better treatment by nobles. Sir Myles had to threaten to report all three debaters to Lord Wyldon before they would be quiet.

Lalasa threw Kel twice, once in December and once in February. In January, no less a person than Queen Thayet commissioned a dress from Kel's maid. Kel was able to tell Lalasa that she could now afford a dress shop of her own.

Joren seemed to be many places that Kel was after Midwinter. They didn't fight; they traded greetings if they passed in the hall. He watched her at mealtimes and Sunday night battle lessons, though. She would look up to find those level blue eyes fixed on her. She would walk around a table model and bump into him. Once, eerily, she felt a touch at the back of her head as the class broke up one night. When she turned, only Joren was near, and he was walking away.

She might have thought she imagined it, except that Neal and Owen saw it, too. Neal wanted to tell Joren his behavior was rude, but Kel and Owen talked him out of it.

Apart from those memories, she felt as if she went to bed one night before Midwinter and awoke at the end of March. The winter had fallen away. Nobles and other important folk were arriving at the palace in droves, preparing for the congress that was held every two years. Lord Imrah came from Port Legann with Prince Roald in tow; Sir Inness returned with Cleon. The first thing Roald and Cleon said to the fourth-years on their arrival was, "Are you ready for the big exams?"

13

THE TEST

"Lalasa, stop fussing!" Kel ordered her maid at her last fitting before the big examinations. "If it fits any more perfectly, I won't be able to take it off!"

Lalasa removed the pins she'd been holding in her mouth. "I just want you to look your best, my lady," she explained in all seriousness. "Though there's little I can do with this cursed gold and red. I don't think anybody really looks good in it."

"Well, I'll look better than anybody else, that's for certain." Kel began to remove her tunic, and promptly stuck herself with a pin.

"Here, miss—best let me." As Lalasa slowly drew the tunic and its pins over Kel's head, she added, "If you don't mind, I'm going to Tian's for a bit tonight. I've a week to finish her majesty's dress for the opening of the congress, and Tian's agreed to hem whilst I work on the bodice. I'll be home before you go to bed, doubtless."

"That's fine." Kel changed into breeches and a shirt, then opened the lower shutters. Summer had come early, and her room was stifling when they were closed.

Two strangers, men in the rough clothes of commoners, were in the courtyard. That surprised Kel: the pages' wing was tucked well out of the way for visitors. Only servants, teachers, and nobles came there.

"Are you lost?" she inquired.

One of them, a burly man who needed a shave, snatched off his hat. After a moment his smaller companion did the same.

"Saving your presence, your lordship, but we was supposed t'meet our boss in the entry hall." They think I'm a boy, Kel realized, amused. Her loose shirts still concealed her figure. "Witless, here"—the big man elbowed his companion—"got us turned about."

"I was sure it was this way," the little man whined. He leered as Lalasa came to stand beside Kel. "Miss."

Jump leaped out the window and trotted over to the men. They backed away.

"It's all right. He's just not used to strangers." Kel swung over the window sill and dropped onto the courtyard flags. Her sparrows, hovering about their nests in the eaves, called greetings. "I'll show you to the entry hall. It's easy to get lost here." As Kel passed Jump, she realized the dog was acting strangely, cocking his bulky head this way and that as he looked at the men. He seemed unsure of something. "Jump, stay with Lalasa," Kel ordered. "If you men will follow me?"

She led them to the entry hall and received their thanks, then returned home. It was supper time; she was hungry. Telling Lalasa to have a good time at Tian's, she went in search of her friends.

After supper the boys and Kel visited the royal menagerie to while away the hours until bedtime. To their surprise, they found their teacher Lindhall Reed, his living skeleton Bonedancer, Numair Salmalín, and Daine visiting the small tribe of pygmy marmosets. Since Daine was present, the keepers allowed the tiny monkey-like creatures out of their enclosure. They climbed all over the pages, clearly as fascinated with them as the pages were with the marmosets.

It was late when the pages returned to their rooms, swearing they wouldn't be able to sleep. Kel saw no light burning behind Lalasa's screen and was glad her maid hadn't waited up for her. Kel herself wasn't nearly ready for sleep. She quietly closed the dressing room door, lit a candle, and read a history of King Jasson's battles until she was ready to sleep. When she turned in, she left the shutters open for Jump. The dog seemed to have gone off on a ramble, as he did now and then.

The next day, exam day, Kel was up before dawn as always. She opened her shutters, admitting the sparrows. They tumbled in as much as they flew: it was windy. Hurriedly they pecked at their seeds and flew out to feed the nestlings. They would be in and out all day. Kel started morning exercises—just because the big examinations were today was no reason to slack off, she thought.

She was half done when a sense of something not right made her stop in the middle of a strike. The sun was rising. Lalasa should have come out by now. And Jump was nowhere in sight.

Kel opened the dressing room door. The lamp was still unlit. She heard nothing that sounded like her maid getting dressed.

"Lalasa?" she called. She couldn't believe the older girl would sleep in today, of all days. Was she ill?

There was no reply. Frowning, Kel looked behind the wooden screen. Lalasa's bed was as neatly made as ever, her plain cotton nightdress laid across it. She had not come home the night before.

Kel stared at the bed and nightgown. She'd heard stories about servants who crept away for a night or two, but this made no sense. Lalasa had never done such a thing; why start now? She had seemed fine the afternoon before. They had talked about finding her shop together over the summer—Lalasa had been excited about that. Besides, she had asked Kel for permission to attend the big exams, to watch her mistress prove herself before the world. She wouldn't have asked that if she had meant to run away.

I'm not going to panic, Kel thought. If she stayed later at Tian's than she realized, she might have slept there so she wouldn't wake me coming in. Probably when I get back from breakfast, she'll be here. I hope she *and* Jump will be here.

Kel washed her face and hands in cold water, dried, and dressed in breeches and a shirt for breakfast. She wasn't about to get food stains on her gold tunic by wearing it while she ate. It would be just her luck to wear it to breakfast and drop bacon on her lap.

When she joined her friends in the pages' mess, she

grinned. Neal looked absolutely green; Merric, Seaver, and Esmond were pale. "Eat something," she ordered, spooning porridge into her bowl. "You'll need it."

"How can you *think* of food?" asked Merric. Neal picked up a slice of toasted bread and began to shred it.

"Because I don't want to faint just as we go from classroom tests to weapons," she said. "Remember? Like Ragnal of Darroch fainted last year?" Prodding and teasing, she got them to eat, and said nothing of her maid. They wouldn't be interested; Esmond had even told her months ago that servants weren't important enough to be worth the time Kel spent thinking about hers.

"Don't take forever to primp," Neal urged Kel as she finished. "You know I hate to be late."

"We won't be late," she told him. "Comb your hair and stop running your fingers through it. You'll do fine."

"You have no nerves," he said bitterly.

"Just as well, because you have too many," she retorted, and carried her tray to the servants.

The man who took it winked at her. "Luck, Lady Kel. From us all." He nodded to the other man and the woman who served the food and took dirty dishes away. The other man grinned; the woman curtsied.

Kel smiled. "Thank you," she said, touched.

Lalasa had not returned.

Kel looked for Gower—he wasn't in his room. Worried, she went to Salma's. To her relief, Gower was having breakfast with the woman who ran the pages' wing. At first Kel was reluctant to mention Lalasa's absence before Salma. Only when she remembered that Lalasa answered to her alone did she ask Gower if he'd seen his niece.

"Not since yesterday noon," he replied, dark brows raised. "Is there a problem?"

"She didn't come back last night," Kel said flatly. "She was to visit her friend Tian, my sister's maid, but she said she was coming back."

"My lady, it's common for girls to stay out overnight," Salma informed her. "If she has a lover—"

"I'd know if she did, I think," replied Kel.

"Did you quarrel? It happens, and she is young. She might think to punish you," Salma pointed out.

Kel shook her head. "We didn't quarrel. She was looking forward to today."

"She's a good girl," Gower commented slowly. "And that grateful to Lady Kel." He got to his feet. "I'll go see Tian," he told Kel and Salma. "See what she knows."

As the door closed behind him, Salma remarked, "Unless you want to get the girl in trouble, don't mention her absence to the guards. They'll apply the penalties for runaway servants, and you'll have no say in the judgment that's handed down on her."

"I wouldn't anyway," Kel replied. "Lord Wyldon made it clear when I hired her that she's my responsibility, not the palace's."

"I'm sure there's a reason for this, milady," Salma commented as she showed Kel to the door. "She *did* say she wanted to watch you prove how good you were before the gods and everyone else."

When Kel went back to her room, there was still no sign of Lalasa, and Kel was running out of time. She looked around for the uniform she was to wear today and got a most unpleasant surprise. It lay on the dressing room worktable, every pin still in place. That was not right. Lalasa would never have gone to Tian's with this tunic unfinished—she always did Kel's work before she did anything else.

A knock called her to the door. Kel opened it, the pinned tunic in her hand. There stood Gower and Tian.

"She never came last night," the maid said, clutching a balled-up handkerchief. "I waited and waited. I thought— we quarreled, but Gower says she told you she meant to visit me." Her eyes were red and swollen, as if she'd been crying.

"She did. She said you were going to hem the queen's dress while she did the bodice." Now all Kel's instincts clamored that something was very, very wrong. Other maids would lose their tempers and cause their mistresses and friends anxiety—not Lalasa. After three years Kel knew her as well as she knew anybody. If Lalasa was not here, if she hadn't been where she had said she would be, then something had happened.

"Gower, will you check the servants' infirmary?" she asked. "If she took sick, perhaps..."

Gower nodded and left them.

"Please, Lady Kel, what might I do?" Tian asked. "My lady's off with her husband to Port Caynn. I've the whole day free."

Kel tried to think, while part of her mind cried that she had to get ready for the big examinations right *now!* Her parents would be there; Numair and Daine, the two

Shangs, Master Lindhall, and Stefan from the stables. She hadn't much time.

"Try palace stores," she suggested. "The drapers, and the tailors. Maybe she just got me a new uniform." It seemed unlikely—the pins in the tunic she held were an argument against that—but it was all she could think of.

"Thank you, my lady." Tian dipped a curtsy and ran down the hall.

Anxious, Kel shut the door. She could change clothes, at least. Her other uniforms were presentable, if not as perfectly fitted as the one she held. She found the freshest uniform and started to change.

The sparrows had picked up on her tension. Those birds not ferrying seed to the nestlings fluttered around the chamber and courtyard, as if they expected to find Lalasa in a crack in the walls.

"Where's Jump?" she asked them. "What happened to him?"

The birds whirled and spun in a frenzy. All of them suddenly halted, coming to rest on her bed. "You don't know," Kel guessed.

Crown hopped forward one step and gave a single peep. Kel had a feeling that her guess was right.

"Look for them, those who can be spared?" she asked. "I know you've the nestlings to care for, but…Find Lalasa? Find Jump?"

Crown chattered. She and half the birds on the bed took to the air and flew away. The rest went back to the seed dishes.

Kel had just pulled her tunic over her shoulders when she heard a low scraping sound near the door. Had someone like Joren thought to make her late by laying a messy trap outside, as people had done in her first year? When she opened the door—carefully, in case a bucket of water was rigged to drop on her—she saw only pages. She examined the flags in front of her door for puddles of urine or oil, but saw nothing. Turning, she found a sheet of parchment on the floor. She'd heard it being slid into her room.

The handwriting was bold, the message unmistakable.

She is in the palace.
You can find her if you look.

At the bottom of the page there was a further note:

Tell anyone and we will hurt her.

Kel's hands began to shake. Slowly and carefully, she folded the parchment in half, then into quarters. Why kidnap a maid?

To hurt her mistress.

When she had finished her probationary year and won Lord Wyldon's permission to continue, she had thought it would be the end of people trying to make her quit. Now she knew they had only been waiting. They had committed a crime to stop her from taking the big exams.

It won't work, Kel thought grimly. The tests usually end by the second bell after noon, with no halt for lunch. Once they're over, I'll be able to search wherever I want.

"I knew you would come," Lalasa had whispered, that night Vinson had scared her. "I never knew anyone who would fight for me." Lalasa, creeping about like a mouse for a year or more, terrified of her own shadow. Now she was a vivid and happy young woman, and she gave Kel credit for the change. Of course she would understand that Kel had to take the big exams first. She always thought Kel was more important than she was.

She would be frightened, Kel was sure of that. And she must have been so throughout the long night.

Someone pounded briskly on her door. It was not Gower or Tian, but Neal, Merric, Seaver, and Esmond, all dressed for the examinations, hair neatly combed and plastered into place with water or pomade. "Reporting for inspection, sir!" Merric said, trying to grin. They all saluted.

What could she do? She let them in and did the requested inspection, tugging at collars and hem lines, checking their hose for wrinkles, patting a stiffened clump of hair into its proper place. "You're as lovely as a field of daisies," Kel assured them when she was done. "Why don't you go on to the assembling room? I'll be there in a moment." She had to *think*.

Neal did not leave with the others. "What's the matter?" he demanded, holding her eyes with his. "You have your Yamani face on."

When had he gotten so short? Kel wondered, distracted briefly. He had towered over her once. Now he was just an inch taller, and he was almost nineteen.

"Kel, what's wrong?" Neal demanded, gently shaking her arm.

The note had said tell no one, but they could hardly spy on Kel here, in her room. She unfolded the note and gave it to him.

"Who are they writing about?" Neal asked.

"Lalasa. She never came home last night, and Tian

says she never arrived there, where she said she was going. Jump's missing, too."

Neal returned the note. "Tell the palace guard. They'll find her."

"Did you read the whole thing?" Kel asked him, shocked. "They'll hurt her!"

"They wouldn't dare," Neal told her stubbornly. "If they torture her on top of kidnapping, in the *palace* to boot, they'll get no mercy from the royal courts, and they know it. They just want you to be late." He searched her face, his green eyes feverish. "Kel—no. You're not going to— That's what they want. You'll repeat a year, two— maybe all four. You can't! Not after all we've been through!"

Kel wiped her eyes. They were wet, for some reason. "Neal, she trusts me. She's my responsibility. And she'll be so frightened...I have to find her." Until she heard herself say it, Kel hadn't realized she was really going to do it, really going to turn her back on the big exams and repeat however many years Lord Wyldon gave her. She fought to smile. "I just want to be the second-oldest page in living memory, don't you see."

"No, you won't." He drew a deep breath; his wide mouth trembled. "We're friends. I'll help. Between the two of us—"

"Absolutely not," she said fiercely. "No, no, *no!*" The last four years had been torture for him. Now he wanted to do it all again for her? She couldn't let it happen. It would kill her to see Neal either give up a knighthood or repeat his page years. "They win twice then, don't you understand? Now get to the assembly room!" He looked down and away. Kel grabbed his arm and towed him to her door. "You can be my knight-master when I do take the exams, if you want to make it up to me. Neal, please. Don't make me feel responsible for you both! She wouldn't be in this trouble if not for me!"

She thrust him out her door, where Gower caught him. "Excuse me, master," the manservant remarked, setting Neal on his feet. To Kel he said, "She's not in the infirmary. Miss, you must get to the examinations."

If she told Gower, he too might argue. "I'll catch up to you," Kel told Neal, glaring at him, silently warning him to go along with what she said. "There's a stain on one of my hose. I have to change it. Gower, would you check the room where they're holding the exams? Maybe she decided to get there early, before the seats were taken." Neal still hadn't budged. Kel took a deep breath. "Neal, if you are my friend, *go.*"

He left at a run. Gower frowned at Kel. "I really think, miss—" he began.

"Do as I say," Kel ordered him curtly, fresh out of the ability to both lie and be polite. She closed the door in his face and waited, listening. Only when she heard his slow footsteps moving away did she leave the door. She had her belt knife. Her benefactor had sent her a brace of wrist knives; she put those on now. The birds were looking already; it was time for her to do the same. She closed the lower shutters and locked them. The sparrows who stayed with the nestlings continued to flutter in and out through the upper windows.

Before she opened her door again, Kel stopped, and rested her forehead against it. Right now the fourth-year pages were gathering. Lord Wyldon would be on his way to inspect them before they entered the examination room. She could still do it. She could still go if she ran, and she'd be on time. If she came in after the training master, all she would have to repeat would be a year. Surely that wouldn't be so bad. Look at how quickly this last year had gone.

Once they entered the examination room, though…

Wetness trickled down her face. Impatiently she wiped her eyes. Maybe Lalasa would escape her kidnappers. She was clever. If they didn't frighten her too badly, she might get away. Maybe Kel would open this door, and there she would be.

Kel opened the door. Tian was trotting toward her, more upset than ever. "Lady Kel!" she cried. "No one has seen her in stores." She hugged herself, eyes huge in her drawn face. "Did Gower find her?"

Kel shook her head.

"And you're off to the examinations?" Tian inquired.

Kel sighed. She didn't want to worry about Lalasa's friend with so much else on her mind, but Tian looked as if she needed something to do. An idea occurred to Kel. "Do me a favor, unless you have other duties?" she asked.

"Nothing," Tian whispered. "I can't even work on the queen's dress. Lalasa has it."

Kel opened her door. "We'll shoot two arrows from one bow, then," she said cheerfully. "The queen's gown's on a stand in the dressing room—why don't you work on it? Stay here in case Lalasa comes in. Tell her I'm not angry, and make sure she waits for me." After all, Lalasa might get away, or her kidnappers would free her once Kel was so late that she'd have to repeat all four years or give up completely. "And if you work on the dress, then she won't be late in getting it to the queen."

Tian thanked her passionately. Embarrassed, Kel shooed the older girl into her room.

Her list of places to search began with those she knew who wished her ill. Joren should have been at the top of it, but he had been so odd for the last two years that Kel wasn't sure about him.

Vinson, on the other hand, was definitely someone to look at, and Joren's room was on the same hall. Kel trotted upstairs to the squires' rooms, on the floor above the pages.

Kel rapped hard on Vinson's door, once, then twice. She heard nothing when she put her ear to the wood, and saw nothing when she peered through the keyhole. She tried Garvey's room next, then Joren's. No one answered either knock. The hall itself was as silent as if all the squires were on the road with their knight-masters. She knew that wasn't the case; almost everyone had stayed to attend the congress.

Next she tried the pages' and the squires' armories, the storerooms where supplies were kept for their part of the palace, and the catacombs far beneath the palace. There was no sign of Lalasa anywhere. Sweating, covered with smutches from the dusty catacombs, Kel made her way up to the ground floor again. She emerged in a quiet area between two wings of the palace and sat on a bench out of the wind to catch her breath. Next she would try the area of unused sheds where Lord Wyldon had schooled them in city fighting. Those empty buildings made perfect hiding places.

And if she's not there, where will you look? demanded her shrill and frightened self. Garrets? Storage barns? Stable lofts? The palace is *huge*. Better to go to the examinations now, and save yourself a year or two!

I'll look wherever I must, thought Kel stubbornly. She had to find Lalasa. The kidnappers might decide to remove a witness to their crime, and kill her.

She heard a fountain splashing nearby. It might be a good idea to cool off before she resumed her search. The brisk wind turned the water cold on her face, but it helped to clear her head. She was drying her hands on the underside of her tunic when the sparrows arrived, flapping around her head as they screeched.

"You found her?" Kel asked them, trembling. "You know where she is?"

Crown hovered in midair, something in her beak. When Kel stretched out her open hand, the sparrow lit on it and dropped several long black hairs on Kel's palm. Freckle came next. His gift to Kel was a small clump of short, fine white hairs.

"Both of them? Lalasa and Jump? Where?" Kel asked. "Show me where."

The sparrows lit briefly on the fountain's rim, getting a quick drink. When they took to the air again, they flew ahead of Kel, swooping and bobbing on the gusty wind, leading her through a courtyard and across a small garden. When a long shadow fell over Kel, she looked up, and stopped in her tracks. They had brought her to the building that formed the base of Balor's Needle. Now they flew straight up, dancing in flight around the fragile-looking iron stair that twined around the tower.

14

NEEDLE

Kel's vision went gray. A bubble of panic rose in her throat. Why am I surprised? she wondered. Whoever did this wanted to be sure I would fail.

I don't have to, though, she thought. I can tell someone and they'll get her and Jump. I won't have to climb those stairs. I could look around instead and see if I can find out who did this.

"I knew you would come," Lalasa had told her.

Wasn't finding where she was enough?

It wasn't. She knew it wasn't. How could she face Lalasa—or Neal, or Owen—knowing she had turned her back? How could she face herself?

Kel bit trembling lips and forced herself to smile at the birds who had perched on the outer stair railing. "Your opinion of my courage is higher than it should be," she told them. "I'd as soon have my fingernails pulled out than go that way." She laid her hands on the doorknob and twisted. The great wooden panel swung open. Air scented with old incense and candles poured over Kel as she stepped inside the Needle.

The big chandelier was unlit. A lamp burned on a table just inside the door; beside the table was a box full of torches. "I guess they don't light the chandelier for just anyone," Kel murmured, picking up a torch. She held it over the lamp. As soon as the end started to burn, she uttered a quick prayer for courage and began to climb.

Oddly, the job was easier in the near-dark: there were no windows in the Needle. The torch could illuminate only so much. The great open gap at the tower's heart and the gaps in the ironwork steps were just shadows, ones Kel could ignore. She stayed close to the wall and climbed.

At last she reached the top. She set the torch in a holder beside the door, took a deep breath, and raised the latch. Opening the door was a struggle. The wind fought her, pressing against the wood. Kel braced her shoulder against the door and shoved. Slowly the door inched open.

Air buffeted her as she slid through the gap onto the platform. When she let go, the door slammed shut again.

Hysterical barking met her ears. There was Lalasa, bound, gagged, blindfolded, and tucked against the waist-high railing, protected from the wind. Three feet from her, tied to the railing by a rope so short he couldn't turn to chew it, was Jump. The dog howled to see Kel. He leaped into the air, only to be yanked down by his leash. Kel took a step toward them and met the wind's full blast.

Well, no one can see me but Jump. He won't think less of me if I crawl, thought Kel. She got down on all fours, below the railing that circled the platform. Now she was out of the wind and able to crawl to Lalasa.

"It's me," Kel shouted over the wind as she drew her knife. The older girl's flesh was red and swollen around her bonds. "Hold still. I'll have you loose in a wink!"

First she cut away the blindfold and gag, then the ropes. The moment she was free Lalasa threw herself at Kel, clutching her weakly. She sobbed, her face already puffed and dirty from crying.

"Yes, it's all right. Let me get Jump," Kel said in her ear.

Lalasa nodded and let her go, wiping her eyes on her sleeve. Kel crawled over to Jump, who kept trying to lick her face as she cut his leash. There was a raw red circle all around his thick neck where he had pulled against the rope. He'd been hurt—he could barely rest his weight on one hind foot—but his spirits were as boisterous as ever. Kel hugged him quickly, then said, "Come help with Lalasa."

They crawled back to the maid, who was trying to move her wrists. Like Jump, she showed signs of a long fight against coarse rope in the bleeding welts around her wrists and ankles. Kel chafed one wrist while Jump briskly licked one of Lalasa's ankles. "How long have you been out here?" Kel asked. "Can you stand?" She already saw Lalasa couldn't make her hands close.

"I think they brought us up here near dawn," was the sobbed reply. "I'm so cold!"

There was a burlap bag on the platform. Kel wrapped it around Lalasa's shoulders and returned to chafing the maid's wrists. Jump switched ankles. "What happened?" Kel wanted to know. She had to lean close to Lalasa to hear the answer over the wind.

"It was those two men we saw. They came back, and they said they had a message for you. When I opened the door, they grabbed me. They said they'd kill me if I screamed. Jump tried to stop them—he was so brave! But they threw a blanket on him. They would have killed him—they were kicking him—but I said he belongs to the Wildmage. If anything happened to him, Daine would hunt them with every animal in the *world*. They believed me. They wrapped him in the blanket—later they put him in this bag." Lalasa clenched her teeth, shuddering.

"What's wrong?" Kel asked.

"Cramps," she replied, trying to move her legs.

Kel began to massage them, feeling the muscles hard under her hands. Tied in that position since dawn, of course they'd knot, she thought, remembering they still had a stair to descend. "Flex your arms before they seize up," she ordered. "What happened then? Getting you out of my rooms without being seen must have been a job and a half."

Lalasa shook her head. "They gagged me and changed into palace uniforms, and then they fetched one of the large baskets we use to take sheets to the laundry. They had everything, Lady Kel—it was so well planned!" Lalasa opened one arm, and let Jump tuck himself against her side, then wrapped the sack around both of them. The pain of cramping muscles made tears roll down her face, but she spoke not a word of complaint. "They put us in the basket and carried us somewhere. That place was private—they didn't care if Jump barked. They put the blindfold on and let me use the chamber pot—that's when they stuffed Jump in the bag. They took us one other place and kept us there forever, it seemed. Then they brought us here. They said if I wiggled I'd drop out through a hole in the floor. I could hear Jump, so I knew he was all right. He marked them, my lady. He marked them well. We can have the watch on them quick as lightning with all those bites to show." She wiped her face on her apron. "Are the big examinations over?"

"I've no idea," Kel told her. "Try to straighten your legs."

Lalasa tried, but her legs were still too knotted. She shook her head. "Needles and pins, miss. I'll manage."

"You can't manage if you can't stand." Kel returned to massaging Lalasa's thighs and calves. She concentrated on her work grimly. If she thought about what those men had put Lalasa and Jump through, she would go racing off to find and kill them. That was not a good idea. These two had to be taken off the Needle first, to see healers and the palace watch.

At last Lalasa was able to crawl. Keeping her own body between her maid and the opening where the outer stair touched the platform, Kel led the way to the door. She reached up, grasped the latch, and pulled. The door didn't move. Kel sat up on her knees, grabbed the handle with both hands, and tugged hard. The door refused to open. She yanked on it with all her strength; the door would not give so much as a hair.

Gods curse you, she thought to her unknown enemy.

Curse you and all that you do with fire, and sword, and—
and a plague of horseflies.

"It's locked," said Lalasa, her voice shaking. Jump
whined and sniffed around the door. "Who locked it?"

Kel rested her forehead against the rough wood.
"Someone who thinks I won't do what has to be done."

"Lady?" asked the maid.

Kel looked at the opening in the floor just three feet
away. From this angle it offered a view only of empty air
and a distant roof. "We have to take the outer stair, I'm
afraid." Her voice sounded distant and tinny in her ears.
At least it didn't sound like she was terrified witless.

"Lady Keladry, I can't do that." Lalasa shook her head,
her mouth tight, her eyes wide. She seemed to have used
up the last of her courage. "You go. I'll wait here."

Kel gripped her maid's shoulders. "You're not thinking," she said, setting her thoughts in order before she
spoke them. "What's to stop them from coming back for
you when they see me on the stair? They're watching
us"—she waved at the door—"we know that."

"Then let's all three wait!" cried the older girl.
"Someone will come—"

"We're *witnesses*," Kel told her. "We can point them
out. Kidnapping is a crime." Lalasa turned away, hiding
her face in her hands. Jump licked his fingers. "If it *isn't*
them, how long until someone comes? How often do people make this idiotic climb?"

The gods have run mad, she thought as Lalasa shook
her head. They've put me in a spot where I'm begging to
go down that dreadful stair.

"Jump can't do it," Lalasa said, reaching down to rub

one of her calves. Her mouth was set in a stubborn line. "You can see for yourself he can't manage that hind leg. We can't leave him here."

"I'll make a sling out of that sack and I'll carry him," replied Kel. "All you'll have to do is walk down yourself. Come on," she pleaded, tugging Lalasa's arm. "Just try."

First they made a sling out of the coarse sack, checking and double-checking the knot before they risked fitting the dog into it. Jump let them do it, tucking himself into the cloth with only a small whimper for his sore hind leg. They arranged the sling on Kel's back so she could see where she put her feet.

"Don't start wiggling," Kel ordered. For the first time she was grateful for three years of the harness—she barely noticed the dog's weight on her back. "Lalasa, come on."

They got as far as the opening before Lalasa shook her head and rolled away, pressing her face to the platform. For a moment Kel, dizzy from that look at open air, wanted to slap her, and was promptly ashamed of herself. Lalasa had shown her courage in the hands of two kidnapping strangers; she had saved Jump's life.

"You can do this," Kel said. "You survived your brother and the raiders and the road to the palace. What's a stair against all that?"

Lalasa met Kel's eyes. "We really have to do this?"

Kel nodded. "I don't want to be here if they decide they don't need witnesses."

"All right," the older girl whispered.

I have to go first, Kel realized with a gulp. *I have to lead.* "Watch how I do this," she ordered. Lalasa nodded.

Getting on her hands and knees, turning her head

until she saw the opening at the edge of her vision, Kel backed up until both feet touched empty air. I can do this, she told herself firmly. I did it dozens of times climbing cliffs this last summer. "Jump, stay very still," she warned the dog on her back. She groped with one foot until she touched the first metal step. She tested it, making sure she could rest her weight on it, before she set her other foot down. Carefully she straightened her legs. Once again she backed up several inches until there was enough of her in the opening to try for the second step. Now she reached with a foot, groped, and found it. She tested it first, then stepped down. The platform opening was now around her waist, and strong winds plucked at her hose.

Kel took the next step down. "Let's go," she ordered.

Lalasa slid across the platform on her behind, not caring that the wood pulled threads from her skirt. Her lips were pressed so tightly together that a white rim showed around them, but she still obeyed Kel. Together they maneuvered until Lalasa's feet were on the second step and Kel was on the fourth.

Gods help me, I have to turn, Kel realized. I have to see where I'm going. "Wait," she told Lalasa.

Kel flexed her hands. Time to stop dancing and just *do* this, she decided. The sweat that poured down her front was instantly chilled and snatched away by the wind, making her shiver. At least her back was warm—carrying Jump was like carrying a small oven.

The sooner I get it started, the sooner it's done. Putting it off just makes the whole job take longer.

Kel shut her eyes, gripped the platform's edge with one hand, and groped until she could feel the railing with the other. She grabbed it with both hands, turned into the wind, and opened her eyes. Below her the palace swayed; the edges of her vision went dark.

Cliffs are so *solid,* she thought giddily. I never realized it before.

She bit the inside of her cheek hard, until it bled. Her faintness evaporated. She looked at the stairs before her. Like those inside, they had been worked in the shape of flowers, with openings in every step.

When I reach the Realms of the Dead, she vowed grimly, I'm going to find the genius who designed this tower and I'm going to kill him a second time. Horribly.

"Hold the rails with both hands," she shouted. "We'll do this *carefully.* Test the step before you put all of your weight on it. If we're slow, if we're steady, we'll be fine."

I am such a liar, she thought weakly, watching over one shoulder as Lalasa turned. The older girl faced front and took hold of the railings.

Kel gripped the rails so hard that she expected to find the imprint of the iron vines on her palms for the rest of her life. At each step she waited for Lalasa to come down behind her. Of course, her treacherous knees were quivering; they always did when she rose higher than three feet and looked down. Her leg muscles felt watery.

The wind was the worst. It shoved and tugged, yanking the girls' clothes, slamming them into one rail or the other. It thrust at Kel's shaky knees, until she was sure she would fall. Lalasa was no more than one step behind, so close that she often jostled Kel and Jump.

At first Kel ignored her fear by naming the members

of her family, from Great-Aunt Bridala all the way down to her nieces and nephews. When the wind hit the stair with a blast that rattled the whole thing, Kel turned to imagining the tortures she would inflict on the architect who had built the Needle, starting with the evil fingers that had drawn the plans for it.

She was so occupied with this that she didn't see the reddish brown stain on a step a third of the way down. As she rested her left foot on it, the foot slammed through, dropping into empty air. Broken iron gouged deep through her hose and into both sides of Kel's left leg.

Lalasa screamed and lurched forward, bumping into Jump and Kel's back. Kel gritted her teeth and hung on to the railings with all of her strength, supporting Lalasa's weight as well as Jump's and her own for a horrible moment.

"Sorry," cried Lalasa, shifting herself back until her weight rested on her own feet. "Sorry, sorry!"

Kel remained where she was, locked in place, not daring to move. Her leg throbbed; it bled heavily. She looked down just once to see her blood drip onto roof tiles sixty feet below. Closing her eyes, she ordered herself not to look down again.

"My lady, you're bleeding!" cried Lalasa.

"I know," Kel replied. "Will you do me a favor? Just— sit, right where you are. Sit, and—and—let me think."

"Yes, yes, of course," Lalasa said. She sniffled. "Forgive me." Kel felt the stair bounce slightly as Lalasa sat. "May I take Jump?"

Kel nodded. "That would help."

She felt Lalasa fumble with the sling on her back. Jump didn't wriggle, but let the maid ease him out of the cloth. Kel felt better without his weight putting her off-balance.

Once Lalasa had the dog, Kel made herself look at the step that had given way. Carefully she drew her leg out of the hole, trying not to catch it on jagged metal. When she was free, she sat on the step behind her, her back against Lalasa's shins. Then she rested her face in her hands.

The trickle of blood on her skin was an annoying reminder that she couldn't just sit and shiver. Forcing herself to look at the wound, she saw that she had gotten off easily. The cuts were ugly, but they had missed the big veins in her left leg.

A ripping sound made her look back. Lalasa was grimly tearing strips from her petticoat, working around the dog curled up in her lap. She handed a section of cloth to Kel, who used it to bind up the shallow scrapes on the lower part of her leg. "I think I'll need your apron, too," she called.

Lalasa draped Jump over her shoulder to untie her apron. "What happened?" she asked.

"A step gave way," Kel replied.

"Gave way?" whispered Lalasa. "How?"

"Rusted."

Lalasa passed the apron to Kel with hands that shook. Kel folded it neatly into a long bandage. "Are more steps rusted?" Lalasa wanted to know. "Are we trapped?"

"No—no, we're not. I just have to watch where I'm going," Kel said firmly, wiping her forehead on her sleeve. She didn't feel firm, not in the least. Her muscles had turned to water. At any moment she expected the tower to bend, dumping them off the stair.

Focusing on her task, she settled the thickest pads of the apron over the deepest wounds. Then she wrapped the cloth as tightly as she could, and bound it in place with a hard knot. With any luck—though she felt they might be short on that—she'd put enough pressure on the gashes to stop the bleeding. She would need a healer in a hurry, though, to kill infections caused by rust and dirty iron.

"I'll take Jump back," Kel said. "We need to go."

She held still as Lalasa settled Jump in the sling. Gripping the railings, Kel glanced at the step she'd gone through. She didn't dare trust it, but the one beyond looked safe enough. Kel knew they had to go forward, but her nerve was gone. She ought to stand, but no matter how sternly she ordered her traitor body to get moving, it remained where it was. After a little while she realized Lalasa was talking.

"—like any other noble, not caring for anyone but yourself. Servants see the worst of people, even of other servants. We just don't count. Sometimes folk are nice at the start, but sooner or later a noble will treat us bad. It can't be helped. It's natural. After a year fighting off men and being slapped by women, I thought working for a page would be no different. I knew sooner or later your nice mask would come off, only it never did. Think how frustrated I was."

Kel couldn't help it. She had to smile. As if he felt the change in Kel's attention, Jump began to wash the back of her neck.

"I wanted to box your ears when you were forever after

me to fight and learn this grip, and that hold," Lalasa continued. "But then, in the servants' mess, I taught them that wouldn't hear 'no' what it meant. And when I could hold off a squire, a strong, brawny fighter...Well. You taught me all that. You taught me to be near as brave as you are."

After that, what could Kel do? She levered herself to her feet. "Watch for rust," she cautioned. "Just step over that broken stair. And go slow and careful."

There were more rusted steps. Three in a row were the worst: it meant having to use the railings as their sole support as they swung their bodies out and away from the traitor steps. Kel's knees buckled when she touched down, but she stiffened them for Lalasa and Jump. When she almost backed off her step as she helped the other girl to put her feet down, Kel's head spun. She took a deep breath and steadied Lalasa.

When they reached the stone courtyard, Lalasa collapsed, huddling at the stones of the tower's base. Sparrows swirled around her and Kel, shrieking madly.

"Get Daine," Kel ordered, lifting the sling that held Jump from her back and placing him gently on the flagstones. "Jump's hurt."

The sparrows zipped out of the courtyard, piping their shrill alarm call.

Much to Kel's surprise, Tian ran into the courtyard. "My lady!" she cried. "Lalasa! You're all right!" She burst into tears and fell to her knees beside Lalasa, gathering her into her arms.

"How did you know we were here?" Kel asked, tucking the sack-sling around Jump to keep him warm.

Tian fumbled in her apron pocket and gave Kel a

square of parchment. The handwriting was the same as on the first note she had received. This time it read:

Try Balor's Needle.

"Someone stuck it to the door," Tian said. "Gower saw it when he was leaving. My lady—he went to fetch the watch."

Kel nodded absently. There was something she had to report, something very important. She turned to look up at the spidery length of iron that had led them here. "I'm going to tell the king about that," she said, wiping trembling hands on her tunic. "It's not safe."

15

CONSEQUENCES

*T*hings happened quickly after that. Daine arrived at a run, the sparrows fluttering around her. She tended Jump as Kel held him in her lap, healing the dog's bones and bruises, telling him that he was the best dog in the palace.

After Daine left, Kel looked up. More people had come while Daine tended her dog. Gower crouched on Lalasa's right while Tian clung to her friend on the left. A man in the uniform of the palace watch questioned Lalasa as other men in the same uniform milled around the courtyard and searched inside the Needle for clues.

Once Kel got to her feet, still holding Jump, she and Lalasa were taken to the watch's offices. There Kel was questioned—she wasn't too clear on what was asked. A healer came to examine her leg. Kel only noticed when the ache let up. Right about then she stretched out on a bench, waiting for them to be done with her.

Suddenly a furious Jump catapulted off her chest, jarring Kel into wakefulness. She sat up as Lalasa cried shrilly, "That's them! That's the ones that grabbed me!"

"Get this dog!" cried the smaller of two chained men flanked by watchmen.

A sergeant clutched Jump, who tried to fight his way to the kidnappers. One of the men showed a bite on the cheek; both had bandages on their arms.

"I should let you at them," the sergeant told Jump in a kind voice. "I think you're right about them." He looked at the two captives. "So here's another dog what hates you two. Whatever did you dungballs get up to, that so many dogs want to rip you to bits?"

Kel rubbed her eyes. "Why are those men here?" she asked stupidly.

"Well, milady," the sergeant explained over Jump's snarls, "we found them a bell ago, cornered by a pack of the palace dogs. Since they couldn't give no good reason for being here, and they were all chewed up, we thought we'd hold 'em awhile."

Kel nodded—that made sense—and lay down again.

Some time later a familiar deep, musical female voice said, "Why was it necessary to search the palace to find my youngest daughter? And why is she sleeping on a bench instead of in her room?"

Kel struggled to sit up. Someone mentioned "having questions" and "the whole story."

"And have you obtained your answers and your story?" demanded Ilane of Mindelan, hands on her hips.

Kel heard a muttered reply.

"You may ask further questions tomorrow, if you do

not have *real* answers by then," Ilane said coldly. "You will find my daughter in the pages' wing." She looked at Kel, worry in her eyes. "I would appreciate some assistance for her, if you please."

Someone hoisted Kel on his shoulder with a grunt. Kel remembered bobbing through hallways, then falling onto softness. Birds shrieked in her ears as she fell asleep.

A man's voice entered her dream of flying: "Keladry. Time to wake up."

She had to obey that voice. Kel furled her wings and dropped, opening her eyes. Lord Wyldon sat on her bed, leaning over to look into her face.

"Well," he said, "there you are." He looked up. "Stop glaring, Ilane."

"I'm not at all sure that she ought to leave her bed," replied Kel's mother. "From what her maid tells me, she's exhausted. Did you know she rises before dawn every day? *And* she fits weapons practice into every spare moment she has. The idea is to train them, not to kill them, Wyldon."

"It's the training that keeps them alive in the field," Wyldon replied calmly. "Page Keladry, you have things to do."

"Is this the Realms of the Dead?" Kel asked thickly.

"No. You've slept awhile, and you had a healing," Ilane said. She sat on Kel's other side with a mug. "You know healings tire you."

Lord Wyldon helped Kel to sit up with firm, comfortable hands. Her mother held the cup to Kel's lips: it was tea, warm but not hot. Kel gulped it down, and felt her head clear. Once all of it was gone, she sat up completely, rubbed her face, and checked her right side again. Lord Wyldon was still there.

"Jump?" she asked, before she remembered she was not allowed to have pets.

"Sleeping yet," the training master replied. "He seems particularly devoted to you."

Kel looked down, blushing.

"The watch captain asks me to assure you that whoever paid those men to kidnap Lalasa will be found." Wyldon's tone was odd, almost gentle. "I will make sure that is so—I want to learn what manner of creature would do so infamous a thing."

Kel nodded. She would like to know that, too. She bunched her fists. If she was lucky, perhaps she would get a moment to talk to the person who had caused all this, alone. She looked at her mother. "Mama, it *is* you. When did you get here?"

Ilane smiled and brushed Kel's hair back with her fingers. "You do remember your father and I came to the big examinations. When I heard you'd been found, I went to see what was going on."

"Sorry, Mama," Kel whispered, hanging her head. "I'm sorry you came for nothing."

"Wash up," said Wyldon, slapping Kel's knee briskly. "It's time for supper. You will feel more the thing once you have eaten."

Kel did as she was told, happy to use the basin of hot water in her dressing room to get some of the fear-sweat off her hands, arms, and face. She could hear Lord Wyldon and Lady Ilane talking quietly as she changed into fresh clothes. After she combed her hair, she went into the other room. Lord Wyldon had Jump in his lap; Lady Ilane fed sparrows from her hands.

"All set?" asked Wyldon. He put the dog on the hearth rug. Jump yawned, twisted himself into a new position, and went back to sleep. Lord Wyldon opened the door. "Come along," he ordered. Kel waved to her mother and followed him into the hall.

They walked in silence for a few moments before Wyldon asked, "Well? Aren't you going to explain why you did not attend the big examinations today?"

Kel stopped and stared up at him. "Sir?" Why did he of all people ask her that?

Wyldon halted, too, and folded his arms over his chest. "The question is straightforward. Have you an explanation?"

"You always say explanations are excuses, my lord," she reminded him. "You don't want to hear them."

He regarded her fixedly for a moment. Finally he asked, "What do you mean to do, then?"

"Repeat the four years, I suppose."

"Do you expect me to believe you are looking forward to that?"

Kel shook her head. "No, my lord. But I was very late. That's the penalty." She bit the inside of her lip, thinking, I will *not* cry.

To her astonishment, Lord Wyldon clasped her shoulder warmly. "Gods, Mindelan," he said, "I would you had been born a boy." He let her go. "Come. You need to eat, and to reassure your friends, though I did have Ezeko brief everyone when we got the full story. No sense in allowing all kinds of wild rumors."

When he walked on, Kel followed, thinking, But I *like* being a girl.

Inside the mess hall, Kel gathered a tray and utensils, then went to the servers. When she passed the squires, Garvey jeered, "I bet she hired those men to get out of the exams!"

"I knew she'd crumble at the last moment," added Vinson. "Females always do."

A good Yamani would have bowed and planned revenge for a more convenient time. I suppose I'm not a good Yamani anymore, Kel thought as she faced the squires. "Who could be afraid of the big exams?" she asked Vinson and Garvey. "After all, you two passed them."

Cleon and Balduin of Disart guffawed; Yancen of Irenroha snorted.

"When do you leave?" Joren asked coolly. He sat not with Vinson and Garvey, as Kel might have expected, but with Zahir and Yancen.

"I won't," Kel replied.

"You expect us to believe you mean to do all four years again." There was a mocking smile on Joren's lips.

Kel shrugged. "Believe what you like." She turned her back on them and went to get her supper. As she passed the squires' tables on her way to her friends, Cleon touched her wrist. "I'm all right," she told him, surprised by the touch.

"Of course you are," he said. "You're the best." Prince Roald, seated across from Cleon, gave her a warm smile.

When Kel put her tray down at her usual table, she slid into the space left for her by Neal and Owen. As soon as she was settled, Neal hugged her fiercely. Owen did the same; he was crying.

Kel fumbled for her handkerchief and gave it to him, saying, "At least I get to spend another year with you, anyway, whelp." That got a watery grin out of him. She turned to Neal and demanded, "So, did you pass?"

"Of course we passed, and it's a miracle," retorted Merric from his place across from them. "You could have said you had to save Lalasa!"

"I told you, they threatened to hurt her," Neal said firmly. He pressed a cup of fruit juice into Kel's hands. "Drink up. You look like you need the sweet. You had a healing, didn't you?"

Kel nodded.

Lord Wyldon had come to the lectern for the evening prayer. They all scrambled to their feet.

"Mithros and Goddess, we pray you, grant your blessing," Wyldon said, his clear, cold voice cutting through the whispers. The pages and squires bowed their heads. Kel wondered if she was the only one who had noticed that for the first time since her arrival here four years ago, Lord Wyldon had included the Goddess in the nightly prayer. "Strip the veils of hate from our eyes, and the grip of bitterness from our hearts. Teach us to be pure in our souls, dedicated only to service, duty, and honor."

He lowered his hands. His audience murmured, "So mote it be."

Kel stopped the boys from asking more questions by asking them about the examinations. As she listened to them, she kept thinking that something was very wrong. Shouldn't the fourth-years have walked to the squires' tables by now? And while the meal before them was good, it was still a typical supper. The night the fourth-years became squires, there were always special foods and entertainment for them all.

Halfway through the meal, a servant opened the door. In walked an old man wearing a long, fur-collared, maroon wool robe and a velvet cap with ear-flaps. Over the shoulders of his robe he wore a heavy gold chain of office, its pendant marked with the crossed gavel and sword of the Royal Magistrates. Kel had seen him before, at the big examinations of years past. He was Duke Turomot of Wellam, the Lord Magistrate and chief examiner of pages.

Everyone stood as the old man walked stiffly to Lord Wyldon's dais. The training master came over and bowed to him. For a moment they talked in low voices. Then Lord Wyldon helped Duke Turomot up to the lectern.

The old man glared down at his audience. "Silence," he ordered, though no one made a sound. "Evidence has been given, confession made. Two men were paid by an as-yet-unknown third man to force Page Keladry of Mindelan either to be late for the fourth-year examinations or to be unable to attend altogether. Said coercion being out of the control of Page Keladry or of Lord Wyldon her training master, it is hereby ordained that in two days' time Keladry of Mindelan shall present herself in the First Court of Law of the palace in Corus at the second bell of the morning. There and in the practice courts she will be given the appropriate fourth-year tests by the regular examiners."

The boys cried out in astonishment, filling the room with sound. Kel's Yamani training took hold. It kept her face calm, her back straight, and her knees locked when she might have collapsed onto her seat. She couldn't believe her ears. Neal was pounding her on the back—so was Owen. Iden, Warric, and her first-year friends jumped up and down, cheering.

But I was ready to do it, she thought, gripping the table, wanting to touch something real. I didn't like it; I didn't want it. I would have screamed and wept and hit things once I was alone, in private, as is decent. But I would have done it. I would have been a page four more years.

Duke Turomot pounded the lectern. "Order!" he shouted. "Order!"

The pages slowly calmed down.

Breathing heavily, the old man said, "There was no reason for this unseemly display. If any such occurs on testing day, I will have those responsible ejected from my presence." He glared at them, making sure they'd heard, then added, "Heralds have been sent to announce the new day of testing. Furthermore, the one who perpetrated this defilement of the law and the examinations will be found and duly punished. With the guidance of Mithros, we will achieve a fair solution."

They recognized the cue and replied, "So mote it be."

Duke Turomot left the mess hall, clutching his robes tightly around his thin frame. Lord Wyldon took his place at the lectern. "Provided that Keladry of Mindelan passes her fourth-year examinations in two days, we will hold the celebration for the new squires on that evening. Page

Keladry, report to me when you have finished your meal."

She didn't finish her supper, only gave up on it. She hardly knew what to think. They start out treating me different, putting me on probation, even though they say I'm supposed to be the same as the boys, she thought as she carried her tray to the servers. And now they make another exception for me, then tell me I'm to move to the squires' tables with everybody else. Can't they make up their minds?

Two days later at the supper hour, Lord Wyldon stood at the lectern and announced, "New squires, you are seated in the wrong place."

Kel, Neal, Merric, Seaver, Esmond, and Quinden picked up their trays. Together they walked to the lowliest of the squires' tables as the pages and squires applauded and cheered.

So far, so good, thought Kel as she took her seat. She was tired, but happy. She could still remember the look of pride in the eyes of her parents, her brothers Inness and Anders, and her sisters Adalia and Oranie, all of whom had come for the big examinations. She could remember the grins on the faces of Sir Myles, Lord Raoul, her friends among the squires, Daine, Salma, Gower, and Lalasa. And she meant to enjoy the night, and the fresh cherry pies, and the tumblers hired by Lord Wyldon as a treat for them all.

As she walked out of the mess hall, yawning, a hand reached out to stop her. It was Lord Wyldon. "Congratulations," he said quietly. "You have earned your new status."

Kel bowed. "Thank you, my lord." It meant a great deal, coming from him.

"You should know, it may be a little while before you are chosen as a squire. It's the congress," he said, understanding the question in her eyes. "Most knights will take a little extra time to look the new squires over, since they will be here."

"But you think it would take me a long time to find a knight-master anyway, being The Girl," Kel suggested, surprising herself with her new boldness. Maybe it was that funny, baffled look in his eyes that gave her the courage.

Wyldon smiled crookedly. "I think I will no longer try to predict what will or will not happen to you, Squire Keladry. So far you have proved me wrong on every count. Even I can learn when to quit." He bowed to her, and walked away.

Kel was still trying to decide what he'd meant when she returned to her rooms. She had a guest: Lalasa was pouring tea for Stefan Groomsman. Jump was on his back at the stableman's feet, offering his belly to be scratched. The sparrows had retired for the night, all but Crown, Freckle, and Peg. They were picking on a crumb-covered plate that showed the man had been there for some time.

"I'm sorry," Kel said, upset that he might have been waiting since the time she normally came in from supper. "Lalasa, you should have sent the birds for me...Is Peachblossom all right?" She couldn't think of any other reason that might bring the people-shy hostler into the palace itself.

"No, no, Squire Keladry, Peachblossom's fine." Stefan

got to his feet, shedding crumbs. Reaching inside his tunic, he dragged out a packet tied with string. "I was told to give this to you today."

Kel accepted it with a frown and undid the string. When she opened the packet, she found a handful of folded papers. The top one was a bill of sale for the strawberry roan gelding Peachblossom, marked "paid in full," witnessed by a palace notary, and made out to Keladry of Mindelan, squire. The other papers appeared to be paid bills for feed, care, and palace stabling, all for the strawberry roan gelding Peachblossom, owned by Keladry of Mindelan, squire. The sums listed covered four years. All were notarized, complete with red wax seals. If there was anything more official-looking, Kel didn't know of it.

"I'm that relieved," Stefan commented as the confused Kel looked through the papers a second time. "It broke my heart to think of parting you two, let alone I doubt he'd do near so well with anyone else. Congratulations, squire."

He was headed for the door when Kel said, "Wait! I didn't—who did this?" She leafed through the documents, looking for any names other than her own, Stefan's, and the notary's. "I don't see who paid all this money! Stefan?"

The door closing was her only answer.

At the bottom of the receipts was a folded note. Her mysterious benefactor had written, "Gods all bless, Lady Squire."

CAST OF CHARACTERS

Adalia of Mindelan	sometimes called Adie, Kel's older sister
Alanna of Pirate's Swoop and Olau	the King's Champion, also called "the Lioness," born Alanna of Trebond
Anders of Mindelan	Kel's oldest brother, a knight
Baird of Queenscove, Duke	chief of Tortall's healers, Neal's father
Balcus Starsworn	springtime god
Balduin of Disart	senior page/squire
Bonedancer	living archaeopteryx (dinosaur bird) skeleton
Chisakami, Princess	daughter of the Yamani emperor, former betrothed of Prince Roald, deceased
Cleon of Kennan	senior page/squire
Conal of Mindelan	Kel's third-oldest brother, a knight
Danayne	Archpriestess of the Moon of Truth temple in Corus
Dermid of Josu's Dirk	page
Douglass of Veldine	knight-guardian of Maura of Dunlath
Eda Bell	the Wildcat of the Shang order of fighters
Emry of Haryse	Neal's maternal grandfather, a famed general
Esmond of Nicoline	page, began the same year as Kel
Ezeko, Obafem	sergeant, trainer from the Tortallan army, formerly from Carthak
Faleron of King's Reach	senior page/squire, Merric's cousin

Flyndan	captain, second in command of the King's Own
Gareth of Naxen, Duke	called "the Elder," king's counselor, training master in Alanna's time
Garvey of Runnerspring	senior page/squire, Joren's crony
Hakuin Seastone	the Horse of the Shang order of fighters
Harailt of Aili	dean of the royal university
Iakoju	ogre, resident of Fief Dunlath
Iden of Vikison Lake	junior page, Owen's cousin
Ilane of Mindelan, Baroness	Kel's mother, wife of Piers
Imrah of Legann	Prince Roald's knight-master
Inness of Mindelan	Kel's second-oldest brother, a knight
Isran, Gower	gloomy servant in the pages' wing, Lalasa's uncle
Ivor	Mithran priest, teaches mathematics
Jasson of Conté	"the Old King," Jonathan's deceased grandfather
Jonathan of Conté	King of Tortall
Joren of Stone Mountain	handsome senior page/squire
Kaddar Iliniat	Emperor of Carthak
Kalasin of Conté	oldest princess
Keladry of Mindelan	known as Kel, youngest daughter of Piers and Ilane of Mindelan, first known female page candidate
Kieran of LaMinch	betrothed of Uline of Hannalof
Lalasa Isran	Kel's maid, Gower's niece
Liam of Conté	younger prince
Lianne of Conté	youngest princess
Lindhall Reed	mage, biology teacher
Longleigh, Hugo	senior palace servant

Maura of Dunlath	heircss of Dunlath, ward of Douglass of Veldine
Merric of Hollyrose	page, began the same year as Kel, Faleron's cousin
Myles of Olau, Baron	Alanna's adoptive father, teacher, head of royal intelligence service (spies)
Nariko	Yamani armsmistress/teacher at the imperial court
Nealan of Queenscove	known as Neal, page, Kel's sponsor, son of Duke Baird
Numair Salmalín	mage, born Arram Draper
Oakbridge, Upton	palace master of ceremonies
Oranie of Mindelan	Kel's older sister
Osgar Woodrow	palace smith
Owen of Jesslaw	feisty junior page
Piers of Mindelan, Baron	Kel's father, diplomat
Prosper of Tameran	page
Qasim	Bazhir soldier in the King's Own
Quinden of Marti's Hill	page, began the same year as Kel
Ragnal of Darroch	page
Raoul of Goldenlake and Malorie's Peak, Lord	Knight Commander of the King's Own
Roald of Conté	heir to the Tortallan throne, one year older than Kel
Salma Aynnar	head of servants in the pages' wing
Seaver of Tasride	page, began the same year as Kel
Stefan Groomsman	Chief Hostler, has wild magic with horses
Teron of Blythdin	junior page

Thayet of Conté	Queen of Tortall, commander of the Queen's Riders
Tianine Plowman	known as Tian, maid, Lalasa's friend
Tilaine of Mindelan	Kel's sister-in-law, Anders's wife
Timon Greendale	headman of palace servants
Tkaa	basilisk, immortal
Turomot of Wellam, Duke	Lord Magistrate, chief examiner of pages
Uline of Hannalof	one of the "royal ladies"
Upton Oakbridge	palace master of ceremonies
Veralidaine Sarrasri	known as Daine, called "the Wildmage"
Vinson of Genlith	senior page/squire, Joren's crony
Warric of Mandash	junior page, Owen's cousin
Wyldon of Cavall, Lord	training master of the pages and squires
Yancen of Irenroha	senior page/squire
Yayin	Mithran priest, teaches reading and writing
Zahir ibn Alhaz	senior page/squire, of the Bazhir

GLOSSARY

Balor's Needle: a tower, the highest part of the royal palace in Corus, used mostly by astronomers and mages.

basilisk: an immortal that resembles a seven-to-eight-foot-tall lizard, with slit-pupiled eyes that face forward and silver talons. It walks upright on its hind feet. Its hobby is travel; it loves gossip and learns languages easily. It possesses some magical skills, including a kind of screech that turns people to stone. Its colors are various shades of gray and white.

Bazhir: the collective name for the nomadic tribes of Tortall's Great Southern Desert.

blazebalm: a thick, sticky substance like paste, which burns when lit (either manually or at a distance) by a mage or archer with fire arrows.

Carthak: the slaveholding empire that includes all of the Southern Lands, ancient and powerful, a storehouse of learning, sophistication, and culture. Its university was at one time without a rival for teaching. Its people reflect the many lands that have been consumed by the empire, their colors ranging from white to brown to black. Its former emperor Ozorne Tasikhe was forced to abdicate when he was turned into a Stormwing (and later killed). He was succeeded by his nephew Kaddar Iliniat, who is still getting his farflung lands under control.

centaur: an immortal shaped like a human from the waist up, with the body of a horse from the waist down. Like humans, centaurs can be good, bad, or a mixture of both.

Code of Ten: the set of laws that form the basis of government for most of the Eastern Lands.

Coldfang: an immortal that resembles a giant lizard with pebbled skin. Its colors vary. Its power lies in its ability to track a thief until capture, no matter how cold the trail or how long it takes. Its weapon is bitter cold; its pace is slow but inexorable.

Copper Isles: a slaveholding island nation to the south and west of Tortall. The Isles' lowlands are hot, wet jungles, their highlands cold and rocky. Traditionally their ties are to Carthak rather than Tortall, and their pirates often raid along the Tortallan coast. There is a strain of insanity in their ruling line. The Isles hold an old grudge against Tortall, since one of their princesses was killed there the day that Jonathan was crowned.

coromanel: a flat, crown-shaped piece fitted over the tip of a lance. It spreads the power of a lance's impact in several directions, to make the force less severe.

Corus: the capital city of Tortall, located on the northern and southern banks of the Oloron River. Corus is the home of the new royal university as well as the royal palace.

River Domin: runs through fief Mindelan.

dragon: a large, winged, lizard-like immortal capable of crossing from the Divine Realms to the mortal ones and back. Dragons are intelligent, possess their own magic, and are rarely seen by humans.

Eastern Lands: the name used to refer to those lands north of the Inland Sea and east of the Emerald Ocean: Scanra, Tortall, Tyra, Tusaine, Galla, Maren, and Sarain.

Galla: the country to the north and east of Tortall, famous for its mountains and forests, with an ancient royal line. Daine was born there.

Gift, the: human, academic magic, the use of which must be taught.

glaive: a pole arm including a four- or five-foot staff capped with a long metal blade.

Great Mother Goddess: the chief goddess in the Tortallan pantheon, protector of women; her symbol is the moon.

griffin: a feathered immortal with a cat like body, wings, and a beak. The males grow to a height of six and a half to seven feet at the shoulder; females are slightly bigger. No one can tell lies in a griffin's vicinity (a range of about a hundred feet).

Human Era (H.E.): the calendar in use in the Eastern and Southern Lands and in the Copper Isles is dated the Human Era to commemorate the years since the one in which the immortals were originally sealed into the Divine Realms, over four hundred and fifty years previous to the years covered by *Protector of the Small.*

hurrok: an immortal shaped like a horse with leathery bat-wings, claws, and fangs.

Immortals War: a short, vicious war fought in the spring and summer of the thirteenth year of Jonathan's and Thayet's reign; named for the number of immortal creatures that fought, but also waged by Carthakis (rebels against the new Emperor Kaddar), Copper Islanders, and Scanran raiders. These forces were defeated by the residents of the Eastern Lands, particularly Tortall, but recovery is slow.

King's Council: the monarch's private council, made up of those advisers he trusts the most.

King's Own: a cavalry/police group answering to the king, whose members serve as royal bodyguards and as protective troops throughout the realm. Their Knight Commander is Lord Sir Raoul of Goldenlake and Malorie's Peak. The ranks are filled by younger sons of noble houses, Bazhir, and the sons of wealthy merchants.

K'mir, K'miri: the K'mir are the matriarchal, nomadic tribes of the mountains in Sarain. They herd ponies and are ferocious warriors and riders. The Saren lowlanders despise the K'mir and are continuously at war with them. There is a small, growing population of them in Tortall, where Queen Thayet is half K'mir and a number of the Queen's Riders are also of K'miri descent.

mage: wizard.

Maren: a large, powerful country east of Tusaine and Tyra, the grain basket of the Eastern Lands, with plenty of farms and trade.

Midwinter Festival: a seven-day holiday centering around the longest night of the year and the sun's rebirth afterward. Gifts are exchanged and feasts held.

Mithros: the chief god in the Tortallan pantheon, god of war and the law; his symbol is the sun.

ogre: an immortal with aqua-colored skin, shaped like a human, from ten to twelve feet in height.

River Olorun: its main sources are Lake Naxen and Lake Tirragen in the eastern part of Tortall; it flows through the capital, Corus, and into the Emerald Ocean at Port Caynn.

pole arm: any weapon consisting of a long wooden staff or pole capped by a sharp blade of some kind, including spears, glaives, and pikes.

Queen's Riders: a cavalry/police group charged with protecting Tortallans who live in hard-to-reach parts of the country. They enforce the law and teach local residents to defend themselves. They accept both women and men in their ranks, unlike the army, the navy, and the King's Own. Their headquarters is between the palace and the Royal Forest. Queen Thayet is the commander; her second in command, Buriram Tourakom, governs the organization on a day-to-day basis.

quintain: a dummy with a shield mounted on a post. One outstretched "arm" is weighted with a sandbag, while the other is covered by the shield. The object in tilting at a quintain is to strike the shield precisely, causing the dummy to pivot 180 degrees. The jouster can then ride by safely. Striking the dummy anywhere but the target circle on the shield causes the dummy to swing 360 degrees, so the sandbag wallops the passing rider.

rowel: a star-shaped revolving piece on a spur, which cuts into a horse to make it pick up its speed.

royal ladies: fifteen or so young, active women of noble birth who can ride and use a bow as well as dance and converse with all manner of people. Queen Thayet takes them on visits to small, isolated fiefs or meetings where there is a possibility that they will be needed to help her with danger or handle emergencies that may arise.

Scanra: the country to the north of Tortall, wild, rocky, and cold, with very little land that can be farmed. The

Scanrans are masters of the sea and are feared anywhere there is a coastline. They also frequently raid over land.

Shang: an order of warriors, mostly commoners, whose principal school is in northern Maren. They specialize in hand-to-hand combat.

Southern Lands: another name for the Carthaki Empire, which has conquered all of the independent nations that once were part of the continent south of the Inland Sea.

spidren: an immortal whose body is that of a furred spider four to five feet in height; its head is that of a human, with sharp, silvery teeth. Spidrens can use weapons. They also use their webs as weapons and ropes. Spidren web is gray-green in color, and it glows after dark. Their blood is black, and burns like acid. Their favorite food is human blood.

Stormwing: an immortal with a human head and chest and the legs and wings of a bird, with steel feathers and claws. Stormwings have sharp teeth, but use them only to add to the terror of their presence by tearing apart bodies. They live on human fear and have their own magic; their special province is that of desecrating battlefield dead.

tauros: a seven-foot-tall immortal, male only, that has a bull-like head with large teeth and eyes that point forward (the mark of a predator). It is reddish brown, human-like from the neck down, with a bull's splayed hooves and tail. It preys on women and girls.

Temple District: the religious quarter of Corus, between the city proper and the royal palace, where the city's largest temples are located.

Tortall: the chief kingdom in which the Alanna, Daine, and Keladry books take place, between the Inland Sea and Scanra.

Tusaine: a small country between Tortall and Maren. Tortall went to war with Tusaine in the years Alanna the Lioness was a squire and Jonathan was crown prince; Tusaine lost.

Tyra: a merchant republic on the Inland Sea between Tortall and Maren. Tyra is mostly swamp, and its people rely on trade and banking for income.

warhorse: a larger horse or greathorse, trained for combat—the mount of an armored knight.

wildmage: a mage who deals in wild magic, the kind of magic that is part of nature. Daine Sarrasri is often called the Wildmage, for her ability to communicate with animals, heal them, and shapeshift.

wild magic: the magic that is part of the natural world. Unlike the human Gift, it cannot be drained or done away with; it is always present.

Yama: the chief goddess of the Yamani pantheon, goddess of fire, who created the Yamanis and their islands.

Yamani Islands: the island nation to the north and west of Tortall and the west of Scanra, ruled by an ancient line of emperors, whose claim to their throne comes from the goddess Yama. The country is beautiful and mountainous. Its vulnerability to pirate raids means that most Yamanis get some training in combat arts, including the women. Keladry of Mindelan lived there for six years while her father was the Tortallan ambassador.

AGAINST ALL ODDS, KEL IS NOW A SQUIRE.

But which knight will choose to train her?

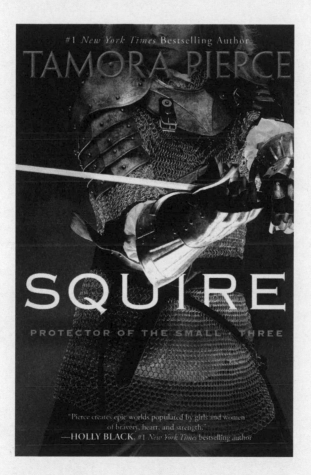

Read on for a peek at Kel's next adventure!

I

KNIGHT·MASTER

*D*espite the overflow of humanity present for the congress at the royal palace, the hall where Keladry of Mindelan walked was deserted. There were no servants to be seen. No echo of the footsteps, laughter, or talk that filled the sprawling residence sounded here, only Kel's steps and the click of her dog's claws on the stone floor.

They made an interesting pair. The fourteen-year-old girl was big for her age, five feet nine inches tall, and dressed informally in breeches and shirt. Both were a dark green that emphasized the same color in her green-hazel eyes. Her dark boots were comfortable, not fashionable. On her belt hung a pouch and a black-hilted dagger in a plain black sheath. Her brown hair was cut to earlobe length. It framed a tanned face dusted with freckles across a delicate nose. Her mouth was full and decided.

The dog, known as Jump, was barrel-chested, with

slightly bowed forelegs. His small, triangular eyes were set deep in a head shaped like a heavy chisel. He was mostly white, but black splotches covered the end of his nose, his lone whole ear, and his rump; his tail plainly had been broken twice. He looked like a battered foot soldier to Kel's young squire, and he had proved his combat skills often.

At the end of the hall stood a pair of wooden doors carved with a sun, the symbol of Mithros, god of law and war. They were ancient, the surfaces around the sun curved deep after centuries of polishing. Their handles were crude iron, as coarse as the fittings on a barn door.

Kel stopped. Of the pages who had just passed the great examinations to become squires, she was the only one who had not come here before. Pages never came to this hall. Legend held that pages who visited the Chapel of the Ordeal never became squires: they were disgraced or killed. But once they were squires, the temptation to see the place where they would be tested on their fitness for knighthood was irresistible.

Kel reached for the handle, and opened one door just enough to admit her and Jump. There were benches placed on either side of the room from the door to the altar. Kel slid onto one, glad to give her wobbly knees a rest. Jump sat in the aisle beside her.

After her heart calmed, Kel inspected her surroundings. This chapel, focus of so many longings, was plain. The floor was gray stone flags; the benches were polished wood without ornament. Windows set high in the walls on either side were as stark as the room itself.

Ahead was the altar. Here, at least, was decoration: gold candlesticks and an altar cloth that looked like gold chain mail. The sun disk on the wall behind it was also gold. Against the gray stone, the dark benches, and the wrought-iron cressets on the walls, the gold looked tawdry.

The iron door to the right of the sun disk drew Kel's eyes. There was the Chamber of the Ordeal. Generations of squires had entered it to experience something. None told what they saw; they were forbidden to speak of it. Whatever it was, it usually let squires return to the chapel to be knighted.

Some who entered the Chamber failed. A year-mate of Kel's brother Anders had died three weeks after his Ordeal without ever speaking. Two years after that a squire from Fief Yanholm left the Chamber, refused his shield, and fled, never to be seen again. At Midwinter in 453, months before the Immortals War broke out, a squire went mad there. Five months later he escaped his family and drowned himself.

"The Chamber is like a cutter of gemstones," Anders had told Kel once. "It looks for your flaws and hammers them, till you crack open. And that's all I—or anyone—will say about it."

The iron door seemed almost separate from the wall, more real than its surroundings. Kel got to her feet, hesitated, then went to it. Standing before the door, she felt a cold draft.

Kel wet suddenly dry lips with her tongue. Jump whined. "I know what I'm doing," she told her dog without conviction, and set her palm on the door.

She sat at a desk, stacks of parchment on either side. Her hands sharpened a goose quill with a penknife. Splotches of ink stained her fingers. Even her sleeves were spotted with ink.

"*There you are, squire.*"

Kel looked up. Before her stood Sir Gareth the Younger, King Jonathan's friend and adviser. Like Kel's, his hands and sleeves were ink-stained. "I need you to find these." He passed a slate to Kel, who took it, her throat tight with misery. "Before you finish up today, please. They should be in section eighty-eight." He pointed to the far end of the room. She saw shelves, all stretching from floor to ceiling, all stuffed with books, scrolls, and documents.

She looked at her tunic. She wore the badge of Fief Naxen, Sir Gareth's home, with the white ring around it that indicated she served the heir to the fief. Her knight-master was a desk knight, not a warrior.

Work is work, she thought, trying not to cry. She still had her duty to Sir Gareth, even if it meant grubbing through papers. She thrust herself away from her desk—

—and tottered on the chapel's flagstones. Her hands were numb with cold, her palms bright red where they had touched the Chamber door.

Kel scowled at the iron door. "I'll do my duty," she told the thing, shivering.

Jump whined again. He peered up at her, his tail awag in consolation.

"I'm all right," Kel reassured him, but she checked her hands for inkspots. The Chamber had made her live the thing she feared most just now, when no field knight had asked for her service. What if the Chamber knew? What if she was to spend the next four years copying out dry passages from drier records? Would she quit? Would paperwork do what other pages' hostility had not—drive her back to Mindelan?

Squires were supposed to serve and obey, no matter what. Still, the gap between combat with monsters and research in ancient files was unimaginable. Surely someone would realize Keladry of Mindelan was good for more than scribe work!

This was too close to feeling sorry for herself, a useless activity. "Come on," Kel told Jump. "Enough brooding. Let's get some exercise."

Jump pranced as Kel left the Chapel. She was never sure if he understood her exactly—it grew harder each year to tell how much any palace animal did or did not know— but he could tell they were on their way outside.

Kel stopped at her quarters to leave a note for her maid, Lalasa: "Should a knight come to ask me to be his squire, I'm down at the practice courts." Gloom overtook her again. As the first known female page in over a century, she had struggled through four years to prove herself as good as any boy. If the last six weeks were any indication, she could have spared herself the trouble. It seemed no knight cared to take The Girl as his squire. Even her friend Neal, five years older than their other year-mates, known for his sharp tongue and poor attitude, had talked with three potential masters.

Kel and Jump left her room to stop by Neal's. Her lanky friend lay on his bed, reading. Jump bounced up beside him.

"I'm off to the practice courts," she said. "You want to come?"

Neal lowered his book, raising arched brows over green eyes. "I'm about to commence four years obeying the call of a bruiser on a horse," he pointed out in his dry voice.

A friend had commented once that Neal had a gift for making someone want to punch him just for saying hello. "I refuse to put down what might be the last book I see for months."

Kel eyed her friend. His long brown hair, swept back from a widow's peak, stood at angles, combed that way by restless fingers. Her fingers itched to settle it. "I thought you wanted to be a squire," she said, locking her hands behind her back. Neal didn't know she had a crush on him. She meant to keep it that way.

Neal sighed. "I want to fulfill Queenscove's duty to the Crown," he reminded her. "A knight from our house—"

"Has served the Crown for ages, is a pillar of the kingdom, I know, I know," Kel finished before he could start.

"Well, that's about being a *knight*. Squire is an intermediate step. It's a pain in the rump, but it's a passing pain. I don't have to like it," Neal said. "I'd as soon read. Besides, Father said to wait. Another knight's supposed to show up today. I hate it when Father gets mysterious."

"Well, I'm going to go hit something," Kel said. "I can't sit around."

Neal sat up. "No one still?" he asked, kindness in his voice and eyes. For all he was five years older, he was her best friend, and a good one.

Kel shook her head. "I thought if I survived the big examinations, I'd be fine. I thought *somebody* would take me, even if I am The Girl." She didn't mention her bitterest disappointment. For years she had dreamed that Alanna the Lioness, the realm's sole lady knight, would take her as squire. Kel knew it was unlikely. No one would believe she had earned her rank fairly if the controversial

King's Champion, who was also a mage, took Kel under her wing. In her heart, though, Kel had hoped. Now the congress that had brought so many other knights to the palace was ending, with no sign of Lady Alanna.

"There are still knights in the field," Neal said gently. "You may be picked later this summer, or even this fall."

For a moment she almost told him about her vision in the chapel. Instead she made herself smile. Complaining to Neal wouldn't help. "I know," she replied, "and until then, I mean to practice. Last chance to collect bruises from me."

Neal shuddered. "Thanks," he said. "I've gotten all the bruises off you this year that I want."

"Coward." She whistled for Jump, who leaped off the bed to follow her.

The practice courts were deserted. Lord Wyldon, the training master, had taken the pages to their summer camp earlier that week, ahead of the traffic that would clog the roads as the congress broke up. The combat teachers had gone with him; Kel saw only servants near the fenced yards where pages and squires practiced. She'd thought that older squires might come out to keep their skills sharp, but none were visible.

She saddled her big gelding, Peachblossom, murmuring to him as she worked. He was a strawberry roan, his cinnamon coat flecked with bits of white, his face, stockings, mane, and tail all solid red-brown. Except for the palace horse mages, he would tolerate only Kel. Abused when he was younger, Peachblossom was no man's friend, but he suited Kel nicely.

Practice lance in hand, she guided Peachblossom to the

tilting yard. There she studied the targets: the standard quintain dummy with its wooden shield, and a second dummy with a tiny black spot painted at the shield's center. They were too solid to fit her mood. Though it was a windy June day, she set up the ring target, a circle of willow twigs hung from a cord attached to a long arm of wood. It was always the hardest to hit due to its lightness. Today it whipped on its cord like a circular kite.

Kel rode Peachblossom to the starting point and composed herself. It was no good riding at the ring target with an unsettled heart. Six years of life in the Yamani Islands had taught her to manage her emotions. She breathed slowly and evenly, emptying her mind. Her green-hazel eyes took on their normal, dreamy cast. Her shoulders settled; her tight muscles loosened.

Kel gathered her reins and resettled her lance. Part of the bargain she and her horse had made to work together was that Peachblossom would answer to verbal commands and Kel would never use the spur. "Trot," she told him now.

The big horse made for the target at an easy pace. The ring flirted in the air. Kel lowered her fourteen-foot lance until it crossed a few inches above her gelding's shoulders. The lead-weighted wood lay steady in her grip. Her eyes tracked the ring as she rose in the stirrups. On trotted Peachblossom, hooves smacking hard-packed dirt. Kel adjusted her lance point and jammed it straight through the ring. The cord that held it to the wooden arm snapped. Peachblossom slowed and turned.

With a hard flick—the movement took strength, and she had practiced until she'd gotten it perfect—Kel sent

the ring flying off her lance. Jump watched it, his powerful legs tense. He sprang, catching the ring in his
jaws.

A big man who leaned on the fence applauded. The sun
was in Kel's eyes: she shaded them to see who it was, and
smiled. Her audience was Raoul of Goldenlake and
Malorie's Peak, knight and Knight Commander of the
King's Own guard. She liked him: for one thing, he treated
her just as he did boy pages. It was nice that he'd witnessed
one of her successes. The first time she'd seen him, she had
been about to fall off a rearing Peachblossom. That her
mount was out of control was bad; to have it witnessed by
a hero like Lord Raoul, and ten more of the King's Own,
was far worse.

"I'd heard how well you two work together," Lord
Raoul said as Kel and Peachblossom approached. He was
a head taller than Kel, with curly black hair cropped short,
black eyes, and a broad, ruddy face. "I'm not sure I could
have nailed that target." Jump trotted over to offer the ring
to the big knight. Raoul took it, tested its weight, and
whistled. "Willow? I don't think I *could* nail it—the ring I
use is oak."

Kel ducked her head. "We practice a great deal, that's
all, my lord. Jump wants you to throw it for him."

With a flick of the wrist the knight tossed the ring, letting it sail down the road. Jump raced under it until he
could leap and catch the prize. Holding his tail and single
ear proudly erect, he ran back to Raoul and Kel.

"Practice is the difference between winning and being
worm food," Raoul told Kel. "Do you have a moment? I
need to discuss something with you."

ARRAM. VARICE. OZORNE.
THREE STUDENT MAGES
WHO ARE BOUND BY FATE . . .
FATED FOR TROUBLE.

Read on for a peek at book one
in the Numair Chronicles!

CHAPTER 1

❧

August 30–September 1, 435

THE IMPERIAL COLISEUM, THAK CITY,
THE CARTHAKI EMPIRE

Arram Draper hung on the rail of the great arena, hoisting himself until his belly was bent over the polished stone. It was the only way he could get between the two bulky men who blocked his view. He knew it was risky, but he couldn't waste his first chance to see the gladiators when they marched into the huge stadium. His father and grandfather were back at their seats, arguing about new business ventures. They weren't paying attention, waving him off when he asked to visit the privies and never realizing he'd squirmed his way down to the rail instead.

Apart from them, he was alone. There were no friends from school for company. They all said he was too young. He was eleven—well, ten, in truth, but he *told* them he was eleven. Even that didn't earn him friends among his older schoolfellows. Still, he wasn't a baby! If he didn't see the games with his family today, he might never get the chance, and he'd learned only last night he might not see Papa again for two years, even three. Carthak was a costly voyage for Yusaf Draper, and his new venture would take him away for a long time. But in the morning, Arram would be able to tell the older students that *he* had watched the games right from the arena wall!

Already he'd heard the trumpets and drums announcing the arrival of the emperor and his heirs. He couldn't see their faces, but surely all the sparkling gold, silver, and gems meant the wearers were part of the imperial family. He could see the Grand Crier, who stood on a platform halfway between him and the royals. More important, he could plainly hear the man's booming voice as he announced the emperor's many titles and those of his heirs.

"Lookit!" The bruiser on Arram's left bumped him as he pointed north, to the emperor's dais. Arram wobbled and might have pitched headfirst onto the sands twenty feet below if the man on his other side hadn't caught him by the belt and hauled him inside the rail. Without appearing to notice Arram's near fall, the man on the left went on to say, "There's the widow, and her son! She never comes to games!"

"Who's the widow?" Arram asked. "Who's the son?"

The big men grinned at each other over his head. "For all you're a brown boy, you don't know your imperials," said the one who had bumped him. "The widow is Princess Mahira, that was married to Prince Apodan."

"He was killed fightin' rebels two year back," the other man said. "An' the boy is Prince Ozorne."

Now Arram remembered. Ozorne was a year or two ahead of him in the Lower Academy.

From the podium, the crier bellowed that the emperor

would bless the games. Everyone thundered to their feet and then hushed. His voice amplified, most likely by a mage, the emperor prayed to the gods for an excellent round of games. When he finished, everyone sat.

For a very long moment the arena was still. Then the boy felt a slow, regular thudding rise through the stone and up his legs. His body shuddered against the railing. Nearby, in the wall that took up a third of the southern end of the arena, huge barred gates swung inward.

Here came drummers and trumpeters, clad only in gold-trimmed scarlet loincloths. Their oiled bodies gleamed as brightly as the polished metal of their instruments. The brawny men represented every race of the empire in the colors of their skin and hair and the tattoos on their faces and bodies. One thing they had in common: iron slave rings around their throats.

Arram rubbed his own throat uneasily. His original home, Tyra, was not a slave country. Three years in Carthak had not made him comfortable with the practice, not when there were no slaves at his school. He saw them only when he was outside, and the sight of them made him edgy.

The leader of the musicians raised his staff. The trumpeters let loose a blare that made Arram jump, almost tipping him over the rail. The men caught him again.

"You're best off at your seat," the friendly one advised. "Ain't your mamma callin' yeh?"

"I'm *eleven*," Arram lied. "I don't need a mother — I'm a student at the School for Mages!"

The men's laughter was drowned out by a thunder of drumrolls. Arram gave the sands what he called his special, *magical* squint. Now he saw waves of spells all over the arena floor. They sent ripples through the air, carrying the arena's noise even to the people in the seats high above.

"Why do they allow spells on the arena sand?" he shouted at the friendlier of the two men. As far as he knew, magic was forbidden here. Perhaps they allowed only their own magic, just as they allowed the emperor's magic.

"What spells?" the man bellowed. He reached over Arram's head and tapped his friend as the musicians marched past. "The lad thinks there's magic on the sands!"

The other roughneck looked down his flattened nose at Arram. A couple of scars on his face told the boy he may have come by that nose in fighting. "What're you, upstart?" he growled. "Some kind of mage?"

"Of course I am!" Arram retorted. "Didn't you hear me say I'm in the School for Mages?"

"He's simple," the friendlier man said. "Leave 'im be. Who're you bettin' on?"

The other man seized Arram by the collar and lifted him into the air. "If you're a mage, spell me, then," he growled. "Turn me into somethin', before I break yer skinny neck for botherin' us."

"Don't be stupid!" Arram cried. His mind, as always, had fixed on the question of magic. "Only a great mage can turn a person into something else! Even—"

His foe choked off Arram's next comment—that he might never be a great mage—by turning his fist to cut off the boy's voice entirely. "*Stupid*, am I?" he shouted, his eyes bulging. "You moneyed little piece of tripe—"

Arram might have corrected him concerning the state of his pocketbook, but he couldn't breathe and had finally remembered a teacher's advice: "You don't make friends when you tell someone you think he is stupid." He was seeing light bursts against a darkening world. He called up the first bit of magic he'd ever created, after a walk on a silk carpet brought flame to his fingers. He drew that magic from the sands and seized the fist on his collar.

The tough yelped and released Arram instantly. "You! What did you do to me?"

Arram couldn't answer. He hit the rail and went over backward, arms flailing.

He was trying to think of lifesaving magic when a pair of strong, dark brown arms caught him just before he struck the ground. He looked into a man's face: eyes so brown they seemed black in the bright sun, a flattened nose, a grinning mouth, and holes in both earlobes. His head was shaved.

"You don't want to join us, lad, trust me, you don't," he told Arram, already walking back against the line of marching gladiators. The ones closest to them were laughing and slapping or punching the big man on the shoulder. Like him, they wore leather armor. Like him, they were oiled all over. Some were missing ears or eyes. These were the beginners, the midlevel fighters, and the old-timers, not the heroes of the arena. Some didn't look at Arram; they were murmuring to themselves or fondling tiny god-images that hung on cords around their necks.

"Hurry, boy," an older gladiator muttered to Arram's rescuer. "Guards comin'."

WHEN YOU GAMBLE WITH KINGDOMS,
ALL BETS ARE OFF.

Follow Aly's journey
from slave to spymaster in the
Trickster's Duet.

"Tamora Pierce's complex, unforgettable heroines
and vibrant, intricate worlds blazed a
trail for young adult fantasy."
—SARAH J. MAAS,
#1 *New York Times* bestselling author

EMBER   RHCB